BULLETS &DOUBT

A. K. RAMIREZ

BULLETS &DOUBT

MARISSA AMBROSE WITNESS SERIES BOOK 4

4 Horsemen
Publications, Inc.

Table of Contents

Dedication

For my mom.

Chapter 1

Gray, overcast September rain clouds allowed just a bit of light to creep into the room. Most of the summer heat had dissipated, and things were finally cooling off. Stretching out, Marissa rolled to face Mac, who appeared to still be sleeping, his arm draped over her waist. As she started to scoot closer to him, his arm pulled her closer and lazily opened his eyes.

"Good morning," he murmured.

Marissa leaned in and gave him a soft kiss. "Good morning," she responded softly. "Can we just stay in bed?" She nestled into his chest, letting him completely wrap his arms around her. She hadn't slept well. Not nearly long enough.

"I wish we could." It was the expected response. He leaned down and kissed her forehead but made no move to let her go.

"How much time do we have?"

Mac groaned. "Last I looked, we had about an hour before we needed to get moving." She felt him take in a deep breath and exhale slowly.

Now it was Marissa's turn to groan. At the sound, Ellie sat up and crawled over Marissa, trying to see what was going on and effectively pushing her way between them. Laughter erupted in the room as the giant shepherd made her own morning rounds, licking faces and wagging her tail with excitement. Once she was satisfied, she plopped herself down at the bottom of the bed and huffed, looking at the door.

"I'll let her out." Mac sat up, feet hitting the ground.

Marissa was grateful; getting up for her was a much slower process. Chances were, Mac had been lying there awake for a while. Damn morning person.

Once his pants were on, Mac leaned back over and gave her a kiss that left her tempted to pull him right back into bed again before he pulled away.

"We have to," he said firmly, grabbing his shirt and opening the door. Ellie didn't even wait for him to call her before she jumped off the bed and charged down the stairs. Mac stopped in the doorway to look back at her. "Ten minutes?" When she nodded, he smiled. "I love you."

"I love you, too." The words still felt so strange, but she didn't hate them. And there was no doubt in her mind that she meant them.

With a heavy sigh, Marissa rolled back to her own side of the bed and worked on pushing herself into an upright position. She noted the dull ache in the back of her head that was there nearly every morning, and a lightheaded sensation ran over her. She waited a minute for it to pass and put her feet on the floor. As soon as she pushed off the bed and stood on her feet, Marissa suddenly felt all of her own weight, and the ache that had been local to her head traveled through the rest of her body as everything suddenly felt heavy.

Marissa wasn't sure if it was the change in the weather, the constant weight of the stress manifesting, or if it was just another flare-up *just because*, but her body was sabotaging her. She closed her eyes for a moment before swaying on to the balls of her feet and heading into the bathroom. She did her business, washed her face, and threw her hair up in a quick bun. Marissa did her best to avoid her own reflection in the mirror, but her eyes stopped on the woman staring back at her. Marissa had seen better days; in fairness, she had to remind herself she had looked worse a year ago. The section of scar on her chest that showed over the top of her tank top was finally beginning to look less angry. She ran her fingers over it and winced. It started at her clavicle and went down her chest before pivoting down her side.

Where that scar ended, a deeper scar was beside it on her abdomen; that was the one that had almost killed her. The one that was visible, that she had to stare at every day, had just been sick torture. A daily reminder of what she had endured. The section on her chest Marissa had tried to tear off herself in a moment of mania, wanting to remove it from her skin. Thankfully, it had started to heal nicely.

Closer to twenty minutes later, Marissa headed down the stairs, placing her feet sideways as she did, her ankles locking up as she stepped. As she reached the bottom of the stairs, she was met by Kate, who was already dressed and had a Pop-Tart® in her hands.

"Hey!" Kate smiled at Marissa, taking a bite of her pastry before walking into the living room.

Marissa's gaze followed Kate into the living room to see Veronica sitting in the recliner. Veronica raised her hand and waved. "Good morning."

Marissa rubbed her face and nodded. "Morning." She was surrounded by morning people. It was a nightmare. "Thank you for coming over so early. I really appreciate it." Jared had never been a morning person; in fact, during their relationship, Marissa was usually the one who was up and functioning first. Growing up, Melanie had been the closest to a morning person in the family, and she was still always a bitch during that first hour.

"It's cool. I'll get her to school. Just send me a text if you need me to pick her up, too." Veronica gave Marissa an encouraging smile.

"Oh! If you pick me up, can we watch the next *Back to the Future* movie?" Kate asked excitedly, wiggling in her seat on the couch.

Marissa glanced at her phone. "Guys, it's not even seven." She shook her head.

"It's Michael J. Fox," Veronica said defensively.

Marissa couldn't stop herself from smiling at their enthusiasm. Shaking her head, she turned as Mac came out of the kitchen. Ellie was already geared up in her vest.

"You ready?"

"I guess," she said, with as little enthusiasm as she could.

Mac kissed her cheek and grabbed his keys. "We'll be back hopefully this afternoon."

"It should be this afternoon. It's just a meeting," Marissa said, hoping her words were the truth. She looked back over at Ronnie and Kate. "If you guys need anything, just give me a call, okay?"

They both nodded.

Reluctantly, Marissa let Mac lead her outside. She walked around to the passenger side of the SUV, opened the door, and let Ellie jump in and into the back. They had agreed they would take his car and that he could drive. It was too early in the morning for Marissa to drive.

She buckled herself and settled into the seat as Mac did the same. He turned and smiled at her.

"You're going to fall asleep, aren't you?"

Marissa shook her head and struggled to stop the yawn from escaping. "No."

A couple of hours later, Marissa was opening her eyes as Mac put the car in park. "I fell asleep," she said apologetically, rubbing her eyes. Glancing around, she realized they were not at the Seattle Police Department. "Where are we?"

"It's okay," he said, before turning to her. "While we were on the ferry, I got a call. They asked for both of us to be here."

"Where?"

"The home of Derek Murphy."

"Derek Murphy the prosecutor?" Marissa's brain was starting to catch up.

Mac nodded, and she noticed how grim his expression was. She glanced past him to see the cops moving around outside. "Fuck."

Mac again nodded his head. "Yeah."

They both got out of the vehicle, and Marissa was met by Captain Cooper, who looked as sick as she suddenly felt. She looked over to the Crime Scene Investigator van on the other side of the

SUV. There were officers taping off the scene and keeping a growing group of onlookers back.

"Come on." Cooper motioned for her to follow. She waited for Ellie to jump out of the car and closed the door. Marissa glanced over but saw Mac talking to his superior, FBI Agent Nick Walker. Turning back to her own former superior, Marissa let out a sigh and followed him into the house, with Ellie trotting at her side. She nodded at the officers as they made their way inside.

It was a beautiful home; her eyes took in the high ceilings and likely expensive artwork on the walls. She could only imagine how big it appeared when it wasn't full of people.

"No signs of a break-in, or a struggle. He was home alone; his wife had been out of town on a girls' trip. When she arrived home this morning, she found him and made the 911 call." Cooper led her through the open floorplan to a hallway before making a sharp right into the home office. Marissa put her hand out to stop Ellie before entering the room, giving the dog the signal to sit and stay. There, at the desk, were the remains of the former lawyer. He was slumped over his desk, blood spatter covering the oak finish. "First impression, shot at close range, execution-style. It doesn't look like he put up any kind of fight."

There was comfortable familiarity in the way he was running through the scene with her. Despite what was happening, for a moment, Marissa missed it. The crime scene investigators were working around them, photographing everything. The camera flash caught Marissa's eyes off guard, causing her to blink the light back.

Marissa stuffed her hands into her pockets, stopping short before reaching the desk. "Do we think it's related to O'Rourke? Because this isn't exactly his MO."

Cooper turned to look at her and let out a heavy sigh, giving her a quick nod. "Agreed. It's not his MO, and O'Rourke wouldn't have even been on my radar here if he hadn't left a calling card." He motioned to the desk.

Marissa stepped forward to look at what Cooper was pointing at. Trying hard not to focus on Murphy's slumped over, blown-out head, she looked at the papers that were clearly staged by his hands, sprinkled with blood spatter. One was a newspaper clipping of Murphy speaking to the press after O'Rourke was sentenced. There was a giant X marked over the clipping. Besides that, Marissa saw other clippings: one of his arrest, with a picture of Marissa leading him to the police car in handcuffs; another clipping of Cooper speaking to the press, with their old captain standing to one side of him and Mac standing to the other side, the officers involved, herself included, standing behind him. There was also a clipping that pictured one of their informants from O'Rourke's inner circle. They were spread strategically around the crossed-out clipping.

"Fuck," Marissa mumbled under her breath, stepping out of the way of the techs who were beginning to bag things up. "I guess we *have* to have that meeting now, then?" She looked up at Cooper, who nodded grimly.

"We're going to need to push our meeting back just a little. Need to finish up here."

"Yeah," she said with even less enthusiasm and started backing out of the room, but her eyes were still on the body of what used to be Derek Murphy. She had met with him several times before the trial and remembered him being a real nice guy who was very passionate about the case. On the desk beside his outstretched hand was a picture of him and his wife; Marissa couldn't imagine what she must be feeling right now.

"Ambrose?" Cooper paused, watching her.

"Sorry," she said softly before turning to leave the room. She passed the coroner on the way out of the room and found Mac and Nick Walker standing in the doorway at the front of the house.

Mac turned and gave her a half-hearted smile before turning back to Nick and nodding his head. "We'll see you there."

Nick nodded and headed back to the office Marissa had just left, tipping his chin to her in a silent greeting as he passed by. Marissa nodded back and walked over to Mac, who put his arm around her. "Come on." He gave her shoulder a squeeze as they headed for the car, Ellie on one side and Mac on the other.

The drive to the precinct was silent. Marissa still had the image of the crime scene burned into her mind. The whole reason they were out here in the first place today was to have a meeting about Johnny O'Rourke. It had been about a couple of months since he had skipped out on his house arrest and disappeared. They had met early in the beginning, but it was a case for the FBI; Marissa hadn't been a part of that. There hadn't been any sightings or rumblings about him at all until a week earlier when he had made a phone call to the precinct with some heavy threats. He had promised to repay the debts he owed; he was just trying to figure out who to visit first. Clearly, he had made a decision. O'Rourke had called from a burner phone, which they had found two blocks away from the precinct.

They had all received the call, putting everyone on high alert, but this was supposed to be the day they were meeting. The delay was in concern that having everyone in one place was what he was aiming for. Sadly, they had made the wrong decision.

Marissa was staring out the window as they pulled into the parking lot, and she felt Mac take her hand. His touch snapped her back into the moment.

"Hey," he said gently.

"Hey." Her own voice was quieter than she had intended. She gave him a half smile.

"It's going to be alright."

She shook her head. "Tell that to Derek Murphy." Marissa sighed.

"Don't. Don't go down that road right now. We all made a conscious choice to wait."

"It was the wrong one." She sighed again and closed her eyes, leaning back into the seat for a moment. Marissa took in a deep breath and opened her eyes. "I'm sorry, I just…" she trailed off.

"Yeah. I know," he said softly. He gave her hand a squeeze while exhaling. "Do you want to wait inside or stay here?"

Marissa shrugged her shoulders. "Let's just wait here."

Chapter 2

Marissa leaned back in her chair and swayed slightly from side to side. Ellie sat beside her with her head propped on the arm of the chair, enjoying ear scratches from Marissa, who stared at the top of the table while everyone talked around her. She had napped in the car earlier, but it hadn't been restful; she'd woken up feeling even more drained. The dread began to spread from the pit of her stomach throughout her body.

The only one who was in the room that hadn't been a part of that investigation was Nick Walker. There had been a different agent in charge back then, and he was no longer with the bureau. They had been working on tracking him down, but he had moved out of the country after retirement. Marissa stared at the table, remembering the feeling of accomplishment they had all shared when they'd made that arrest of O'Rourke.

Now that the group was all there, the mood was definitely not the one they'd shared the day of his arrest. They were all talking over each other, arguing and making excuses. She closed her eyes. Their voices all melded together, losing their arguments within one another; it all felt pointless. She kept her eyes closed and listened to the noise for several minutes before she couldn't take it anymore.

Marissa opened her eyes and shook her head. "So what exactly is the plan here? Because, and no offense," she looked directly at Nick Walker, "but the FBI doesn't seem to have a great track record right now." Her voice broke through all the men's voices in the room, and they fell silent, all eyes on her.

"Marissa—." Cooper started, but Nick Walker interjected.

"Ideally, putting you all up in safe houses feels like the right answer."

"Why are you even here? You weren't there for any of this." The man to Marissa's immediate right glared at Walker. He was a tall, lanky officer she recognized as Brett O'Brien, one of the officers who had assisted Marissa on the arrest.

Nick ran his fingers through his hair and shook his head. "Because the bureau put me in charge out here, and this is a top priority."

"I, for one, will not hide in a safe house," Captain Cooper chimed in. "We need to get ahead of this and bring Johnny O'Rourke back in."

"I'm with him," Marissa said, looking at her old lieutenant-turned-captain before glancing back at Walker.

"Of course you are," she heard Walker mumble as his hands landed on his hips. He waited a moment before he addressed the room again. "Alright, if you are all going to refuse a safe house, I, at least, want protective detail on all of you at all times." He looked over each of them, not bothering to hide his annoyance.

"What we need to do is find him. We should be working the case." Cooper hit the table. "He should never have been allowed out." Cooper glared over toward Walker but spared a momentary glance at Mac.

Agent Walker let out a long breath before answering, his tone dripping irritation. "The last thing each and every one of you should be doing is working this case. There are good men on it. They will bring him in."

"Should we be concerned about Agent Spencer?" O'Brien said after a moment, but Walker shook his head.

"He has been notified and has declined the safe house and security. He's not currently in the country." Walker huffed in frustration. He knew he didn't have the room, but he was giving it his best effort anyway. "We have a special task force dedicated to finding and bringing in Johnny O'Rourke. You may be refusing the safe houses, but none of you are going to go looking for him on your own." His eyes fell on Mac and Marissa intentionally.

Marissa offered the smallest of shrugs, determined not to agree to anything. Mac shifted in his chair uneasily before speaking.

"I understand the danger, but doesn't it make sense to have the people who were brought in the first time on said task force?"

Walker glared at Mac before turning his eyes to the tabletop. "Were you there this morning? Did you see the newspaper clippings? The ones with your faces circled?" He dug around in the folders in front of him before he tossed a few enlarged photos of the clippings from earlier at the crime scene. "Here. In case you missed it. *This* is what we are dealing with. He is specifically calling out each and every one of you in this room. So no, I don't think putting you on a task force that is focused on finding him is the smartest move we can make."

Mac opened his mouth to argue, but Walker held up a hand.

"I'm not saying that your insights and knowledge aren't welcome or needed, and as it stands now, the plan is to sit down with each of you individually to go over everything—."

Marissa sat up in her chair abruptly. "What about our CI?" A heavy weight suddenly landed on her shoulders. She couldn't believe that she had even forgotten. If it hadn't been for their informant and his testimony, they would have never found him. And the papers had said as much.

Walker shook his head. "We haven't been able to locate Mr. Douglass. We've tried." He spoke with a defensive tone that hadn't been there a moment before.

Marissa narrowed her eyes at him, feeling like he probably hadn't tried hard enough. Not like she would have. They likely had only been searching since the phone call they'd all received. Zeke Douglass would have gone underground as soon as he heard O'Rourke was on house arrest. The pit of her stomach burned hot. Zeke had been her informant, but no one had asked her where she thought he might be. That burning sensation had begun to rise up through her chest, inching its way into her throat. She might not have been responsible for the team—everyone at the table had been there to do a job, and they had done it well—but they all knew the risks. Zeke Douglass had been her responsibility; Marissa had been the one to convince him to testify.

Marissa shook her head, staring at the top of the conference table as Ellie nudged her knee. Her faith in the justice system was rapidly deteriorating. Swallowing the burning sensation down, she couldn't listen to this anymore. She and Mac had just done this, gone over all the details they could cover from that fucking case. She got to her feet and waited for Walker to trail off.

"I'm done. I've got somewhere to be. I'm sorry we aren't meeting under better circumstances." She glanced at the familiar faces before her eyes landed on Walker. "I am officially declining the offer of a safe house. I will accept your security, but I doubt it's going to do much. If you need me, you know where to find me." She flashed Mac and Cooper an apologetic look before turning for the door, holding it open long enough for Ellie to follow her through, and slamming it shut behind her.

She headed directly to the bathroom. After checking to make sure the two stalls were empty, she locked the door behind her and let out a long breath. Leaning against the sink, she turned on the cold water, waited a moment, and splashed her face. She could feel the tightness building in her chest. The icy water on her face sent a shock through her, but it quickly dissipated … without breaking up the panic that was growing; this was not the time or place for this.

When Marissa stepped out of the bathroom, she needed to walk across the building and into the interrogation room where Daniel Fryer was waiting. She needed to shake off all the feelings from this morning and get herself in the right headspace. If there was a right headspace to be in.

When she became a homicide detective, she never expected so much time to be spent playing mind games with a serial killer. A serial killer who had almost killed her. Serial killers were not nearly as common as television shows and movies made people believe. It had only been a handful of years, and she had already dealt with more than one.

She turned off the water, looked up at the reflection staring back at her, and let out a heavy sigh. Straightening up, Marissa fixed her bun and tucked her red shirt back in. Her eyes drifted to the scar on her chest. A year ago, she couldn't bring herself to wear anything that let it show. Usually, she would at least put cover-up over it, making it less prominent and pronounced. Today, she hadn't. It had been a deliberate choice, although if asked why, she wouldn't have been able to put it into words. Marissa let her fingertips brush across the top of it, wincing. Not because it hurt, but because she couldn't feel it at all. There was only a little sensation, mostly a feeling of pins and needles.

Stepping back from the sink, Marissa straightened out her shirt and tried to shake off the morning. She pushed down the aggravation and feelings about O'Rourke, Nick Walker, all of it, and braced herself for the interview to come.

Glancing down at Ellie, who was sitting at attention directly at her side, looking up at Marissa, she sighed. "I just want to go back to bed," she muttered to herself and the dog, shaking her head.

As she unlocked and opened the door, she saw Mac standing there, typing something on his phone.

He immediately looked up, obviously relieved. "You okay?"

Marissa shrugged her shoulders, adjusting Ellie's harness before she stepped out of the doorway and walked over to him. "I guess."

She inhaled deeply and walked into his arms, not even processing how strange it was for him to give her a hug in the middle of the precinct. Their relationship wasn't a secret anymore.

"Everything is going to be okay," he said with so much confidence, she almost believed him.

She rested her head on his chest and nodded unconvincingly. "I just hate all of this," she said finally as he tightened his arms around her. Once upon a time, Marissa used to work cases that had nothing to do with her. She wasn't a victim; she wasn't a target; she was the hero. She was the one working to make people feel safe. It had been a lifetime ago. Of course, there were risks that came with the job, but this was not what she'd signed up for. It left her feeling exhausted, down to her bones. Not just tired but crushing exhaustion.

"I know," he said, resting his chin on the top of her head. "But we'll get through it. It will be okay." He turned his wrist to glance down at his watch. "You've got some time before Fryer. Why don't we go outside and get some air?"

She nodded her head, still leaning against him. Ellie snorted and nosed her leg as though in agreeance.

"Come on." He pulled away slightly but took her by the arm and led her out of the precinct. He walked them over to the SUV parked right out front and leaned against the wall, letting her go. With a bit of effort, she hopped on the front hood of the SUV and let out a heavy sigh, looking at Mac across from her. She dropped Ellie's leash, and the shepherd sat down right in front of the vehicle to watch Marissa's every move. Mac gave her a small smile, and she felt her stomach flip, bringing a smile to her own lips.

"What if we just left?" she said suddenly, as the thought ran across her mind. "What if we packed everything up—the dog, the cat, Kate—and we just left?"

He raised an eyebrow at her. "Is that something you really want to do?"

"Kind of, yeah." She meant it. "Just disappear. Leave everything behind and go start over somewhere."

Now a smile grew from the corners of his lips. "Where would you want to go?"

"Ireland," she said after a moment. "Surrounded by water. Small populations. Accents. Guinness. We can change our names."

"Well, that's easy enough." He laughed. "And what would we do?"

She shrugged. "Whatever we wanted to." She laughed. "We could have a farm."

He raised his eyebrow again. "You on a farm?"

"What?"

He pushed off the wall and walked up to her, putting his arms around her. "You know that means you'd have to wake up at the crack of dawn every morning?"

"Okay. Maybe not a farm." She put her arms around his neck.

He sighed, his smile replaced by a frown. He hesitated before he spoke again, his voice lower. "What about your mom?"

Marissa winced, dropping her head between them. She hadn't forgotten, but for just a moment, she had pushed this idea back. She went to say something, but only a sigh came out.

"I'm sorry," he said finally. "I just know you would never forgive yourself if you left now."

And he was right. Her mom needed her. Her sisters needed her. Her mom's stage-4 cancer diagnosis had taken everyone by surprise, except maybe her mom, who had found a lump but hadn't wanted to be a burden. Now it was just too late to do anything about it.

"No, you're right," she said softly. "I just … it's nice to imagine sometimes, you know?"

"I know." He kissed her forehead. "Do you want to reschedule the interview? Today's already been a lot."

Marissa considered it for a moment; it had already been a long day. But she shook her head and let out a sigh, leaning back. "No. We're already here." She kicked her feet in visible protest, but she knew it was the responsible thing to do.

Mac nodded, backing up to give her the space to slide off the car. She looked over at the door to the building and let out a heavy breath. Mac, with one hand in his pocket and the other taking hers, pulled her into a hug. Marissa closed her eyes, grateful for the closeness as she held on.

A moment went by before she took a breath and a step back, shaking her head. "It's weird to be back here, in this head space. The O'Rourke case was so long ago. I can't believe we have to do this again."

"But this time." He gave her a half smile and squeezed her hand. "We know who we're looking for. We don't have to play catch-up. We just have to find him."

She dropped her head back into his chest. "Ugh. I just want to go back home." She huffed and straightened herself up, although wiggling her shoulders in small protest.

Mac looked her over and shook his head. "Let's reschedule. We have to come back to the city, anyway."

Marissa went to argue, but the words wouldn't come out. She knew she wasn't up for this today. "Okay," she said finally, and Mac leaned forward to give her a kiss on the forehead.

"I'll go deal with it. Why don't you get into the car?"

Marissa nodded and watched him go back inside the precinct. Despite how drained she felt, a smile formed on her lips as she shoved her hands in her pockets and headed toward the SUV.

Chapter 3

Despite her attempt to stay awake and keep Mac company, Marissa passed out again before they made it on the ferry. When she opened her eyes again, they were parked in the driveway, Mac's hand on her knee. "Hey, hon. We're home."

Marissa straightened her back and wrapped her hand around his, giving Mac an apologetic look. "Sorry, I don't know why I'm so … tired…" She let her words drift off, the excuse feeling weak as it came out of her mouth.

"You have nothing to apologize for." He shook his head, keeping his eyes locked on hers. "You've sort of had a lot going on lately. Being tired is not shocking." He gave her hand a squeeze and motioned toward the outside.

Marissa reluctantly let go of his hand and got out of the car, holding the door open for Ellie to follow. The shepherd jumped down, ran straight up the porch steps, and sat down at the door, waiting patiently to be let inside. Marissa paused as she walked up the last step, looking around the porch to see if there were any packages or letters waiting.

As they walked in, Marissa noted the empty living room. A glance at her phone told her it was only 2:30 and Kate would be in school for another hour. She opened her messages and sent a text to Ronnie.

[We're home. We'll grab Kate from school. Thank you so much!]

It only took a moment for a response to come through.

[Ronnie: Of course! I hope everything went well. Tell Kate we will continue *Back to the Future* next time!]

Marissa smiled at her phone before shoving it back into her back pocket. As if on cue, because Marissa was talking about Kate, Wicket appeared, rubbing her tail against the wall on the stairs before sitting down on the second step. She flicked her tail in disappointment.

"She'll be home soon," she said to the cat, who, Marissa was sure, if she could emote anything more, would be wearing a disapproving frown. Wicket had been her best friend, Allison's, cat. When Allison died, Marissa hadn't hesitated to bring her home. Wicket liked Marissa well enough, but she loved Kate. It had been one of the many bonuses to Kate's return a few months ago; the cat was no longer depressed.

She leaned down, unbuckling Ellie's service vest and taking it off. The shepherd shook herself off, letting her tail sway in a slow wag. "Good girl." Marissa gave her head a pet before hanging up the vest and leash in the entryway. She let out a heavy sigh and turned to go into the kitchen where she knew Mac was already in the fridge. He would be looking for something to make for lunch.

Marissa was about to say something when her phone rang. Pulling it from her back pocket, she saw Greg's name flash across the screen. Sucking in a breath, she answered and put the phone to her ear. "Greg? Is everything okay?" She kept her tone as gentle as possible, knowing that Greg was still taking shit from her sisters.

"Hey, Marissa. I know you were planning to come by today, but your mom is having a pretty rough day. Chemo isn't really agreeing with her."

Marissa leaned her elbows on the counter, dropping her head. "She asked you to call?"

This was becoming pretty routine. Her mother didn't want anyone to see her struggle; she had always been one of the strongest women Marissa knew. She had raised three girls on her own, had run her own business, and even though there were definitely hard times, her mom never let it show. Cancer was another beast; the past few weeks of chemo had been rough on her. If she could have, she probably would have sent Greg packing, too, keeping her vulnerability to herself. Marissa could relate, although she hadn't done a very good job of it lately.

Greg paused. "She did."

Poor guy. He had been in their mom's life for nine years, but he was still new to Marissa and her sisters. Marissa was grateful that she had met him before word about her mother's illness came out. Melanie and Madilyn, on the other hand, had met him for the first time at the hospital, and it hadn't gone over well.

"Is she there? Can I talk to her?" Marissa asked softly.

"Yeah, give me a minute." He sounded relieved.

"Thanks, Greg." She looked up at Mac to find him watching her, leaning against the kitchen island. A moment later, she heard a faint cough in the background before she heard her mom's voice, obviously arguing about getting the phone.

"Hey, honey." Her mom's tired voice came over the line, and Marissa felt her heart drop.

"Hey, Mom." She tried not to sound disappointed; that felt selfish. "I hear you're not feeling well today?" It had been almost two weeks since she had seen her at this point.

"Not really, sweetie. I'm sorry."

"Can I still come by? You don't have to get up or do anything." She tried not to make her words sound like a plea.

"Maybe tomorrow, honey. I'm just really tired. I need to get some sleep. But I promise. Tomorrow."

Marissa swallowed her disappointment. "Okay," she managed. Clearing her throat, she closed her eyes to avoid the look she knew Mac was giving her. "Can I talk to Greg again?"

Her mother sighed on the other end of the line. "You know, Marissa, I don't need a babysitter."

"I know, Mom. I just have a quick question." She put her hand on her forehead and let out an unsteady breath.

"Love you, hon," her mom said finally.

"I love you too." A moment later, Greg came back on the line. "Is she really okay?"

"Yeah. I think so," he answered before she heard his muffle, as he said something to Marilyn. When he returned on the other end, his voice was a little louder. Marissa assumed he had gone to a different room. "She's just really tired. The treatment is wiping her out."

"Okay." Marissa rubbed her eyes, which were still closed. "Okay. Just call me if she needs anything. If anything changes. Just … call me."

"I will, Marissa, I promise."

She opened her eyes and clicked the End Call button on her phone, straightened herself up, and shaking her shoulders, as though she could shake off the heaviness she was suddenly left with.

"Everything okay?" Mac asked, though Marissa was sure he was just trying to fill the uncomfortable silence. He knew the answer already.

"Not really," she managed. He made his way around the counter and wrapped her in his arms, pulling her into a hug. Marissa didn't make a move for a minute, trying to keep the tears at bay, but as they started streaming down her cheeks, she found herself holding him like her life depended on it.

When he let her go, Mac brought his hand under her chin and lifted it so she would look at him. He gave her a sad but reassuring smile. "We'll get through this. Together."

Marissa could only nod her head. It didn't feel like it would be okay, but she was glad he was there. "I need to go lie down," she said finally, a sudden rush of exhaustion washing over her as she wobbled in place. Mac held her arms, trying to steady her. The pain had been there the whole time, but the throbbing had grown more unbearable since hanging up the phone.

"Upstairs, or you want to lay down on the couch?"

"Couch." She nodded her head. The idea of trying to traverse the stairs gave her a headache. Ellie, as though on cue, was right at her side, with her nose gently nudging the side of her thigh.

Everything was flaring up. She would have to deal with the waves of sudden exhaustion that knocked her off her feet, the dizzy spells, the headaches. The only thing the doctor had been able to suggest was to lower the amount of stress she was dealing with. Marissa had laughed in his face—something the older man had not appreciated. Large patches of her skin would often feel like they were on fire, sometimes completely invisible to the eye. Other times, she would wake up, and her skin would be splotchy with red hives. Her doctor had recently reaffirmed the conclusion they had both come to nearly a month ago: It was the stress. There wasn't much they could give her to help fix it. She wasn't treatable either. The stress had held her in a constant state of flaring up.

As Mac helped her get settled on the couch, Ellie jumped up and made herself comfortable on Marissa's legs, prepared to keep her resting in place. Marissa reached out and scratched her ear and looked up to see Mac gazing down at her with a small smile.

"What?" she asked after a moment, unable to stop herself from smiling back.

He shook his head, his smirk growing just a little wider. "Nothing. Nap. There will be food when you wake up." He leaned down and kissed her forehead. "I love you." His lips lingered for a moment before he straightened back up.

"I love you too," Marissa responded with ease, watching him for a moment before her eyes closed again.

The next thing Marissa knew, Kate was shaking her gently and leaning over the couch. "Marissa, I'm really sorry to wake you," the teenager spoke quietly, her big, blue eyes worried.

"What's wrong?" she asked groggily, blinking and trying to focus. She had slept hard. The kind without dreams, where she was almost confused about where she was.

"Ms. Parker is here, and she wants to talk to you and Mac." Kate paused, sitting on the coffee table in front of the couch. "But I think she wants to send me to another foster home."

That was all it took to shake the sleep off Marissa. Sitting up, she noticed that the room had grown dark, and the blinds were already closed. The only light was from a corner lamp. Rubbing her face, she dropped her feet to the floor. "What time is it?"

"It's after seven."

"Why did you guys let me sleep so long?" The question came out before she even thought about it. She hadn't meant to sleep so long; in fairness, she hadn't meant to sleep at all.

"Mac said you needed sleep." Kate shrugged her shoulders. "We weren't going to wake you up except to make you go upstairs."

Marissa raised an eyebrow. Mac really must have thought she needed the sleep if he wasn't planning on waking her up for dinner. "Okay, where are they?"

"The kitchen."

"Okay." Marissa pushed off the couch and got to her feet, which were still unsteady. It was the first time she noticed that Ellie was no longer in the living room. Chances were the shepherd was getting all the head scratches she could.

Marissa walked toward the kitchen, a sick feeling growing in her stomach. She had known this conversation was coming. Kate had been with them for almost five months now. She had spent the summer there and had started school with them. They had all fallen into a comfortable routine, despite the dangers that were always lurking.

Ms. Meredith Parker was sitting at the table, with a glass of what looked like tea sitting in front of her. Mac was still on his feet, leaning against the kitchen island with his arms crossed in front of his chest. They both turned as she and Kate entered the room.

"Hello, Marissa." Ms. Parker smiled at her, pushing her green-rimmed glasses back up the bridge of her nose. The social worker had been working with Kate since Marissa and Mac found her last winter, less than a year ago. She had already placed her once, but Kate had run away and back to Marissa. "I'm sorry for the late drop-in, but this was an important matter I wanted to speak to you both about as soon as possible."

She looked at Kate and let out a sigh. Ms. Parker was clearly trying to decide if this was a conversation she wanted to have in front of Kate. A moment passed before she broke the silence again.

"A possible placement opportunity has opened up, and I think it would be a pretty great fit." She folded her hands together on top of the table. "A couple who have taken older foster kids before. Their oldest just went off to college, and they are looking to add to their family. They only live thirty minutes away."

As Ms. Parker spoke, Marissa pulled out the chair across from her and sat down at the table. Licking her dry lips, she glanced at Mac, trying to read his expression. He kept his eyes on Ms. Parker, his expression remaining still. Looking to her other side, she saw that Kate was already shaking her head.

"Why can't I just stay here?"

Marissa closed her eyes and dropped her head before meeting Ms. Parker's gaze. "Kate, why don't you go upstairs while we talk this through?" She turned back to Kate, whose steely blue eyes glistened with tears. The fourteen-year-old suddenly looked so young, so vulnerable, trying not to cry. Reaching out, she took Kate's hand and gave it a squeeze. "Trust me, okay?" she said softly, feeling herself break.

Kate gave her a weak nod, shooting a glare at Ms. Parker and giving Mac a similar pleading look before she turned to leave. She gathered Wicket up in her arms before she stomped all the way up the stairs.

Marissa let out a heavy sigh when she heard the bedroom door slam.

Ms. Parker adjusted in her chair, taking a sip of her tea before she cleared her throat. "In fairness to Kate, I have to ask the same question. You seem to have the ideal situation going on here. She's happy with you. She's in school now, and her counselor says she's doing really well."

Marissa nodded, letting her eyes drop to the top of the table. If she could have, there wouldn't have been a question. She would have adopted Kate if she could. She loved Kate. But because she loved her, she couldn't keep her, knowing the danger lurking nearby.

"I want nothing more than to have her stay," Marissa started, wanting to stop right there. "But my job, Mac's job..." She glanced over at him to see his expression still hadn't changed. "There is a *lot* of danger. Real danger that is out there right now." She sighed. "That's why I reached out in the first place. I want her to be safe."

Ms. Parker nodded her head slowly and looked over at Mac. "What about you? Thoughts?"

Mac cleared his throat and looked between Marissa and Ms. Parker before he shook his head. "We really do love her. We just want what's best for her."

Again, Ms. Parker nodded her head. "I'm going to be honest: the likelihood that she'll just run away again is very high. And if she is angry at you when she does, Lord only knows where she will end up. She is doing really well in your care. Her counselor used the word *thriving*." She let her shoulders drop. "This couple would be a good fit, but they would also be a good fit for any other teenager in need of a soft place to land. One less lucky who doesn't have people who already love them."

The conflict Marissa was feeling was enough to make her dizzy. Nodding her head, she sighed. "Okay. Then let's just wait."

Ms. Parker finished her tea and got to her feet. "Thank you for your hospitality. And truly, I know you only want what's best for her. I still believe that this is it." She put a hand on Marissa's shoulder and gave it a squeeze before she headed toward the front door, Mac following to escort her out.

Once they were both out of the room, Marissa let her head drop to the table, a small pulsing coming from the base of her skull, the headache still in the early stages. A moment later, Mac returned and sat down in the chair beside her.

"How are you feeling?"

"Like a horrible traitor who was trying to find Kate a safer home," she mumbled without picking up her head.

"You wanting her to be safe because you care about her does not make you a traitor." He reached out and took her hand, entangling his fingers with hers.

"I just want what's best for her, and I am not it." She lifted her head, turning to look at him. "There is a serial killer stalking me, sending me threatening letters and photographs. Always right around the corner, but a complete shadow. *We* have a criminal boss who is also out there and promising revenge." She shook her head. "How are we doing what's best for her?"

He gave her a squeeze and his best reassuring smile. "We'll figure it out, Marissa." Of course, he couldn't argue with the facts. "Maybe we will find her somewhere to stay just until we get O'Rourke off the street, and we deal with your stalker."

Marissa used her free hand to rub her face, resisting the urge to explain to him that she was pretty sure the danger was never going to be gone. Instead, she gave him a halfhearted smile. "Maybe."

"Now." He again gave her hand a gentle squeeze. "How are you *feeling*? Any better than earlier?"

Marissa took a minute before answering him, letting herself feel out her body. "A little. I'm starting to get a headache, and I can't believe I'm still tired. I literally slept the day away."

"Well, we're having a roast for dinner, which is nearly done. You want to go grab Kate?"

Marissa smiled at him and nodded. "Sure."

He leaned forward and gave her a quick kiss before getting back to his feet and over to the stove. He had apparently put cooking on hold while Ms. Parker was there and was more than content to get back to it.

Marissa gave Ellie a reassuring look as the shepherd lifted her head from where it had been resting. She had made herself comfortable beneath the table, lying at Marissa's feet.

Marissa headed up the stairs, holding on tight to the railing for support as she did so. She was light-headed by the time she reached the top of the stairs and had to stop at the landing to let the feeling pass before she headed down the hall to Kate's room. Knocking at the door, she didn't wait for a response before she turned the knob.

"Hey Kate?" There was no answer, but as Marissa pushed the door open, she saw Kate sitting on her bed, leaning against the wall, holding Wicket close to her.

"Do I have to leave?" She seemed so small in the moment, Marissa just wanted to hug her. Instead, she leaned against the doorframe.

"Not today, sweetheart." She let a smile slip onto her lips.

Kate let Wicket go, getting to her feet and hurrying over to wrap her arms around Marissa, burying her head into her chest. "I just want to stay with you."

"I know," she whispered. Marissa's heart ached as she watched the long-haired cat glare at her for a moment before stalking over to the pillows at the head of the bed and making herself comfortable again. Wrapping her arms around Kate and holding her close, Marissa let herself enjoy the moment, breathing easy for a second before she pulled back. "Come on, dinner is ready." She deserved a fucking moment.

Chapter 4

Marissa couldn't stop herself from wincing as she tried to adjust her position on the couch. She rubbed her arm anxiously. Ellie looked up and huffed at her.

"Sorry, girl," she said softly, slightly smiling down at the shepherd before she gave Dr. Bailey a forced smile. "I'm sorry." She wasn't sure what she was apologizing for, but the words just fell from between her lips.

Dr. Susanne Bailey gave Marissa a sympathetic smile in return that just made Marissa want to apologize again.

She let out a long breath of frustration. "You know, I never used to apologize. My mom would always get on my case and called me prideful, but the words *I'm sorry* implied that I was wrong." She shook her head, loose hair that had fallen from her ponytail falling in front of her eyes.

"What happened?"

Marissa shrugged a shoulder. "The warehouse." It was the only way Marissa could verbally refer to it. She couldn't say *kidnapping. Abduction.* To say anything else made her feel at fault somehow.

"Do you feel like what happened at the warehouse gives you something to apologize for?" Dr. Bailey furrowed her brow.

Marissa just shrugged. She was honestly as confused by the facts as her therapist was. "I don't know."

"Do you still feel like you are at fault somehow?"

Again, Marissa shrugged. "I really don't know."

"Okay." Dr. Bailey wrote something down and changed the direction of her next question. "It's been, what? Three years?" she said slowly, watching for Marissa's reaction.

Marissa blinked before she glanced at her phone, which rested on the arm of the couch. *September 18.* Marissa's breath caught in her throat, and she could feel the knot in her chest tighten. "I didn't even realize," she said quietly. "Three years today."

"You may not have consciously recognized it, but your body certainly remembers." Dr. Bailey paused, giving Marissa a moment to sit with the realization. "How have you been feeling? Physically, I mean."

Marissa shrugged. "Exhausted. I feel like I can't stay awake lately." *That's an understatement,* she thought to herself, as she remembered having to pull over to the side of the road because of exhaustion after her last doctor's appointment in Port Angeles. She had to take a catnap before she could finish the drive home. "My eczema has been flaring up lately." She gestured to her arm, which was still splotchy red. "Haven't had much of an appetite, which has been hard because Mac is always cooking…" she trailed off.

The truth was that the list was very long. She hadn't given it much thought though, because these symptoms always raised their ugly heads, unwanted and uninvited.

"Have you been experiencing nightmares?"

"No," she lied. She wasn't sure why, but the lie came out with ease. "I've been too tired to dream about anything."

"And how have you been feeling emotionally?" Dr. Bailey asked without looking up from the notes she was taking.

"I'm overwhelmed." The words came out, and with it a visceral shudder that touched every part of her. She met eyes with Dr. Bailey, who was now watching her, giving her the space to keep going. "There are too many balls in the air."

Marissa wrapped her arms around herself, feeling the knot in her chest tighten. She looked down at Ellie, who had crawled into her lap, and lowered her voice, not trusting herself not to break into tears.

"The stalking, the serial killer, O'Rourke. The teenager in my house. My mom. The constant panic knowing that someone is always watching. And for what?" She let out a shaky breath. "It's a lot."

"That would be a lot for anyone."

"It's like..." She let her eyes drift down onto the dark hardwood flooring, focusing on a long scratch, probably from when the desk was moved into the office. "Being in a small room, where the walls are closing in. Just slow enough so it isn't obvious. And the room is spinning, like that ride at the fair." Her eyes shot back up to meet Dr. Bailey's. "The one where you let gravity take over and you're stuck to the wall while it spins out of control. But it never stops."

The therapist behind the desk waited a beat, either wanting to see if Marissa was going to add anything or trying to think of what to say in response. A long moment later, she adjusting in her chair and broke the silence.

"If you had to pick one thing that sits at the forefront of that..." She paused, considering her words. "Which ball in the air is the biggest, the heaviest?"

Marissa let out a laugh, but there was no amusement or humor behind it. "Does it matter? I feel like they're all pretty fucking heavy."

"I can imagine they would all be heavy. Let's try a different approach." She paused, clearly thinking. "If you had to pick the lightest one, the one that worries you the least, which would it be?"

Marissa thought about everything she had just listed off. "Kate," she said finally. "I worry constantly about her being in danger just by staying with me. But having her around—I don't know how to put it into words." She shook her head. "I had contacted the social worker a couple of weeks ago about getting her placed, because with O'Rourke and the constant threat of Ben, it's too big a risk. But when she showed up with a possible placement, we kept her with us instead."

"You said 'with us.' Do you mean Mac?"

Marissa nodded. "Honestly, Mac didn't say much. He just agreed with me." Marissa was pretty sure it was because he couldn't openly endorse the idea of a teenager staying where there was potential risk. "According to Ms. Parker, the counselor says she's not just doing well, she's thriving with us. Her grades are good, although school just started. She's enthusiastic. She's adjusting so well." Marissa shook her head in frustration.

"That all sounds wonderful. What are you shaking your head at?"

"Because if it wasn't for the looming fucking threats, I would keep her with me. She's such a good kid, and she's gone through so much shit. She deserves to be happy. And I want nothing more than to make that happen for her." Marissa shifted on the couch, trying to shake off the pins and needles she was beginning to feel in her feet. "I called Ms. Parker a few weeks ago and told her we needed to get her into a new foster home. And then when she came, I just lost all the conviction to do so." She sighed. "Kate said she just wants to stay."

"So, I assume that Ms. Parker is at least aware of the O'Rourke situation, since it's in the papers."

Marissa nodded. "She is."

"But not the stalker, serial killer part?"

She shook her head. "No. If I had told her that in the beginning, she would have never let me take Kate home. Which is probably the way it should have happened."

"I understand you don't want her in danger. And you have a lot that complicates your life." She seemed to be choosing her words carefully. "But I think it says a lot that you were able to take this traumatized teenager and make her feel comfortable. That is no easy feat, especially with a teenager. You deserve to recognize and give yourself some props for that."

Marissa dropped her shoulders. She didn't feel like she had done anything except show the girl kindness and give her a bedroom. It had been a rocky start, but that had mostly just been Marissa with herself more than anything. Melanie had put doubts in her that she had any ability with kids or knew what she was doing. She still missed her nieces; she had only seen them once since she and Mel had "made up." Now that relationship was fragile.

"How are things going with your mom?" Dr. Bailey asked, her voice softening slightly.

The question alone brought unwanted tears to her eyes. Marissa shook her head. "It's been … hard. The radiation has been really rough on her. She's constantly sick. The only time I've been able to see her is when it's been my turn to take her to the hospital. We've tried to come to the house, just to see her, but she will call and cancel the day of. I tried just showing up one day, but she was sleeping." Her body involuntarily shuddered. "She doesn't want anyone to see her in the condition she's in. Like she's ashamed or something."

"Well, based on everything you've told me about your mom, she is a strong lady. Accepting that she's not at her best and that she needs help can't be easy for her."

"I guess." Marissa leaned her head back and let out a couple of slow breaths in quick succession.

"I don't want to push you or make you feel pressured to talk about it if you aren't ready," Dr. Bailey said gently.

"I'm really not." She wasn't going to be. From the minute they had been told their mom had cancer, her entire world had come crumbling down.

"Have you received any more letters?"

Marissa shook her head. "Not since the last time." It had been about two months since Marissa had received anything. It was almost unsettling, because it wasn't that they were gone, whoever they were. There was likely a reason they had gone silent. Mac had suggested it was because of O'Rourke.

"That must be unsettling." Dr. Bailey must have been reading her expression.

She nodded. "It is. Knowing they are still out there. Waiting for the shoe to drop at that moment." She shuddered. "It's not over." She thought back to the note on the back of the photograph she had found on the last batch she had gotten. *Soon.* The word echoed in her mind often. The threat was clear.

Leaning forward a little, Dr. Bailey sighed. "And O'Rourke. How are things going? I heard something on the news about a murder he's connected with?"

Marissa nodded her head. "I can't talk much about it, and it's not even my case, but I can tell you that he is going after everyone who played a part in putting him behind bars. Unfortunately, he got to the prosecutor, Derek Murphy, in his home."

"That's awful."

"Yeah." Marissa had been to a lot of crime scenes. There was nothing more gruesome or worse about this one, but the connection made it feel like it had been someone she was close to. "It's not great. The intent is clear, and we're all in danger."

"Are they giving you extra security? Or a safe house?"

Marissa sighed. "A safe house was what was suggested, but I can't do that. Right now, with my mom…"

Dr. Bailey nodded. "Right. That does make it complicated indeed." She gave Marissa a sympathetic smile. "I'm so sorry that you're going through all of this. It's a lot." She paused, glancing down at her notes and flipping back a couple of pages. "I want to go back just a little bit. We talked about all the things that are going on, and we talked about how you're feeling…" Her eyes were scanning over the pages, clearly searching for something. Finally, she stopped and looked back up, meeting Marissa's gaze. "How are you coping with all of that? I know previously that some of the methods to deal with those things tended to be on the more destructive side."

Marissa couldn't stop herself from frowning. *Destructive* was one way to put it. She often missed how numb the alcohol and pills made her feel, especially when she was on the constant verge of panic all the time. It had been almost nine months since they had gotten rid of the opioids and the hard liquor in the house. There were also self-harm tendencies. It had been maybe six months since she had done anything outright, but the small things were destructive, too. Digging her nails into her skin, biting her lip until it bled, pulling on her hair: those little things were still going pretty strong. Not that she wanted to admit it. Instead, she just shrugged.

Dr. Bailey began listing things off. "Suicidal ideation?"

Marissa shook her head.

"Drinking or using drugs?"

Again, Marissa shook her head.

"Self-harm?"

This time, Marissa paused. "I still chew my nails down far enough until they bleed. Or pull at my hair. Those kinds of things."

"Nothing big like cutting or burning yourself?"

The thoughts were always there, but they had quieted enough to be ignored. The scar from where she had bitten down on her own arm still sometimes surprised her. But again, she shook her head. It was a lot different from that original intake session where she had to say yes to pretty much everything the doctor listed off. So at least there had been growth.

"Okay," Dr. Bailey said as she finished writing something in her notes. "We talked about journaling a while back. Have you been able to give that a try?"

Marissa opened her mouth and almost lied, but shook her head instead. "No. I haven't. I bought a really nice notebook for it. Shades of blue and purple with a butterfly on it."

"But?"

Marissa shrugged. "I don't know. I'm not much of a writer."

Dr. Bailey gave her an encouraging smile. "You don't have to be a writer to put your feelings down on paper. They don't need to be grammatically correct, or rhyme or sound like poetry. You just write down your thoughts. They don't even have to be full sentences. You could make lists even. Just something to let everything out." She straightened in her chair, putting her pen back down and adjusting her glasses on her face. "Because if you keep holding it all in, you are going to self-destruct. It's not a matter of if; it's a matter of when."

Marissa swallowed, nodding her head slightly in acknowledgment. She had already experienced a few breakdowns this year. What was one more?

"Try it. Before our next appointment. Just see if it gives you any kind of relief. If not, we'll find something else, okay?"

This time, Marissa managed to smile before nodding. "Okay." She couldn't imagine what she would write. Her feelings were simple: She didn't want to do this anymore. She didn't want to die; she just didn't want to be in her life anymore.

Chapter 5

Marissa sighed, leaning back in the chair again as she waited. Now she wished she had taken Mac up on his offer to come with her for company, even if he wasn't going to be in the room when it was finally her turn. The drive to Gig Harbor had been a beautiful one, not far from Tacoma, where Kate's mom had previously lived. Marlene was here somewhere, too, as part of the system and looking at life in prison. Marissa had been there many times to visit with Marlene since her arrest; she was doing her best to try to help, for Kate's sake. Marissa wished it was Marlene she was coming to visit with today.

Instead, she was here to see Laura Seaver. Laura, among other things, had been Marissa's therapist the previous year. Arrested on three counts of murder, the former psychologist would likely never see freedom. Marissa had made weekly trips to see Laura for almost three months before she stopped. The visits weren't getting her anywhere. Laura had all the leverage in the room; she knew what Marissa wanted, and she had all the power. There was nothing Marissa could offer. It had been six months since her last visit, and honestly, she wasn't sure why she was back. Not much had changed.

The door opened, and Laura was escorted in, cuffs on her hands and her feet. Despite the grayish-blue jumpsuit, she looked like the same put-together woman Marissa had known. Her hair wasn't tied back like she had always worn it, and it actually made her face look softer. They had run in the same circles since high school. Laura had dated Marissa's best friend, Allison, on and off for years before she murdered her in a fit of jealousy and rage nearly a year ago. It would have been nice to never be in the same room with her again, but Laura Seaver had come face to face with her serial killer stalker. Or his accomplice. She wasn't actually sure.

The ownership in the phrase sent an icy chill through her. *Her serial killer, her stalker.* Marissa didn't have much time to sit on it, though, as Laura gave her a smirk from across the table.

"I'm not going to lie. I didn't expect to see you again, Marissa."

If she'd had it her way, she wouldn't have. "Same," she said plainly. She adjusted her shoulders and tried to force herself to put on a polite smile. "How have you been?"

"You know, I can't honestly complain. Three meals a day, room and board that I don't have to worry about. Could be a lot worse." There was amusement in the woman's eyes that reminded Marissa just how much she hated talking to her. Marissa wanted to slap her across her perfect face. "What brings you here, detective? Is there something I can do for you?"

Marissa let out a sigh before she could stop herself; the woman sitting across from her absolutely knew why she was there. "I want to talk to you about the man who brought you back to Port Townsend."

"Why do you assume it's a man? Clearly, women are just as capable of awful things." Something Marissa had considered, but Laura had already confirmed it had been a man. She was just trying to walk Marissa in circles.

"Laura." She clenched her jaw, her teeth grinding. "Enough with the fucking mind games already. Just tell me who caught you on the boat."

"What do I get out of it?"

This was why Marissa had stopped doing this on a weekly basis. It never went anywhere. It was bad enough she had to play games with Daniel Fryer; she didn't want to give the woman who had murdered her best friend anything.

"I know you have regrets, at least as far as Allison is concerned." The mention of Allison's name wiped the smirk right off Laura's face. "Consider it a part of an atonement."

She seemed to be considering Marissa's words. Marissa held her breath, feeling the smallest spark of hope in the pit of her stomach when the woman across the table shook her head, her brassy, blonde hair falling in front of her face.

"Even if I wanted to, Marissa, I can't," she said simply, clasping her hands together.

The tiny spark of hope dissipated, and in its place came the disappointment she had expected from this visit. Trying to keep her expression neutral, she held back another sigh. "Why? What's stopping you?"

Laura met Marissa's gaze, her cold, blue eyes searching for something she didn't find. Finally, she shrugged her shoulders. "If I could answer that, we wouldn't be having this conversation. I would have told you everything you wanted to know months ago."

Marissa grumbled under her breath and cracked her neck to the side. She was tired of dead ends. "There's nothing I can say or do to change your mind? Nothing I can offer?"

Laura raised her eyebrow. "Short of getting me out of prison, no."

Not even a consideration. Dropping her gaze to the table, Marissa opened and closed her fist, biting the inside of her cheek. It wasn't until she felt those icy, blue eyes from across the way boring into her that she let out the air she had been holding in.

"What?" She had intended to snap and let out the frustration she was feeling, but the words came out quiet and weak.

"Some things just never change." Laura shook her head, leaning forward on the table slightly. "You're still that same insecure, damaged girl you've always been. Even before everything happened. You used to mask it with false confidence and a bitchy demeanor. It's why your relationship with Jared never worked out. Because you could never get past your own insecurities and self-loathing. You can't love anyone else if you can't love yourself."

She took a breath and smirked before continuing. "Allison was the one who put all the effort into your friendship. When you moved away, she was always the one initiating the calls, always the one making the effort to go visit. And the only other friends you had, real friends, were your sisters. And that was familial obligation more than anything else."

She shook her head, shoving the hair that kept falling in front of her eyes behind her ear. "Now you don't even bother trying. You go through the motions, but you're not really here. You aren't giving yourself to anything or anyone. You might as well still be locked in that warehouse." She laughed. "You aren't any better off now than you were before I ended up here."

Marissa glared across the table, trying to ignore the sting of her words. She opened her mouth to retaliate, but Laura continued. Ellie sat up, resting her head on Marissa's knee quietly. Marissa took her hand and buried it into the shepherd's fur, giving her neck a grateful scratch.

"Honestly, I think it was the wrong place, wrong time. Or right place, wrong time, depending on who you're talking to. The obsession with you has less to do with you and is more circumstantial. You were just the object that all of that energy could go into."

Again, she shook her head. "There isn't anything special about you, Marissa. The only thing that makes you stand out from the next woman is the depth of your brokenness."

"Says the woman who probably won't see the outside of these walls ever again," Marissa snapped, but it may as well have been shouted into a void.

Laura didn't miss a beat, leaning back in the chair, her look of amusement still holding on strong. "And let's talk about the men in your life." She paused, likely for dramatic effect. "You attract men with a white knight complex. They just want to save you, not knowing that there isn't a chance in hell. Jared, because he fell into a pattern, and whether it be that he is tenacious or stupid, he doesn't know how to give up. Even though he knows he can't save you, at the end of the day, he will always show up and try. It never worked out because of *you*. You were always the one who gave up. You were the one who didn't try. On the other hand, your FBI agent doesn't know any better. I'm sure he's got some idea because he deals with people all day long, but right now, he thinks he can come to your rescue. Literally. There is an actual threat against you versus yourself. He thinks he has a chance. Too bad all he's going to find is disappointment."

"Fuck off." Marissa pushed back from the table, startling Ellie, who had been resting beside her. "Stop playing the therapist role." Marissa would like to have said Laura's words had lost all meaning when she killed Allison, but Marissa knew there was truth to them. She just didn't want to hear them. She motioned to the guard that the interview was over, and he went to get Laura's escort.

"Hit a sore spot, did I?" Her lips had widened into a full grin, as though she could see physical wounds inflicted by her words. "You are nothing more than just a broken human with a storm around you that makes collateral damage for the people who want to try to love you. I'm willing to bet if *he* ever got his hands on you, he'd be collateral damage, too. Assured mutual self-destruction." She got to her feet as the guards came in. "He's probably closer than you think, Marissa."

Marissa blinked and watched the officers escort Laura out of the room, getting to her feet. Ellie also got to her feet, her ears flat as she watched the prisoner leave the room. Marissa took a couple of breaths before giving the guard a nod as she started heading out the door.

Later, Marissa sat in the car, one hand on the steering wheel, one elbow propped in the window, and her hand in a fist against her temple. This visit had been a mistake. Mac had told her as much when she'd left the house that morning. Nothing good was going to come from it, and he was right. Glancing in her rearview mirror, she watched as Agent Starr adjusted in his car. He was dressed in casual clothes, jeans, a dark-colored shirt, and black sunglasses over his eyes. Jacob may not have been in a suit, but he was still clearly FBI. It was almost comical, squeezing into a compact Honda as a big six-and-a-half-foot man. It really wasn't new; he had been moving around like a silent, giant body-guard for months now. At least now he could be obvious about it. Everyone, her sisters and mother included, understood the O'Rourke situation.

Marissa looked down at her phone. She had three missed calls and several messages. One call had been Mac just checking in. Another had been Jack asking about getting lunch. The third was Sean Boswell, asking to schedule a meeting. She had placed the phone in the middle console of the car and left it on silent. She didn't want to talk with anyone at the moment.

Marissa looked over at the passenger seat where Ellie sat, staring at her expectantly. She held eye contact with the shepherd for a moment before reaching over and giving her an affectionate pat.

"Hey, good girl, you want to go for a walk by the water?" Marissa glanced at the clock on her radio display before turning on the car. She rolled her window down all the way, opened Ellie's window about a third of the way, and then pulled out of the spot. As she drove out of the lot, she watched to make sure Jacob was following behind her. She was sick of shadows, but it wasn't his fault. She didn't want to make his job any harder. Jacob had become such a regular face in their lives now; they were all on a first-name basis. He had even cracked a joke or two in her presence now.

Getting on the I-16, she headed east, rather than heading toward home, and made the fifteen-minute drive over the Narrows Bridge, toward Titlow Beach. She parked along the street and took off Ellie's vest, but left her leash on. They headed down the path to the spot called Hidden Beach, Jacob trailing behind.

It wasn't exactly hidden or a secret, but before noon on a Tuesday, the beach was pretty empty. They followed the path to a bridge that hovered over the train tracks and continued to an opening to a boat launch before hitting the woods again. She took the right that led down to the water, and instead of continuing to the main beach, she made another right. It meant climbing quite a few concrete structures, but it opened up to a smaller beach, right in view of the Narrows Bridge they had just crossed.

Marissa sat herself down on a large rock only a few feet away from the surf coming in. Ellie, in rare form, pounced on the water climbing up toward them, her tail swaying in circles. The puppy-like behavior brought a smile to Marissa's lips and, for just a moment, the weight dissipated. She watched the black shepherd and the water, looking out to the calmness of the water under overcast skies. Glancing over her shoulder, Jacob was trying to look casual, like he wanted to be there looking at the water. Marissa smiled before turning back to the Puget Sound.

But as quickly as the weight had gone, it came back heavier than it had been as Laura's words seeped back into her thoughts. Despite all the bullshit she had spewed, there was a truth to her words. In a lot of them. Her description of Marissa before had been right on the nose. Like all the mean girls before her, it had been a mask for her own insecurities. It was also true that she wasn't trying now. She was going through the motions—always holding back.

Letting out a heavy sigh, Marissa rubbed her face. The overwhelming need to just get in her car and drive washed over her. Everyone would be better off. Most of her family was already on board with cutting her out. Jared wanted nothing to do with her anymore, not really. She and Ellie could just pick a direction and disappear. People disappeared every day.

But then there was Mac. And there was Kate. The guilt swallowed her as she thought about how they would feel if she just took off. And there was her mom. No one knew how long she was going to have. She couldn't leave without an explanation. At least Mac would know why. Her mom wouldn't. And it wasn't likely Kate would understand.

Ellie whined and nudged Marissa, bringing her back to the moment. While she had been lost in her own thoughts, it had started to rain. Not hard, but enough that it was already soaking through the shepherd's coat. Marissa wiped her face and nodded, getting to her feet. "Let's go." She had to hold back a laugh at the look of relief that washed over Jacob's face.

As she approached Jacob, she couldn't help but smile. "Not a fan?"

The big man shrugged his shoulders, shaking the rain off as he started walking alongside her. "I don't do large bodies of water."

Marissa made a face at him. "Not at all?"

"Nope." Jacob shook his head with more enthusiasm than Marissa was sure she had seen in all the months she had known him. "No one knows what's down there. Nope. No, thank you."

Marissa blinked. She couldn't imagine being afraid of the water; it was the thing that brought her comfort. And considering how often they rode on the ferry together, she felt for him.

Jacob interrupted her thoughts, directing her back toward their vehicles. "Not a fan of rain, either. Let's get back to the cars."

She realized in that moment how badly she didn't want to go back. Marissa didn't want to get back in the car and drive home, where someone was bound to be waiting to drop yet another letter on her doorstep. She didn't want to go home to the struggles with her sisters over their mom. The drama with O'Rourke. Marissa just wanted to disappear. Digging her heel into the sand, she looked back out toward the Sound like the waves held the answer.

Only ... Mac and Kate weren't with her. She let out a long, heavy breath before turning back toward the trail.

"Come on." The small, kind smile on the giant agent's face made Marissa think that he had a clue as to what she was feeling at that moment, and she was grateful for his company. Nodding, she started walking again.

They hurried back, both getting thoroughly soaked by the time they made it to the cars. Marissa let Ellie in the back so the shepherd could shake off on the backseats. She got into the front seat and peeled off her coat, tossing it on the passenger side floor and running her hands through her wet hair, pushing it from her face. She turned on the car, blasted the heat, and looked down at her phone, which was still sitting in the center console. The screen lit up, and it buzzed where it sat as Mac's name scrolled across the screen.

"Hey." She hoped her voice sounded more upbeat and lighter than she felt.

"Hey. How is it going?" He was trying not to sound concerned, but he wasn't convincing either.

"It's going. We're getting ready to head back now." Marissa glanced back to see Ellie rubbing her back along the seats, trying to wipe the water off.

"Okay, good." He paused. "But how did it go?" he pushed gently.

Lowering the heat to a more tolerable temperature, she sighed. "You were right. It was a complete waste of time." She stopped herself before going into detail. There was no point in rehashing what Laura had said. "She didn't have anything helpful to offer. Ellie and I are heading back now."

Sitting on her third porch step was a familiar manila envelope. Marissa had noticed it right as she pulled into the driveway. She had gotten out of the car and just leaned against the hood of the Mini Coop, folding her arms across her chest. Jacob was doing a perimeter check, and Mac was standing on the porch, watching her as they both waited for the all-clear. Ellie sat next to her, whining softly, confused as to why they weren't going into the house, but she stayed by her side, nonetheless.

The drive back home had been a quiet one, just a little over two hours with the traffic. Marissa had turned up the music, trying to tune out Laura's words, and kept the window down, enjoying the cool, sunny weather. She had almost worked herself out of the mood the visit had put her in when she had pulled into her driveway.

Marissa met Mac's gaze and let out a sigh, running her hand up and down her shoulder. She wanted nothing more than to already be on the porch and in his arms, desperate for a hug that could make her feel safe. She didn't care that she was supposed to wait, and she took a step forward, but Jacob appeared and shook his head.

"*Now*, we're all clear. I've called Walker."

Mac was already moving toward her, pulling her into that hug she so desperately craved before leading her up the porch. He paused on the step and grabbed the envelope, motioning for Jacob to follow them as they went inside.

Chapter 6

Marissa stared at the envelope they had set on the kitchen table. Mac stood next to her while Jacob paced in the kitchen on his phone. Again, she found herself wondering what the consequences would be of just not opening it, not looking through its contents at all. But the truth was another woman could be in trouble. At least as long as she kept playing the game, the status quo remained the same. No one close to her was likely to end up dead.

With a huff, she ripped the manila envelope open and dumped the contents on to the table. Out came a few pictures, a letter, and some flower clippings. Marissa didn't recognize the dried, dead flowers but found the strip of paper with the description—

Black Dahlia. Doom.

—simple, short, and to the point. Marissa blinked, trying to remember the last time flowers had been part of the package. It had been a while, for sure. Pushing the flowers and the paper that went along with them to the side, she grabbed the letter. Something else she hadn't received in a minute.

Marissa,

> *I know you're distracted while someone else is hunting you. I can't blame you—it's a dangerous threat. But I can assure you, no one else will get within five feet of you. I will make sure of it. Put your mind at ease. I'm watching over you.*

> *I admit, we've also been distracted. But you have our full attention now.*

> *It's been a while. Have you gotten your affairs in order? Time is on my side now. I'm counting down the days.*

Marissa shuddered involuntarily, shaking her head as she shoved the letter to the side, which allowed Mac the chance to snatch it up to inspect. Turning her attention to the photographs, she realized there were fewer than last time. There was one of her, from within the last week. There was one of Mac, one of Jared. And one of the mysterious brunette they had yet to identify. And that was it. As though there hadn't been time to dabble in photographs.

Again, she shuddered. The way the sentences read, *"Put your mind at ease. I'm watching over you,"* were written as though she was supposed to find comfort in the words. Marissa ran her hand over her face, spending extra time rubbing her eyes. When she opened them again, she looked at Mac standing beside her, making no effort to hide his concern.

Before she could say anything, Kate walked into the kitchen, and Marissa whirled around.

"You're back!" Her smile faded, though, as she eyed the obvious FBI agent pacing around the kitchen on the phone, throwing out a *Yes, sir* every few minutes. "Is everything okay?"

Marissa forced a smile, pushing herself away from the table to the kitchen entrance to pull Kate into a hug. "Everything is fine." She felt herself relax a little when the teenager hugged her back. "We are dealing with a work situation though so—."

"I should go back upstairs till dinner?" Kate offered, eyeing Jacob before looking at Mac and then back at her.

Marissa gave her a grateful smile. "I'll order pizza. And we can watch something, okay?"

Kate nodded, giving a half wave to the men standing by the table before smiling back at Marissa and turning back to head up the stairs. She stopped to scoop up the cat at her feet and disappeared.

When Marissa heard her door close, the smile vanished from her face, and she turned to the two men standing by her kitchen table.

"You okay?" Mac asked after a moment.

"Not even a little bit." She walked back into the kitchen but went to her hutch, opened one of the glass cabinet doors at the top, and grabbed the unopened bottle of wine that she had left from when she had purged most of the other bottles of alcohol. A glass of wine now and then was not something to be concerned about; it was for once in a blue moon, to celebrate or to help her get some sleep. Tonight, it would hopefully make her feel like less of a passive victim. She avoided Mac's gaze as she filled a glass and knocked half of it back before she came back to the table and sat down, the letter and photos strewn in front of her.

By the time Marissa had finished her second glass, Nick Walker had appeared in her kitchen, led by Jacob. She took note of Mac removing the bottle before Walker had a chance to look around the room.

"Where is it?"

Marissa was grateful they were skipping pleasantries and small talk, at least.

Gesturing widely with her hands at the table in front of her, she didn't bother saying a word. Or moving any more than she already had.

He stepped beside her and leaned over the table, inspecting the photos, letter, and flower clippings they had organized.

Marissa leaned against the back of her chair and crossed her arms, staring past the table, lost in her thoughts. A year ago, this felt less complicated. She received photographs on an inconsistent basis, usually just in time to remind her that she was always being watched. But there wasn't any FBI security detail. In fact, there hadn't been anyone else in the loop until she had told Allie and her brother-in-law, Brian. And then Allie was gone. It hadn't been fair to drop such a bomb on Brian, though. It was the only reason Jared knew the truth now. How many other people knew? Her old precinct in Seattle, the ones who had treated her like she was crazy after, the local precinct in Port Townsend, and Sheriff Jackson.

And if she was honest with herself, she hadn't cared much about what happened to her back then. She hadn't been especially careful, although she was always looking over her shoulder. Marissa had worked so hard to keep herself numb, and now she missed that feeling. The last nine months had changed her in just about every way now. It wasn't just about her anymore. Mac may have been there in the beginning to keep her safe, but it was so much more now. And she had—*they* had—Kate to think about. Even though she had pushed Mel away, Madi was back and trying to build relationships with everyone she had previously left behind. So, to Marissa, where they were today compared to a year ago was almost comical: with the same stalker, *plus* criminal boss O'Rourke back out on the streets.

Laura Seaver was right. No matter how hard she'd worked on herself over the past year, *some things just never change.*

She glanced at her wineglass and twirled it between her fingers, wishing it wasn't empty. It had been about six months since she had had a full glass of wine, let alone two. She jumped at the sound of Walker's voice when he finally broke the silence.

"It's odd how he changes between 'I' and 'we.' I assume we got nothing on camera?" He looked up at Jacob and Mac, still ignoring Marissa. She was fine with it. Both men nodded at their superior, who groaned and clenched a fist. "How does this keep happening?"

Unfortunately, no one had an answer.

After a long moment of silence, he pulled out the chair to Marissa's right and sat down, folding his hands together on the table. "Alright. Let's bag all of this up and get it to evidence." He finally turned his attention to Marissa, his eyes lingering on the wineglass for a moment before meeting her eyes. "You have a meeting with Fryer tomorrow?"

Marissa nodded. "I do."

He sighed heavily, dropping his head momentarily. "Okay. I want *both* Mac and Agent Starr with you at all times." His eyes shot up to Mac, who nodded his head once. "And we should get someone to stay with your girl when you aren't here."

Marissa raised an eyebrow, surprised at what almost seemed like thoughtfulness. "One of the PT officers, she's a friend of mine. She usually stays with her when we can't be here," Marissa said.

"Another pair of eyes and trained with a gun can't hurt. The SP officer, Trotter ... he's actually applied to the academy. He's young. He's capable. I think it would be good for him."

Marissa shrugged a shoulder, although she was sure Ronnie would be less than thrilled. "I guess."

"I'm going to stay across the street tonight and probably for the foreseeable future until we figure this out."

Marissa instantly hated that but bit the bottom of her lip, so it wasn't obvious on her face. When she looked back up at Mac, he didn't look thrilled, though.

"What about the O'Rourke case?" Mac asked, putting a hand down on the table and leaning slightly toward his boss.

His superior's frown deepened, and he clenched and unclenched his fist. "Right," he said finally, sighing. "Well, I'll be over there tonight, and we'll figure something out moving forward. I know a safe house is out of the question."

Marissa tensed up at the word but remained quiet.

"But we needed to figure something else out. Because the security camera and eyes across the street and even eyes in the house haven't made a difference."

Marissa resisted the urge to yell *"Obviously!"* in his direction.

Instead, Laura's words burst into her mind: *You aren't any better off now than you were before I ended up here.*

She pushed back from the table, nodding her head at Walker before getting to her feet. "Okay. Well, if that's it..." She waited until he got back to his feet, taking the hint that she was absolutely kicking him out.

Walker rose but didn't make a move to leave the kitchen yet. "I want Agent Starr to stay here, though."

Marissa stared at the man before letting out a sigh of acquiescence. "I have a guest room I can set up for you." She turned to Jacob, who just silently nodded. "Do you have any preferences for pizza?"

He shook his head. "No, ma'am. Anything is fine." She wanted to *again* explain that he did not need to call her *ma'am*.

Looking back at Walker, she forced a smile to her face. "If there is nothing else..."

Now he took the hint to leave and stepped away from the table.

Now you don't even bother trying. You go through the motions, but you're not really here. Laura again, and she was right. Again.

"Wait," Marissa said suddenly, surprising even herself. Laura's words continued to stretch across her mind. *Some things just never change.* Not that she hadn't been doing anything to help herself, but Marissa felt like maybe she hadn't been proactive enough. Once the FBI got involved and Marissa had gone back to work, her own case had definitely been moved to the back burner. "Would it be possible to get copies of all the letters I've given to you tomorrow when we are in Seattle?"

Walker raised a curious eyebrow at her before looking over at Mac. Mac just shrugged his shoulders, just as confused. "We can make that happen. And we will figure this out."

Marissa stared at the table as he made what she was sure was an empty promise—good intentions or not.

The rest of the evening was uneventful. Marissa ordered pizza, Kate came down, and they all had dinner in the living room and watched television with Jacob. Marissa couldn't focus, her mind continuing to wander back to the letter. The photographs. Looking over at Kate, she found herself feeling beyond grateful that the teenager remained untouched by his threats. The kids could be seen in the background of pictures here and there, but they had never been a focus. At least there was some kind of comfort in the idea that the kids were off-limits.

Marissa paused. No, kids weren't off limits. There was a little girl out there who would never know her dad. She hadn't been a target, but Evelyn Disher was a victim, nonetheless.

As the movie came to an end, Mac turned the light on and got to his feet. Marissa stretched and also got to her feet, smiling at Kate. "Alright. It's nearly midnight. You need to get to bed; you have school in the morning."

Kate nodded and bounced off the couch. She gave Marissa a hug as she walked by. "Good night!"

Marissa double-checked that Jacob was set for the night. Sheets, pillows, and a blanket, since it was getting cold again, and she showed him what was now the new guest room, since Kate had taken over what had been the old guest room. Once Mac did his routine check of the downstairs and Ellie had gone out, he headed upstairs and met her in her bedroom.

She was sitting at the foot of the bed, the muscles in her arms screaming. She looked up as Mac came into the room and gave him a half-hearted smile. Things had gotten so much better since Mac had come back into her life. Everything felt a little lighter when he was around, and every time he looked at her, the butterflies in her stomach fluttered. But when Marissa closed her eyes, she saw the newly delivered picture of Mac flash across her mind again.

"What's wrong?"

His voice of concern brought her back to the present. "I can't keep doing this," she said, dropping back onto the mattress to look at the ceiling and avoid his eyes.

"Doing what?"

"Any of this. All of this. I don't want to do it anymore."

"Marissa." His tone was serious now. "It's going to be okay."

"No, it's not. And I really need everyone to stop telling me that it will be. It's not okay, and it won't be okay." She sat back up to see him leaning against the dresser in front of the foot of the bed.

Mac raised an eyebrow at her, folding his arms. "That's a little dramatic."

"If you want me to be dramatic, I can be fucking dramatic. I'm just being a realist. The FBI has been on the job for how long now, and absolutely nothing has improved?"

Mac just stared at her, expressionless. So she continued.

"The police can't do anything, the FBI can't do anything. I'm just done, Mac. I can't do *any of this* anymore." She gestured wildly with her hands.

Mac watched her for a long minute before he shook his head. "No," he said finally.

Now Marissa raised an eyebrow. "No, what?"

"I know what you're doing." He shifted his weight where he stood, his stance now firm. "I'm not going anywhere. I don't care if I'm a target."

Marissa refused to meet his gaze, defiant. "I could not live with myself if anything happened to you," she managed finally, her eyes locking on an invisible spot on the carpet.

"Nothing is going to happen to me. I am a trained agent of the FBI. I'm a sharpshooter. I'm not going to let anything happen to you. Or Kate. Or myself."

"You know, all those other men were pretty sure they were going to be fine, too. They are all dead, in case you're wondering."

"You can't push me away." He took another step toward her, now standing right in front of her. He put his hand on her chin and guided her gaze to meet his. "I love you. I'm not going anywhere."

She wasn't sure when the tears had begun, but they were trailing down her cheeks as she shook her head. "I love you, too. But I won't be able to live with myself if anything happens to you."

"And I won't be able to live with myself if something happens to you." Mac leaned down and kissed the tears on each cheek before he placed a third gentle kiss on her lips, only stopping enough to whisper in her ear. "I love you."

She didn't say it, but it was because he loved her that he was in danger in the first place.

Chapter 7

He was already in the room and sitting there, as always, staring down at his hands, which were cuffed to the table. Daniel Fryer looked a little more disheveled than usual, his hair and beard grown out and unkempt. He also looked tired. The circles under his eyes were more pronounced than the last time they had spoken, and his lips were together in a tight, thin line. Marissa turned away from the one-way window and, as she reached the door, she fixed her face to remove any evidence of a frown. She entered and took one of the empty chairs across the table from the serial killer. Mac took the other, while Jacob stood against the wall beside the one-sided mirror. His presence in the room wasn't a common thing, but it wasn't interesting enough for Fryer to comment.

He must have noticed Marissa's hesitation and shook his head. "Not my best look, I know." He studied her for a moment before raising an eyebrow. "You look a little rough yourself, detective." He acted as though Mac wasn't there, which had become the norm.

"It's been a very Monday-like Tuesday," she said, settling into her chair. As she looked up at him, Marissa noticed he was sporting a dark bruise just beneath his right eye, which disappeared behind the wild beard.

Fryer shrugged his shoulders and, seeing her notice the bruise, he let out a chuckle that sent a chill down Marissa's spine. "I'd say you should see the other guy, but there isn't much left to see."

Marissa did her best to shake off the uneasy feeling he was clearly trying to give her. He didn't plan on making it easy.

"How are things going? Still getting pictures in the mail?" His tone was serious despite the amused expression on his face.

"At this point, I don't feel like it's necessary to dignify that with an answer." She leaned back in her chair, already tired of being in this room. "Can we just get on with it?" Although she had every intention of dropping the copy of the most recent letter on the table, she didn't want to start there.

"Alright." He gave her a smug smile and shrugged again. "An answer for an answer. Last time you were here, I asked you what you were going to do now. Do you know yet?"

Marissa held back a groan. "Not yet."

"Aren't you running out of time?" he asked with a grin that made her uncomfortable.

Marissa blinked. The letter she had just received talked about time being on his side. Nine months earlier, she had received the letter that had "granted her time." *Ben* had called it a gift. Marissa tried to keep her face as still as possible. "As I recall, there was no timeline given."

Fryer shrugged as though it was no big deal. "I wouldn't expect it to be more than a year. When did you receive that letter?"

"My birthday." There was a long pause before she clarified. "Christmas Eve."

"Then yeah, I'd say you're running out of time." He shook his head, his lips forming into a smirk. "A Christmas baby, huh?"

Marissa glared at him for a long moment, staring down his dark gray eyes. She shuddered as an icy chill ran through her. She was staring into nothingness: no expression, no thoughts, no soul sitting behind those eyes.

"Okay." She did her best not to show how unsettled she was. She was also pretty sure he was right. Marissa had done a pretty good job not thinking about it all this time. "You owe me a name."

"Becky Anderson," he said after a moment but didn't offer up more information. He just watched her, purposely drawing out the silence. "She was out camping near Ashford." He let out a contented sigh. "My turn."

Marissa grumbled and braced herself. She hated this game; the serial killer in the room had all the power, and it was absolute bullshit.

Fryer had a strange look on his face, one that made her feel even more uncomfortable than she already was.

A long moment passed before he shifted in his chair, leaning forward and clasping his hands together. "Tell me how you ended up on the Couples Killer Case."

Marissa's eyes widened, and her mouth opened and closed. Ellie remained lying down, but nudged Marissa's foot. She took a moment, adjusting in her seat as she regained her composure. "It was assigned to us."

"Why? What made you and Detective Tom Disher experienced enough, worthy enough, to take on a serial killer case?"

Marissa narrowed her eyes before she blinked and tapped the top of the table. The sound of Tom's name coming out of his mouth made her skin crawl. Mac must have sensed the disturbance because he stopped taking notes to glare at the man across the table, and beneath it, he gave Marissa's knee an encouraging squeeze before he picked up his pen again.

Swallowing down the bile rising in her throat, Marissa shook her head. "It was assigned before it was a serial killer case; it was just a homicide then. We were on it from the very beginning when Miranda Harris turned up dead—."

"Not her boyfriend?" Fryer raised an eyebrow.

Marissa shook her head. "No. His body was in someone else's district. We didn't put it together until we were looking through Ms. Harris's reports before her death." She paused, licking her lips, which had gone dry. "Why are we talking about this?"

Fryer watched her, the corners of his lips curling up into a cold smirk. "Because I think it's relevant."

Marissa huffed, kicking her foot out in frustration but keeping the rest of her body and her expression as still as possible. "Can you tell me why?"

"I could. But I don't think I will right now." That smug expression returned to his features, and Marissa wanted to slap it right back off. "How long did it take you to learn about the boyfriend?" He glanced over at Mac, still smirking as he said the word *boyfriend,* before looking back at Marissa.

Marissa frowned. She couldn't see how this was relevant, but the way he stared her down made her almost think he was trying to tell her something. "Maybe a day or two into the investigation? When we started looking into it, we immediately found the reports they had both made about the pictures. We had put an APB out for him, and the precinct that found him reached out because he matched the description."

"You mean he wasn't identified?" He was trying to lead her to a point.

Marissa huffed in irritation. "No. He was found with no ID or personal belongings. No one had reported him as missing yet."

"Interesting."

"How interesting can this be? *You* killed him."

"Now, now. I've already told you. *I* did not kill any of those couples. Was I an accomplice? Absolutely. Did I have a little fun? Definitely. But I didn't kill any of them."

"Then why is this even relevant?"

"I just think you need to pay attention to *all* of the details." He sighed heavily when it was clear she didn't understand what he was trying to tell her. "Your turn."

Marissa blinked. Whatever question she had planned on asking was no longer there. She wanted to keep following wherever he was trying to lead so she could figure out his point. Instead, she opened the folder Mac had put on the table when they'd entered the room. She pulled out the copy of her most recent letter and passed it across the table.

"I got this yesterday."

She watched his eyes light up and hated that she was offering him anything that he could take joy in. As he read it, Marissa looked over at Mac, who gave her a small smile. She could hear his voice in her head, insisting everything would be okay. She still didn't believe it. She then glanced over at Jacob, who acknowledged her with the smallest movement of his head before shifting his weight from one foot to the other. Looking to her other side, she saw her dog curled up beside her, still alert, her ears flicking back and forth.

Finally, Fryer let out a breath, pushing the letter back. "Well, that's new."

"What?" Marissa asked, not bothering to hide her confusion.

"He's letting his partner be on the page. It's only two sentences, but right there in the middle, when it changes from 'I' to 'we.' And then he goes back to 'I.'" Fryer let out a quiet but shrill whistle. "That's new for him." He shook his head. "I take it that other threat is O'Rourke?"

When Marissa looked surprised, he rolled his eyes.

"I may be in jail, but I can still get the news. I know your history; it was the case that took you from junior detective to the detective who gets put on serial killer cases." He let his eyes linger on Marissa long enough to make her shudder, and then he continued. "I would be very concerned about your timeline. Whatever his master plan is, it's coming up fast. I would say O'Rourke being out there might work a little bit to your advantage. He's less likely to do whatever he's going to do if there's any chance anyone else could take credit for it."

Marissa needed the focus off her. "Can you tell me more about Becky Anderson?"

Fryer gave her a disappointed look before he eventually answered. "Not much to say. I strangled her, drove her out toward Coville, and dumped her body in the woods." He leaned forward on his elbows. "What are you going to *do*, detective?"

Marissa glared at him as he stared back, still wearing that stupid, smug smirk. When she said nothing, he spoke again.

"Come on, Marissa, I'm rooting for you. I know you're smarter than this."

Marissa held her breath before she stood up suddenly, pushing the chair back. "I'm done. I can't do anymore today." She got a little enjoyment at the shock on his face.

"Already? We're just getting started." He didn't bother covering up his surprise and confusion. "You already rescheduled this visit. You can't just cut it short."

"I absolutely can. Maybe think about what you feel like sharing. I'm tired of the cat-and-mouse game, the guessing game. I'm just fucking tired."

The guard came over and got Fryer to his feet as Mac stood up beside her.

"I'm trying to lead you there, Marissa, but you have to follow me," he said, and she could've sworn he was frustrated with her. "It's right in front of your eyes."

"What is?" She stopped, waiting for an answer she was sure would never come.

"Everything. All the answers you're looking for are *right there*, Marissa. You haven't been listening."

She shook her head. "Now you're just speaking in riddles. This is getting me nowhere. If you can't give me a straight answer, why should I keep wasting my time?" Marissa nodded to the guard to wait a moment, ignoring his irritated grumbling.

The serial killer met her eyes and stared, releasing a long, drawn-out breath. "Because I've never lied to you. And I'm doing my best to get you there. Let me help you." She was beginning to lower herself back in the chair, preparing herself for round two with Fryer, when Walker swung the door open, motioning for the guard to take Fryer back to his jail cell. Marissa glared at Walker, but he just stared at her, seemingly clueless about why she was annoyed. She snatched the copy of the letter as Ellie stretched and got to her feet, and they exited the room, Mac following right behind her. Once the door was closed, Marissa let out a heavy breath and shook her head in frustration.

"Hey—," Mac started, but Walker interrupted as Clyde Bennet came over.

"I think that was a good call," Walker said, and Marissa couldn't help but roll her eyes.

"I need to go home." She held up her hand as Bennet went to say something. "I can't be here right now. I'm sorry."

Once they were back in the Mini Coop, Marissa with both hands on the steering wheel, Mac put a hand on her knee. "Are you okay?"

With unwanted tears in her eyes, she shook her head. She wasn't sad. She was angry. And tired. And overwhelmed. It had already been overwhelming, and they had crossed over to the point of no return. She couldn't breathe. "It's just all too much," she admitted, dropping her head as a sob escaped from her. Everything felt like it was closing in on her.

"Okay," Mac said gently, pulling her into his arms as best he could with the middle console of the car between them and holding her close. She cried into his chest, unable to hold it back. It wasn't even one particular feeling—it was all of them, all at once, weighing her down. She was trying her best not to suffocate, trying not to drown in everything.

After what felt like forever, she pulled back from the safety of his arms and straightened herself in her seat. The car's clock showed only about ten minutes had passed, but she felt like she had been crying for hours.

"I'm sorry," she said, wiping her face and taking in a deep breath, trying to regain her composure.

"You don't have anything to be sorry for. It's a lot. It's more than any one person should have to take on."

Marissa nodded and once again put both of her hands on the steering wheel.

"Do you want me to drive?" he asked gently, clearly already knowing the answer.

"No. It'll make me feel better," she said, giving herself a little confidence that the statement was true. She turned on the radio and cracked her window open, backing out of the small city parking lot.

It was still early enough that the two-and-a-half-hour drive would be within daylight, although as they got close to home, the sun had begun to set. She couldn't stop her brain from jumping through all the things actively happening in her life: stalker serial killer, criminal boss out for revenge, her mom dying, isolation from her family, a teenager taking refuge in her home, frequent conversations with her almost-killer. She couldn't begin to figure out how to compartmentalize anything; it was all important. It all required her attention, and she felt like she was going crazy.

Mac allowed the silence to sit over them, letting her play her music as loud as she needed without complaint. Even Mac was part of the overwhelm she realized, as she glanced over at him. He was too good for her. And she was going to get him killed. The thought brought fresh tears to her eyes, which she quickly wiped away before he noticed. Because he noticed everything. He was thoughtful and kind, and he loved her. He wouldn't allow her to push him away like everyone else had.

Along with the sadness and overwhelmed and frustrated feelings she was battling, there was anger boiling there, too. Rage, complete with impatience and indignation, kept rearing its ugly head. It was becoming harder and harder to tamper down. Marissa wasn't sure where it was coming from. Anger had never been her go-to. She always pushed her feelings down—or to the side—and moved on to the next. She wasn't a people person like Melanie, always trying to fix things for everyone else, but she cared more about what others thought than Madilyn, who would simply shrug with indifference and move on.

"What can I do?" Mac asked between songs.

Marissa let out a breath and lowered the music. "I don't know." She put her elbow against the window and rested her head against her fist. "I wish..." She hesitated. "I wish he would stop asking me what I'm going to do. I wish I didn't have to figure out what I need to do."

"One thing at a time." Mac tried to soothe her.

She shook her head. "But where am I even supposed to start? What fucking thing takes priority?"

"Marissa," Mac said her name gently, and she felt hot tears start falling down her cheeks again. "Breathe."

Marissa took a deep breath in and wiped her eyes, nodding her head. She opened her mouth to argue about why breathing wasn't going to help but just closed it again. Words were failing her. A ringing had started in her ears, and her head felt like it might explode.

Mac sighed heavily, and when Marissa glanced over, he looked like he was searching for words of his own. A beat or two passed between them before he finally spoke. "Something was different about today."

"I know, I'm sorry. I just—."

"No, that's not what I mean. I mean Fryer. His direction today was … odd."

Marissa wiped her eyes and nodded her head, swallowing the lump that had risen in her throat. "Was it, though? Because it feels like he's always running us around in circles."

"It was a little weird." He adjusted his seatbelt. "He was kind of obsessive about your first victim's boyfriend."

"He was…" she said slowly. That had been odd. And Fryer didn't ramble about useless information. She looked back to switch lanes, the basic motion of turning her neck sending an ache down her spine.

"What do you remember?"

Marissa paused, trying to think. "Not much, but we could probably call the precinct and get the files?"

"Agreed." He paused. "Tomorrow."

"Should we really wait?"

"Tomorrow, Marissa." His tone was serious, and Marissa couldn't help but smile slightly.

"Yeah. Okay," she agreed, although reluctantly. Surprisingly, Walker had made good on his promise, and she had copies of all the letters she had received. She had planned on pinning them up in her office and trying to find something she had missed, but she had the feeling that was also going to be left to tomorrow, too.

Letting out another sigh, she turned the music back up and tightened her hands on the steering wheel, focused on getting home. It took more effort than it should have.

When they got home, Mac ushered Marissa upstairs and into her bedroom. "Go soak in the tub for a little bit. Kate and I will make dinner. You need to relax."

"No, I need to—," she started, but Mac put a finger to her lips and shook his head.

"There is nothing that can't wait until tomorrow," he insisted. "You need to try to relax. Take a minute for you. Close your eyes and breathe."

"The sentiment is appreciated, but Mac, I can't just turn it off and relax. I—."

Again, he shook his head. "For tonight, you are fine. Nothing is going to be solved tonight. You need to just take a minute for yourself."

She went to argue, but couldn't. Maybe one hour wouldn't hurt. "Okay. But just for a little bit."

"I'll be right downstairs if you need anything."

He leaned down and kissed her, running his fingers through her hair. She leaned into him and into the kiss. He pulled back just enough to kiss her forehead and gave her waist a small squeeze before stepping out of the bedroom. Marissa lingered where she stood for a moment and watched him turn to head down the hallway and back down the stairs. Despite how tight her chest had felt all day, for a moment, it was a bit lighter.

She headed into the bathroom, and instead of turning on the light, she grabbed the lighter from the counter and lit the two candles on either side of her large, clawfoot tub. She knelt and started the hot water, plugged the drain, and grabbed the Epsom salt from beneath the cabinet, adding two generous handfuls to the tub.

Ellie came into the bathroom, tail wagging. "Hey girl," she said softly, taking the shepherd's head into her hands and then hugging the dog. With a sigh, Marissa got back to her feet and started pulling off her clothes, tossing them to the side. Once the tub was full, she turned off the water and slowly lowered herself into it.

A jolt shot through her, the water burning her skin as it covered her body. She took her time, letting her body adjust to the temperature until she was almost completely submerged. Ellie stretched out and made herself comfortable on the bathroom mat beside the tub. Marissa closed her eyes and just let the feeling of the hot water run over her. Her skin tingled, and she knew it was probably a little too hot for her to be sitting in, but she didn't care. Marissa let her head fall back against the back of the tub and tried to let the weight of the day wash off of her. But as the quiet sunk in, she heard Fryer's voice in her mind. *What are you going to do?* She had no answer, and as he had reminded her a few times that day, time was running out.

Chapter 8

The rest of the evening had been quiet. Marissa hadn't felt any more relaxed, but she did feel grateful that she had been given a minute to breathe. When she returned downstairs, Mac informed her Walker had dropped off the files from the Couples Killer case. Then they had a delicious dinner—because Mac didn't know how to make any other kind—and then they had gone to bed.

For the first four hours, she had slept like a rock. But around 3:30 a.m., she woke up in a cold sweat, panic overtaking her. Mac was right there with water and anti-anxiety meds, and he held her in his arms, giving her safety and comfort. And she had fallen back asleep. For another hour. After that, she woke up every hour, feeling restless. Marissa had reached the point where even the pills weren't helping sedate her.

After Mac got up, there was no hope of her getting additional rest, so she got up, too. She had only made it into a seated position by the time he had come back upstairs with coffee for her. He readied himself for his morning run, reminding her that Jacob was still in the house if she needed anything. Likely, one of the agents would already be waiting downstairs on the front porch to take a run with Mac.

When she finally managed to slink out of bed and get to her feet, Marissa found herself in her office. She took the evidence bag they had received from Walker the night before and started sorting things.

Marissa took a step back from the wall that she had pinned the letters to. She had removed the candid pictures taken by Ben from the wall to make room. Leaning against her desk, she examined her work and considered for a moment how crazy she must have looked. She frowned. There was nothing consistent about any of the letters she had received. Nothing consistent about the flower clippings. Even the number of photographs per delivery varied. She bit her lower lip, reading each of them.

The first two were short ... simple. Not even letters, but warnings? Threats?

I'M STILL HERE.
I'LL BE SEEING YOU.

This was likely the man who had her in the warehouse.

The next letter... two paragraphs and a sentence.

MY LOVE.

Marissa shuddered. Despite the shift in tone, she was still pretty confident this was the same man.

The next letter, however, was addressed to *My Dearest Marissa.* This didn't feel like the same man. There was anger at her attempt to "play house," but mostly the letter was a taunt about the torture Brenna Thompson had endured. If Fryer was to be believed, this was the new partner.

The next letter was less of a letter to her and more of a plea for her attention. Even though he still had Brenna at this point, there was nothing new there.

The letter that followed saw the return of flower clippings, which in itself was an odd touch. But this one, also short and to the point, felt like the angriest.

I'M TRULY DISAPPOINTED. YOU SHOULD KNOW BETTER. WHAT DO YOU ACTUALLY KNOW ABOUT THE MAN YOU'RE LETTING SHARE YOUR BED?

This one felt like the man from the warehouse again. There was nothing to back that up, just a feeling deep in her gut. The way everything knotted up inside her when she read it. Each word felt infused with a sort of fury the other letters lacked.

After this letter, it had been quiet. Photographs still came. But no flowers, no letters. Until the one arrived that simply said *mistakes happen.* This was the new guy. This was the man who killed Brenna Thompson in Chicago.

And then, once again, it seemed like it had gone silent for a moment. But on the back of one of the photographs of her, the word *soon* had been written in bold, black handwriting. She wouldn't even have noticed if the picture hadn't fallen off the board and landed face down.

Now, the most recent letter felt ... disjointed. As Walker and then Fryer had both pointed out, the letter switched from "I" to "we" and back to "I" again.

"There's nothing here," she grumbled to herself, wanting to rip them right back off the wall. Instead, she folded her arms across her chest and continued staring at them. She had briefly considered pulling all the pictures out and trying to spread them out again, too, like she had during her manic episode all those months ago. But she had handed most of them over, and there were just too many of them. She did, however, have the newer batches, which offered fewer photos but had very specific subjects.

A photo of Marissa had the word *soon* on the back. Marissa took the newest photo of herself and turned it over, only to let out a breath of relief to see it was blank. She pinned the picture back to the board and stared at the three others, hesitating before she grabbed the photograph of the mystery brunette.

Flipping the picture over, she sucked in a breath. Handwritten on the back of the picture in bold, black ink were the words *Who do you save?* And below that, *The Stranger?*

Marissa pulled down the picture of Mac and the picture of Jared and flipped both over. *The Lover?* and *The Hero?*

Marissa put all three of them on the desk, still upside down and displaying the words on the backs. She felt frozen for a moment, before again pulling her own picture down and turning it around, searching for anything more to give her a clue. Was she supposed to make some kind of choice? What kind of fucking mind game was this? Hadn't she looked them over downstairs the night they arrived? Closing her eyes, she had to think. She thought she had checked the backs of them. Even if she hadn't, Mac or Walker would have, wouldn't they? Was she crazy?

"Mac!" she finally called out, stepping back from the desk to give him room to come into her very chaotic office. He appeared moments later, his expression concerned.

"What's wrong?"

She gestured her head toward the desk, words insufficient in the moment.

Mac followed her eyes and took a step into the room and toward the desk. He mouthed each phrase on the backs of the photos before he picked up each one, turning them over to see which photograph was which. *The Stranger,* the mysterious brunette they hadn't been able to identify yet. *The Lover* was the photo of Jared, taken from across the street. His hands were stuffed in his pockets, and he was looking out into the crowd in front of him, as though looking for someone. *The Hero* was the photograph of Mac. He was actually standing in front of Marissa in this photo, unknowingly blocking her from the view of the camera with his hand on her back. He was glancing back, as though he was looking for the danger that captured the photo, just from a different angle.

When he didn't say anything, Marissa shook her head. "I swear there was nothing written on those when we got them."

Mac put them back down on the desk just as she had placed them and looked at her in bewilderment, clearly trying to remember. Finally, he shook his head. "No, I don't think there was."

Marissa blinked, the hair on the back of her neck standing on edge. "What does that mean?"

When Mac didn't respond, Marissa answered her own question.

"It means that at some point yesterday, someone went into evidence and wrote on them." She picked up the closest photo and held it up to the wall of letters, specifically to the first one. "And the handwriting matches."

Mac looked between the two and slowly shook his head, puzzlement morphing into something close to fear that he quickly masked with his professional-but-concerned face.

"Or worse, someone came in and wrote on them while we were sleeping..."

At that, Mac met her eyes and shook his head with purpose. "No. No one came in last night."

Marissa gave him a half-hearted nod before putting the picture back down on the desk. She wasn't really sure she believed him; she was pretty sure there wasn't anywhere safe. It almost seemed more likely that someone snuck into the old house with two FBI agents and a homicide detective asleep inside than into the police precinct.

Glancing back at her wall where she had all the letters pinned up, Marissa let out a long sigh. "There's nothing here. No pattern, no consistency. I don't know what I was hoping to find putting them side by side."

Mac glanced back over at the letters and let out a sigh of his own. "We're going to figure this out."

His optimism at this point was just irritating. She knew he was trying his best, but right now, she didn't want another person suggesting that everything would be okay. The truth was, she had nothing in the way of evidence or anything to even suggest suspects. All she had was a bunch of unanswered questions. She turned her back to the letters and shoved her hands in her pockets, turning her full attention to Mac. He was staring at the words on the back of the pictures, an unreadable expression on his face.

"What's wrong?" She already knew, but honestly, what wasn't wrong at this point?

His eyes lingered a beat longer before he turned his attention back to her and forced a smile. "Nothing."

"Don't lie," she said gently. "I mean, everything is sort of wrong right now, but what is that face for?"

Mac frowned, taking a sideways glance at the pictures. "The names on the back of these ... I'm not a fan."

Marissa took several steps forward, stretching over the files and papers she had spread out on the floor until she was standing directly in front of him, craning her neck up to look at him.

"*I* didn't label them," she said, pushing up on her toes to give his lips a quick kiss. "So don't worry about it."

Mac smiled, leaning down to give her another, slightly longer kiss before he took another look around the room. "So, what is all of this?" He gestured to the disaster that covered her floor.

"This is everything I could find on the Miranda Harris case. And John Bolton. Before it became the Couples Killer case. When it was just two homicides within days of each other."

"You've been busy." He raised an eyebrow, looking over what she had done.

"Well, I messaged Cooper last night about it, and he faxed everything over this morning." She looked around the floor. "I was going to get to it." She took one long look around the room and shrugged. "I was a little distracted with these. I really thought if I put them all side by side, I'd find something."

"I mean, you did find something. These pictures didn't have messages on them two days ago when you received them." He took a look at the letters pinned to the wall before looking back down at their feet. "So everything desk level and higher is the stalking case?"

Marissa nodded. "Yep. And everything on the floor is Harris and Bolten." She grabbed her coffee off the desk, holding it with both hands, grateful for its warmth.

"You need a bigger office," he observed. "Or a better system."

"Na, the system works great." She smirked slightly, knowing the disorganization had to be driving him crazy.

"You're chaotic. You know that, right?"

"It's part of why you love me."

Mac laughed and shook his head. "No, I love you *despite* it." He took a step back, leaning against the door frame. "What exactly are you looking for?"

"Anything that stands out. Fryer said to pay attention to the details, so I want to look at it all over again. It's been just over three years, and I can't even remember the basics."

"Do you want help?" he offered.

"Not yet. But maybe later," she said, sinking down to the floor and crossing her legs to sit, coffee still in her hands. She winced as she adjusted her body, ignoring the ache. Papers were strewn around her, and with one hand, she started spreading them out.

Mac made a face and took a step toward her but shook his head, quickly giving her a smile and pushing off the door frame. "Alright. I'm going to get Kate to school, and when I come back, I'll make breakfast." He paused before leaving. "I love you."

"I love you too." She watched him head back out of the room and heard his footsteps rumble down the stairs. She had half-expected him to comment on her audible wince from pain but was grateful when he chose not to. If he tried to fix her every time something ached or throbbed, he would have no time left for anything else. She didn't deserve him; he was really a bright spot in the dark chaos that was her life.

Once he disappeared, she turned her attention to the files on the floor. She had spread everything out so she could see it all, and she started trying to grab things in order.

First was the first police report of the photographs delivered to Miranda Harris's house. There had been six pictures, all candid photos taken of Harris throughout her day without her knowledge. It had been taken down in a report, but nothing could really be done. There had been no clear threat. The following week, Miranda came in to make another report. This time, the police offered to have a patrol run by her home. The next report, a week later, included Miranda Harris's longtime boyfriend, John Bolten. They had been together for over twelve years, and in the eyes of some states, that would have qualified as a common-law marriage. However, Washington state was not one of those states that recognized common-law marriages. Once again, the report was filed, but no action was taken because no crime had been committed.

By the time this third report was taken, Miranda had been frantic. The notes in the report read: *Ms. Harris was belligerent and loud. She demanded some kind of action be taken. She was advised to get a security system. Said she already had one. She asked to speak with someone in charge. I told her she could get a phone call back. John Bolten, who accompanied her and is the subject of some of the photos, was very apologetic for her behavior and felt someone was playing a prank on them.*

Boy, were they wrong. Next, Marissa pulled over the police report of the John Doe. Harris lived in Queen Anne, but John Bolten was found north of Capitol Hill. He was listed as a John Doe, with no identifying items found with him. It was assumed to be a robbery gone wrong, despite the fact that he still wore an expensive gold watch on his wrist, which Miranda Harris had bought him. That watch was later used to ID him.

John had suffered a gunshot wound to the chest and bled out. A deli worker who had come out into the alley to dump garbage had found him lying face down. He immediately called the police to report it. There were cameras in the back alley, but they were just for appearances, and none of them were actually operating; that had been July 28.

Next was Marissa's own report. They had received a call that Ms. Harris had not been to work in two days, and her coworkers were concerned, considering the photos she had been receiving; that was August 1. Two officers were dispatched to do a wellness check.

Marissa and Tom had arrived within fifteen minutes of the patrol officer's call that they had discovered a dead body believed to be Miranda Harris. The officers walked them through the scene.

"The door was just open?" Tom asked as they stepped up onto the porch of the upper Queen Anne Hill home.

"Yes. I came up to knock, and that cracked the door open. I called out to anyone inside, announced my presence, and then my entrance. Marty stayed on the porch while I entered the home, and I saw Ms. Harris lying there. We immediately called it in and waited here on the porch." Officer Neil Holden was only a few years younger than Marissa, while Officer Marty Abbott was maybe a little older than Tom. Both men looked a little pale, and Holden was anxiously picking at his fingernails while he relayed the story to them.

Marissa moved over to the body, taking a long look around the room. Everything seemed like it was where it belonged. Nothing appeared to be out of place. Miranda Harris was sprawled across her living room floor, lying face down. Her hand was reaching out for something. Looking around, Marissa didn't see a cell phone anywhere. There were no signs of a struggle, just the woman on the floor, dried blood all around her head. This had been brutal. It had been personal, and it had been violent.

Tom came over, nudging her with his shoulder. "You good?"

Marissa had to shake off the unease. "Better than her," she said dryly, wanting nothing more than to be out of that house.

Marissa hadn't thought about that scene in a long time. Knowing what she did now, the fact that she had been held by the same hands that had committed that brutal crime made her sick. A cold sweat swept through her body, and she felt the bile rising up her throat. She stepped over the files scattered over the floor and hurried over to the bathroom, unable to stop the vomit. Ellie whined and sat in the doorway, seeming unsure of what she should do, letting out a few barks. Marissa sunk down on the floor, leaning against the bathtub and rubbing her face with her hands. She shuddered under the cold sweat and tried to focus on her breathing while her heart pounded hard enough against her chest; it felt like it would burst right through. Her hands had gone completely numb, pins and needles spreading through her arms. Pulling her knees close, she coughed, her throat now on fire. Ellie barked again before slinking into the bathroom and sat at Marissa's feet, resting her head on her knees.

A few moments later, Marissa heard Mac coming up the stairs. "Rissa?"

"In here," she answered, winded and out of breath.

Mac appeared in the doorway. "What's wrong? What can I do?"

Marissa took in a deep breath before shaking her head. "Panic attack."

He nodded and disappeared for a few minutes before returning with pills in his hand and the cup from her nightstand and kneeling next to her. She took the pills and forced them down with water, feeling them all the way down. Mac put his hand out and she took it, suddenly very aware that she was trembling. He led her out of the bathroom, down the hallway, and to their bedroom. Once she was on the bed and lying down, he sat on the bed next to her and stroked her hair.

"What happened?" he asked quietly.

She adjusted her legs slightly as Ellie jumped up and rested on top of them. She shrugged a shoulder, still shaking, her hands still pins and needles. "Just had a moment."

He watched her for a long minute before nodding. "Do you want to talk about it?"

She considered it for a moment. The walls between her own kidnapping and almost-death between the previous victims of the same men had collapsed, and it all came flooding in. But instead, she shook her head.

"I just need to sleep."

Chapter 9

"Marissa." Mac said her name gently and placed his hand on her hip. "Marissa, I need to talk to you."

Marissa forced her eyes open, realizing she had slept through most of the previous day. Mac had woken her up to eat, but the pills had left her in a haze. It only took a second now, though, to understand that while his tone was soft, there was something hard behind it. Blinking her eyes open, she was able to focus and saw the conflict in his eyes. He was pale. His body was tense.

"What's wrong?" Her thoughts immediately went to her mom. The worried expression made her heart pound against her chest twice as fast as it should have been, and a knot had formed in her stomach.

"I just got off the phone with Nick." His tone was still gentle but softer now. "It's Cooper."

It took Marissa's brain a moment to catch up to his words as she stared blankly back at him. She blinked, and a new physical sensation began to take over. The knot in her stomach grew tighter, and she shivered, suddenly cold all over. She waited, but Mac, who had dropped his gaze to the bed, clearly had news he didn't want to share. She knew exactly what was happening.

"When?" She could hear the blood pounding in her ears as she waited, her breathing growing shallow.

"They found him in his home this morning. Gunshot wound to the head. No sign of forced entry. Same newspaper clippings."

Marissa had straightened her posture while he had talked and had begun anxiously scratching at her arms. She had let her eyes wander over her bedroom as Mac spoke, unable to meet his sympathetic gaze. She widened her eyes, trying to force the tears back as she realized she would never see Cooper again. He hadn't been her lieutenant for a long time, but he had been as close to family as a member of a precinct unit could be.

Marissa didn't say anything at first; there was nothing to say. Her heart lodged itself in her throat. But then said, "We need to go. I need to see for myself."

"Marissa—."

"No, I need to see for myself," she repeated, shaking her head. "We need to go. I have to go." She got to her feet, ignoring how dizzy she felt. "If you want to stay, I understand. But I need to go."

Mac let out a sigh. "No, we'll go."

Marissa took a couple of steps before stopping. "Kate." It was still strange to have a teenager in the house. "Shit."

"She's at school." Mac paused to think. "We could have Jake go grab her?"

Marissa shook her head. "He's going to insist on coming with us."

Mac nodded his head in agreement. "Veronica?"

Again, Marissa shook her head. "She's out of town for a couple of days, visiting her brother."

"We could see if your sister wants to pick her up?" he suggested.

Her first thought was Mel, but then she realized he more likely meant Madi. She had played babysitter a few times now. "Yeah, I'll ask her."

She grabbed her phone and pulled up Madi on speed dial. She picked up on the second ring.

"Hello?"

"Hey! Madi, I need a huge favor."

She explained the situation and Madilyn agreed—zero complaints. No more explanation needed. She was grateful to have her sister back in the country. They had never been super close, but then they hadn't spent much time together as adults.

Three hours later, Mac was parking the SUV outside what had been John Cooper's home. Walker met them at the car, shaking his head. "You don't need to see this." He was looking at Mac, but he was talking to Marissa. "You shouldn't be here."

As far as she was concerned, Walker wasn't her boss. She saw Henry Ness, who was now chief of police and hardly ever spotted in the field. But when Cooper had been her lieutenant, Ness had been their captain. He gave her a small nod of his head, and Marissa took that as permission and pushed back Walker and Mac, leaving them behind to discuss whether their presence was appropriate or not. Ellie didn't hesitate, jumping from the car to Marissa's side.

John Cooper lived in the Magnolia district of Seattle. He had held on to the house after his divorce. It was a really nice house—and way above his pay grade. Marissa had visited a few times, but not in years.

Henry Ness was an older man, with a lean, naturally red face and white hair. It skipped going gray and had simply turned white, even before he'd made chief of police. He had been one of the bigger defenders of the Couples Killer being a single man, trusting the profile over her word and experience. The sight of him sent her into a quiet rage. Clenching her fist, she let it go as she and Ellie reached the steps.

"Ambrose." He said her name as though he were still her superior.

"Hey, chief," she said quietly, as she met him at the front door. "I didn't expect to see you here."

"Could have said the same about you. Especially since you're a target." He glanced at Mac and Walker, who were clearly arguing. "The FBI seems less than pleased."

She glanced back at them. "I needed to see for myself."

Ness just nodded his head, understanding. He turned and opened the door, leading her inside. She took one more glance back at Mac, who met her gaze, before she walked the rest of the way in. Following Ness through the first floor, which had an open floor plan, she moved around the CI teams, and as they entered the kitchen, she saw the medical examiner, who stopped as they neared and took a step back. "Did you need something else before we move him?"

Ness put his hand up and shook his head before shoving a hand into his pocket. "No, you're good."

The medical examiner, Beth Lightwater, a woman in her late fifties, nodded her head in understanding and gave Marissa a friendly smile. "Good to see you, detective. I wish it was under different circumstances." They had worked together plenty of times when Marissa was in homicide.

"Me too." She gave the woman a small smile, only briefly glancing down at the body that had once been her lieutenant. Marissa felt her stomach drop. Beth's assistant pulled the bag the rest of the way over John Cooper's face before they took the gurney through the house and toward the van.

Marissa felt sick. She hadn't felt well when she arrived, but … this was now something she wouldn't be able to unsee. Turning her attention to the table, and her face away from Chief Ness, she saw the newspaper clippings with all the Xs marked on them. Derek Murphy, John Cooper, and Zeke Douglass, the informant they used during the trial, all had giant red Xs on them.

"Douglass?" She looked over at Ness, who shrugged his shoulder, looking as confused as she felt.

"We haven't been able to locate him since this started. We assumed he went into hiding when O'Rourke was released."

Marissa frowned, turning back to the table. Her eyes drifted to the blood spatter that covered the oak dining room table. She let out a long sigh. Ellie whined and nudged her leg. Marissa scratched the shepherd's ear before looking back at the table.

The truth was Marissa wasn't sure what she was doing there. She had needed to see for herself, but now that she had, she was at a loss. It was like she had never left homicide. The bodies were just piling up. And they were getting closer and closer to home.

"He didn't show up for work last night, and after a couple of attempts to get him on the phone, they sent patrol over. Found the door wide open. No sign of O'Rourke anywhere," Ness said, filling the silence with a report like an old habit.

She noticed Mac and Walker had come inside the home, and both looked equally annoyed. She let out a sigh, certain she was not going to like whatever either of them had to say right now.

"This looks like trouble," Ness mumbled before the two FBI agents reached them.

"The hit list is getting smaller and smaller." Walker walked up, hands in his pockets, his chest slightly out as he stretched his neck. Marissa could only assume he was trying to make himself appear bigger, as Ness was at least a foot taller than him. "We just got word that officer Brett O'Brien was found dead in his home. It looks like he'd been there about three days."

Marissa felt her heart sink. Brett didn't even live in the Seattle area anymore. He had moved south, closer to Olympia, the capital of the state. So he likely had died right after the meeting they'd called after finding Derek Murphy.

"I wish you would consider a safe house," the senior agent said with a huff. At least he wasn't trying to push it again.

"Same scene?" She gestured to the table.

Walker nodded his head, rubbing the back of his neck. "Same scene. O'Rourke is getting around without being seen, despite the whole state looking for him."

Marissa held back a dry laugh. Law enforcement hadn't been living up to their expectations for a long while now, so this wasn't that surprising. This was a system she had believed in with all of her heart only a few years ago; it left her feeling incredibly sad. She shook her head. "He's probably got others doing his dirty work for him. That's what he used to do."

Mac nodded. "He prides himself on keeping his hands clean."

"The only reason we were able to get a conviction was because of Douglass. Without his testimony, he would have walked."

"Yeah, I remember," Ness responded, looking out over the open floor plan. "It's the no sign of forced entry in any of the crime scenes that has me baffled. Considering everything going on."

Marissa's eyes drifted back to the blood spatter. Her relationship with Cooper had been complicated, but he was the one who had made her a detective, both in rank and lessons learned. And now all that was left was his blood splattered across his table.

They had lingered at the crime scene and debated for almost another hour without making any plans or decisions. They had talked in circles. Even Ness had started coming around to the idea that a safe house was the way to go.

Marissa glanced over at Mac as they drove home, who kept his eyes on the road and held a thin frown on his face. She knew he was considering what the men had said about a safe house. Under normal circumstances, she would have considered it, too, but she couldn't. Not with her mom's health where it was.

"I hate everything," she announced, looking away from him and out the window.

Mac sighed but kept his eyes and hands on the wheel. "I know. I just don't know what the answer is."

"I don't either." She watched the trees fly by.

"He shouldn't have been let out in the first place," Mac mumbled, but Marissa turned at his words.

"Agreed," she huffed, adjusting in the passenger seat. Her immediate response was once again to apologize. Of course, they hadn't been the agents who'd lost him, and it hadn't been their decision to let him go on house arrest during his appeal. But the idea, which had started as a whisper, was now screaming through her mind. "Is this our fault?" she asked finally, her heart sinking even without an answer.

Now Mac turned to look at her for a moment before his eyes went back to the road. Reaching over, he took her hand and gave it a squeeze. And while the comfort of her hand in his made her want to relax, his silence said more. Their actions had led to the appeal, which led to the house arrest, which led to his escape. It definitely felt like it was their fault.

The rest of the car ride was silent. Marissa kept her eyes on the trees. A year ago, things felt impossible. She used to feel cornered and alone and completely hopeless. Since then, she no longer felt alone and had also gained hope. It was ... worse than feeling hopeless. Because there had been a time when everything felt like it was going to be okay. And now it no longer felt that way. She could feel it in the pit of her stomach.

Once they made it home, Marissa was relieved to find Madi at the table with Kate, helping her with homework. It was such a strange sight, so mundane and simple. It was reminiscent of when she and her sisters were younger and their mom would help them with homework at the same table, in the same dining room. Marissa had been good enough in school to get by, but Mel and Madi excelled academically. It was usually Marissa getting the help.

"Hey." Madi smiled and gave a small wave.

"Hey! How's it going?" She was grateful for how easily the smile came to her face, considering the scene they had just left.

"You okay?" Madi asked, raising an eyebrow.

Marissa shrugged her shoulder and sighed before glancing over at the schoolwork on the table. "Oh, math." She shuddered. "Math is the worst."

"You're dramatic. It's not the worst."

"Name a worse subject."

"English," Madi said with zero hesitation.

"Washington state history?" Kate offered with a pout.

Marissa nodded. "You win."

Mac came in behind them. "Math is the best." That statement garnered three dirty looks that caused him to raise his hands defensively. "Tough crowd."

Madi finished up with Kate and got to her feet as Mac sat down. Marissa leaned down and kissed his cheek before turning to walk Madi out.

"Thanks so much, Madi." Kate gave her a big smile before turning back to Mac and the homework at hand.

"Anytime, kiddo." She grinned and waved before leaving the kitchen with Marissa.

"Seriously, you good?" Madilyn asked as they stepped onto the porch.

Marissa exhaled and shook her head. "Not really, but it is what it is."

"I'm sorry," Madi said, running her hand through her hair to pull her ponytail over her shoulder. "And for what it's worth, you've got a great kid in there. I know you've got a lot going on, but for both her and for *you,* I hope you can find a way to have her stay."

Marissa resisted the urge to sigh again. In a perfect world, she would have just kept Kate with her. In a perfect world, there wouldn't be stalkers and serial killers constantly revolving around her.

In all actuality, in a perfect world, Kate's sister would still be alive, and her mom wouldn't be in jail for one count of murder in the second degree and looking at a life sentence. At least she would get the option of parole in ten years. The lawyer had tried so hard to get the charge reduced to manslaughter, but considering she had shown up at Matthew Leland's door with a shotgun, arguing it wasn't premeditated had been hard. But she had only been there for a confession. What had come after had been considered out of her control, a mother drawn to the violence in response to learning exactly what had happened to her oldest child. The judge had felt the possibility of parole after ten years was the fair compromise.

"I would love that," Marissa said finally, shoving her hands into the pockets of her sweatpants. "We'll just have to wait something out and see. I really do appreciate you grabbing her from school and helping her out."

Madi nodded. "Anytime." She gave her a smile and started heading down the steps, stopping before she hit the bottom and turning back to Marissa. "You've got Mom's next appointment, right? End of the week, one o'clock."

"Of course." Marissa nodded. At least this way she'd get to see her mom. It felt like it had been at least a couple of weeks at this point.

"Okay, cool." She grinned and bounced off the step, heading back toward her car. "Have a good week, Sis."

"You too."

She watched Madi pull out of the driveway and wave and waited as the car disappeared down the street. She wrapped her arms around herself and glanced around, certain someone was watching her from somewhere. She could feel it now, rather than just letting paranoia create things in her mind. Shuddering, she turned and went back inside, closing and locking the door behind her.

Chapter 10

The next day started off uneventful. It had been a restless sleep, but it was at least free of night-mares. Kate had gotten off to school, Mac had gone for his run, and Marissa had her coffee between her hands and was once again staring at the mess that was her office. She had definitely reached a new level of crazy. Photos tacked to one wall, a board full of messy scribblings and more photos. On her other wall, she had a map of Seattle, Port Townsend, and anywhere else photos had been taken by the stalker. Or stalkers, since they were a team. After putting a lot of the older photos up against the newer ones, Marissa could actually tell the differ-ence between the photographers now.

And then there was the floor. It had started with Miranda Harris and John Bolten. But then Marissa had the rest of the victims' files faxed over to the station and Veronica had brought them over. The entirety of her floor was covered, except the empty circle in the middle where she was now standing to get a different angle. Her desk chair was pushed up against the desk, which was also littered with files from her own case. She had just taken her place on the floor again when she heard Mac coming back up the stairs.

He appeared in the doorway, his face pale and serious. Marissa frowned at him and waited for him to say something, but he just stood there; that was when she noticed the envelope in his hand. It was already open, and she could see a photo peeking out from the other side, beneath his pointer finger.

"You opened it," she said, an ache shooting through her back as she got to her feet.

"It was addressed to both of us," he answered quietly.

"What is it?" she asked when he didn't continue, standing awkwardly in the middle of the room.

He didn't answer but offered the envelope and photographs. Cautiously, she took them, letting her eyes linger on Mac's concerned face. Slowly, she handed Mac her coffee cup, and she started going through the pictures.

There were six photos, and as Marissa went through, she felt like the wind had been knocked out of her, each photo taking more and more of her breath away. They weren't photographs of her or

Mac, but photographs of O'Rourke, standing off somewhere, *watching them*. Every picture was a photograph of Johnny O'Rourke, standing within range of Marissa and Mac. Two outside Cooper's house, two outside the precinct in Seattle, one outside Derek Murphy's home, and one by the ferry in Port Townsend.

"Fuck," she groaned, meeting Mac's eyes. She went to say something when his phone rang in his pocket. He looked at the screen and frowned before answering.

"Agent Mackenzie," he answered, dropping his eyes to the mess on Marissa's office floor before looking out the window. He was avoiding her gaze.

Marissa knew he was on the phone with Walker. She didn't bother trying to listen and looked around her office instead. It was beginning to overwhelm her, and none of it mattered because she was now holding evidence that O'Rourke was nearby, produced and given to her by her serial killer stalker. She took a deep breath and exhaled slowly, wrapping her arms around herself and clinging to the photographs still in her hand. Ellie was curled up by the door on a dog bed in a clear corner, watching her closely.

Mac hung up the phone and let out a sigh of his own. "Nick is on his way here. He also received the photos. We're out of options."

She immediately started shaking her head. "I can't go into a safe house. I can't disappear."

"Marissa, we put everyone in danger by being here. We are exposing them every time we are with any of them."

The worst part of it all was she *knew* it was the right thing to do. But she would be leaving everyone behind, and they wouldn't know why. Her mom wouldn't understand. Her sisters definitely wouldn't understand. And then there was Kate. "What about Kate?"

"She comes with us," Mac said without hesitation.

"But my mom..." She hadn't given her tears permission to form, but they were falling down her cheeks, anyway.

Mac took one large step forward, gracefully avoiding the mess on her floor, and wrapped her in his arms. "I know. But we have to. We have until they get here to pack everything, and then we have to leave. We can't tell anyone."

"Fuck," she snapped, taking a step back from him. She wanted the comfort of his arms, but the anger made her move back. Marissa looked around the room. They needed to get all of this packed up. She met his gaze. "We need to get Kate from school."

He nodded. "We can have Jacob go grab her?"

She nodded. "Someone needs to take care of Wicket." She realized she was shaking.

"We can probably fill Jackson in, so he doesn't think this has anything to do with the other." He was referring to her stalker.

She just nodded, her anger and frustration ready to explode.

"Okay, I'm going to have Jake go grab Kate." He paused before he moved. "I know it doesn't feel like it, Marissa, but this is for the best."

She again just nodded, not trusting herself to speak. Mac disappeared downstairs, where Jacob was waiting. Marissa stared at her phone on the desk, thinking maybe if she texted people really fast, if she could give them some kind of information, they wouldn't just assume the worst. Because, based on her recent experiences, people would definitely think the worst.

She grabbed her phone and opened her contacts just as Mac reappeared.

"Marissa, you can't." He held out a hand, waiting for her phone.

Grumbling, Marissa handed it over. "This is bullshit."

Before Mac could respond, her phone rang in his hand. They both looked at the screen; it was Jackson.

Mac clicked the button and answered. "Hey, Jackson." He met Marissa's eyes, clearly not trusting her to get on the phone without explaining more than she should have. And in his defense, he was probably right.

"Yeah," Mac nodded his head. "We're packing. Walker is on his way."

Marissa frowned, now confused.

"We'll see you in a few." He hung up the phone and put it in his back pocket, sighing. "Jackson also got them. He's on his way to help get things situated."

That was a momentary relief. At least someone would know she wasn't just bailing. She let out a heavy breath and shook her head. "My mom isn't going to understand. My sisters *really* aren't going to understand."

"I'm so sorry, Marissa. But this is it. There are no other choices." He stepped forward and pulled her into another hug. She resisted at first, but after a breath, she leaned into him and wrapped her arms around him. "They know you were part of that case. They'll put it together. Your mom will understand. So will Madi."

If Marissa hadn't been so upset, she would have snorted at the exclusion of Melanie's name when he spoke of understanding. But the idea of leaving just felt wrong.

By the time Walker arrived, Jackson was there, and Jacob was already back with Kate. Marissa had managed to get all of her files into a large duffle bag before she bothered packing her clothes. They had packed up just the necessities and were currently discussing the cat, which Kate insisted come with them.

Meredith Parker had been called and informed of the situation with just enough information so that she knew this wasn't a kidnapping. Even if Kate went with Meredith now, she could still be a target based on her relationship with Marissa and Mac.

Alongside Walker was the Seattle chief of police, Henry Ness. They all lingered in the living room, packed bags sitting by the door.

"It's time for a safe house. For all of you." Walker shot a look at the chief of police, as though in a challenge. Ness didn't look excited to be there either. Marissa expected him to argue. She needed him to.

Instead, he let out a heavy sigh and dropped his head. "Yeah."

Apparently, he had received his own photographs from Ben. Marissa's stalker had been busy, feeling it was his job to let everyone know that O'Rourke was lingering, watching and unnoticed.

Marissa looked between all the men, stopping on Mac, who was doing his best to avoid her eyes. "I can't disappear right now. My mom has cancer. She needs me." She couldn't help but plead with them, despite knowing there wasn't any point.

"You aren't going to be much help if you're dead." She could tell this was Walker trying to be gentle, but Marissa still wanted to hit him. When she didn't say anything, he continued. "We've got two different locations, one for you and one for Ness's family. But we need to go. Now."

Marissa looked over at Mac, but he was still avoiding her gaze. There was no discussion to be had; this was happening, whether she liked it or not. Whether she agreed or not. And she knew, based on the pictures she had received this morning, it was the right thing to do.

"Okay." It was all she could say as she grabbed the two bags she had packed, one for herself and one for Ellie, and her bag full of evidence and files from her office.

"We have to take Wicket," Marissa heard Kate argue again as they were being ushered out of the house.

Walker began to refuse, but Mac stepped in front of him and picked up the cat. "Absolutely. Go grab her food. We'll pick up a litter box and litter on the way out."

Kate nodded, disappearing into the kitchen and returning a minute later.

Marissa followed everyone outside and into an SUV. She looked back at the house before turning to Jackson. "I know you can't say anything at all, but please take care of my mom. And my sisters."

"Of course," he said in an unnaturally soothing tone. It only made her feel more anxious.

"I was supposed to take her to her appointment on Friday," she said, defeated. Jackson didn't respond. There was nothing to say. They had to disappear.

They had been in the car for hours. Mac was sitting up front next to Walker while Marissa sat in the back with Kate. Jacob was in the car behind them with another agent. Ness had gone in a different SUV and had retrieved his family before heading to wherever they were going. Ellie was curled up at Marissa's feet on the SUV's floor, and while Wicket had been in the cat carrier for the first few hours, Kate had pulled her out and held the large cat against her chest. Wicket seemed a little less excited, but mostly relaxed in Kate's arms. She wished she knew what was running through Kate's mind. It had taken Kate less than five minutes to get all her necessities together, and the only thing she was truly concerned about was Wicket. She was silent in the car before she drifted off to sleep. Marissa couldn't stop thinking how she should have just sent her with Ms. Parker into a safer environment and maybe even a permanent home. This wasn't fair to Kate, even if it was what she thought she wanted right now. It wasn't fair.

Marissa stared out the window, watching the trees fly by until she couldn't keep her eyes open anymore. Her mind couldn't stop wandering to her mom, her sisters, and everything she was leaving behind.

She woke with a start when the SUV came to a sudden stop. Opening her eyes, she found it was dark outside, but she could see they were still surrounded by trees.

"We're here," Walker announced, unbuckling his seatbelt.

"Where is here?" Marissa asked out loud, knowing she wouldn't actually get an answer.

"Your home away from home," he mused with a frown.

Marissa looked over to Kate, who had fallen asleep holding Wicket close. The long-haired cat was also asleep, purring in the teenager's arms.

Reaching over, she shook the girl gently. "Hey, hon, let's get Wicket back into the carrier. We're here."

Kate yawned and nodded her head, giving the cat a hug before getting her back into the carrier. Marissa opened the door and stepped down, and Ellie jumped down and stretched while Marissa grabbed her duffle bag of files. She looked up and tried to focus on the house in front of her; it was a plain-looking brick house that seemed very out of place in what appeared to be a forest.

"So Agent Starr and Agent LeBeau will stay with you. This is only temporary, and once we have O'Rourke in custody, we will come retrieve you." He held out his hand. "I'm going to need your phone."

Marissa resisted the urge to point out how getting O'Rourke into custody was working out so far and just nodded her head. "Great," she muttered, slamming the phone into his hand before walking to the house, letting Walker ramble and leaving Mac to listen. She couldn't be bothered.

A tall, thin man walked by her and headed to the door, unlocking it. He must have been Agent LeBeau; she hadn't seen him before. Despite being tall, he resembled a toothpick standing beside Jacob Starr, who looked more like a quarterback.

Marissa motioned for Kate to follow the two men inside and turned to watch Mac and Walker for a minute. They had pulled the rest of the bags out of the car and were in deep discussion about something. Marissa huffed under her breath and turned to go inside.

As they switched the lights on, she could see a mostly empty, contemporary home. She dropped the duffle bag on the floor and sighed.

Mac came in behind her with the rest of the bags and stopped right beside her. She glanced up, taking in just how much taller he actually was than her. Marissa wasn't short by any means, an average height, but FBI agents seemed to have a height requirement. The shortest one of them was Walker, who was only a couple of inches taller than Marissa.

"It's nice, at least?" he offered half-heartedly.

"How long do you think we'll have to be here?" She knew he didn't have the answer, but she needed to ask the words out loud.

"Hopefully not long," he said grimly, and Marissa felt like there had been a discussion pertaining to how long their stay would be and that the outlook didn't look great.

"Cool." She sighed.

Upon further exploration, there were two bedrooms, a pullout couch in the living room, and a recliner. As they settled in for the evening, Agent LeBeau was given a shopping list for things they needed and then disappeared. Marissa felt like the nearest store was probably an hour away. It felt like they were in the middle of nowhere. She regretted falling asleep during the drive.

It was a nice house, though. Plain, open with not enough windows. Exactly what you would look for in a safe house. After throwing her duffle bag of files into the closet of the bigger bedroom she and Mac had claimed, she plopped on the bed and just stared at the ceiling. Mac came into view and sat down on the bed beside her.

"You okay?"

"Not really," she said without much thought, only glancing at him before she looked back at the textured, ugly popcorn ceiling.

"Is there anything I can do?"

She knew he was just trying to be helpful, but she wanted to just pull the covers over her head and give up. She wanted a phone to call her mom and explain everything.

"No," she said instead, closing and rubbing her eyes.

"I know it doesn't feel like it, but it is going to be okay."

"Is it though?" she snapped, then released a frustrated sigh. "Sorry. I don't mean to snap."

Mac didn't deserve that; he didn't deserve any of it. If he had still been in DC, he wouldn't be trapped right now. Of course, if he had been in DC, the likelihood of a relationship ever forming and his appeal process being a thing was super low.

"It's okay. I get it." His voice was soft. "This is just temporary. Hopefully, we'll be back home in a few days," he said with zero conviction behind his words. He was as defeated as she was.

She watched him for a long moment as he looked around the room before his big brown eyes met hers again.

"What?" he asked, an almost anxious half-smile on his face.

"I love you," she said softly.

His expression relaxed, and he leaned down to give her a kiss, pulling away just slightly to say it back. "I love you too."

Chapter 11

Marissa walked into the room Kate had camped out in and knocked on the door gently to get the teenager's attention. Kate was sitting on the bed with her back against the wall, holding Wicket against her chest and petting her gently.

"Hey. You okay?" Marissa knew the answer already. Kate turned to look at Marissa, her expression completely defeated as she shrugged her shoulders.

With a heavy sigh, she sat down on the edge of the bed. "I'm really sorry, Kate. I should have sent you with Ms. Parker. I knew better, and I didn't do what was best for you—." She had started to ramble, which she hadn't planned on doing, but Kate let Wicket go and shook her head.

"No, I wanted to stay with you. I knew the risks."

Marissa looked at the teenager and held back a sigh. She knew that Kate understood better than she should have. She was so much more grown-up than she should have been. But even with as much as Kate knew, she still didn't understand all the risks. She understood the words, but there was no way for her to truly understand the full weight of those risks.

"You shouldn't have to deal with this. You should be going to school, getting a boyfriend, joining sports or clubs or something."

Kate raised an eyebrow at Marissa before shaking her head. "No. It's okay. Things have been way worse. I'm just a little tired." She paused. "The man on the news. He won't find us here, right?"

Marissa forced a smile and shook her head. "No. We're safe here. I promise."

Promises were something you weren't supposed to make as a detective. But in this moment, she wasn't promising as a detective. Whether or not it was actually true, Marissa had to believe it at that moment to say it to her.

Kate silently nodded and pulled the cat back into her arms. Wicked had been eager for attention throughout their conversation, continuously rubbing up against her, most likely unhappy with being removed from yet another home as well. Marissa dropped her eyes to the bed.

"My therapist suggested I write my feelings down in a journal," Marissa said suddenly. "I've been absolutely terrible about it, cause I'm not a writer." She met Kate's gaze. "Would that be something you would want to do with me? Help keep me accountable?"

The teenager perked up a bit. Marissa had figured phrasing it in a way that made it sound as though Kate could be helpful would garner her interest. "Sure!"

"Like, what we write can stay secret. But we can just have a journaling time that we do together."

"I would love that."

Now Marissa managed a genuine smile. "You're a really good kid, Kate. I'm glad you're here."

Marissa headed back out into the living room with Ellie on her heels, ready to go out one last time before bed. LeBeau had returned with pizza for everyone after being gone for nearly two hours. Apparently, the town was pretty far from the safe house. Everyone had now eaten and was settling in for the night. LeBeau was setting up the pullout couch while Jacob was already comfy in the recliner. LeBeau gave her a nod of acknowledgment while Jacob straightened up in his chair. "Hey, you doing okay?"

Marissa paused by the chair and gave him a shrug of her shoulders. "As okay as I'm going to be."

Jacob gave her a sympathetic smile. "It's not forever. We'll be out of here before you know it."

Marissa smiled back and nodded, heading to the covered outside area for Ellie. There was an eight-foot wooden fence with nothing else in sight. Just the cool wind, a lot of trees, and an open night sky. She waited for Ellie to finish and then locked the door. LeBeau was checking the windows in the kitchen and then came around behind her to make sure the door was locked. She held back a grumble; he was just doing his job.

As she walked into the room she shared with Mac, she couldn't help but smile at the sight of him. He was already in his gray tank shirt and gray sweats, sitting on the bed and trying to make the remote for the television work. There were batteries strewn across the bed, and it was clearly a process. He looked up from what he was doing and gave her a smile that she could see reflecting in his brown eyes. "Hey."

"Hey," she said, closing the door behind her. She felt heavy, weighed down by the situation they were in, but still, the butterflies fluttered in the pit of her stomach at the sight of him.

"How is Kate?" he asked, almost nervously. She couldn't blame him.

"She's okay. She'll be alright. She's a tough kid." Marissa plopped down on the bed, Ellie jumping up behind her and making herself comfortable in what would be Marissa's pillows.

"Good." Mac nodded before glancing back down at the remote and batteries and gathering them up. "This may be a lost cause tonight, but we can have LeBeau head to town and get some new batteries. Because these also appear to be dead."

Marissa sighed and dropped back on the bed, almost landing on Ellie, having forgotten she was there. The shepherd groaned and adjusted her head, but otherwise seemed unbothered. "What the fuck are we going to do?"

"What do you mean?" Mac said after a moment. He had gotten up and put the batteries and remote on the dresser before settling onto the bed and lying down beside her, head in his hand, leaning on his elbow. When she gave him a look, he sighed. "I mean specifically."

"Do you remember what O'Rourke was like before his arrest? Do you remember how long his rap sheet and body count were?" She closed her eyes and shook her head, feeling an ache pulse up and down her back.

"I do," Mac answered gently. "But we are literally in the middle of nowhere. We'll be fine."

Marissa groaned. She was really starting to hate the word *fine*. And then there was her stalker. What were the chances that he had followed them out there, that he knew where they were? She was certain they were high in elevation. However, she didn't know if she felt horrified or comforted by the fact that he had spotted O'Rourke following them. But if he had seen them, why hadn't the FBI? It made no sense. She decided to keep those thoughts to herself and rolled over to bury her face in Mac's chest. He wrapped his arms around her and kissed the top of her head.

The first couple of weeks were tough, but everyone started to fall into a routine. LeBeau would leave the house and get the things they needed when they needed things. The first couple of nights, Kate woke up panicked, having nightmares, but a settled routine seemed to help her. Kate started doing schoolwork through correspondence that LeBeau had picked up; the school believed that Kate was traveling. It kept Kate busy and gave her a sense of routine, which she seemed to find comfort in.

Marissa was still having nightmares and struggling to sleep through the nights. She would wake in a cold sweat, or crying, and Mac would hold her close until she fell back to sleep.

Marissa had cast her eyes in the direction of the duffle bag full of files several times, but the bag remained zipped up in the closet. She couldn't bring herself to look at them since they'd arrived at the house. She was sure that, somewhere in those files, there were answers. Answers she had missed. But she was so tired. Crime scenes were burned into her brain. When she thought about Miranda Harris, her mind flashed to the warehouse. A cold sweat overtook her.

One night, which felt like every other night over the past couple of weeks, Mac stepped into the room to find Marissa sitting on the bed, bag sitting in front of her, still zipped up.

"You finally going to open it?"

She jumped at the sound of his voice, lost in her thoughts, and immediately felt attacked. "I'll open it when I'm ready to open it," she snapped, her cheeks growing hot.

"Hey." Mac threw up his hands, a flash of surprise on his face. "That wasn't meant to be a shot, Marissa. It was a question."

Marissa stared at him for a long moment before dropping her eyes back down to the duffle bag. "And it was just an answer." She doubled down, feeling overwhelmed at that moment.

"All I meant was that you've been staring at that bag for days. Maybe if you go through it ... maybe you can finally get some goddamn sleep," he snapped back in a low rumble.

Marissa blinked. Part of her knew that there wasn't any malice in his words, but that part of her didn't respond to him. "If I want to open the bag, I'll open the fucking bag. If I want to fucking stare at it, I'll stare at it. Either way, it's not going to help me sleep at night."

Mac leaned against the dresser and folded his arms across his chest, staring at her for a long moment, breathing slowly. "What the fuck is your problem, Marissa?" he finally asked in a calm, collected voice. His easy demeanor only made her rage blaze hotter.

"My fucking problem is that we are in the middle of nowhere. I can't talk to my family. My mother is going through chemotherapy, and I'm supposed to be there! I'm supposed to be there for my sisters, and more importantly, I should be there for my mother. My problem is that there isn't one murderer stalking me—there is a fucking mobster out there, too. The fucking killer who has eluded the FBI for almost a year was able to find him, not one hundred yards away, watching us. How? Fucking *how*?" She threw her hands around to emphasize her words. "I can't sleep because all I see are dead bodies. All I fucking hear are the echoes of that warehouse. All those letters. All the threats. I'm. So. Fucking. Tired."

At that, Mac let out a slow, heavy sigh. "Marissa—."

"No. Do *not* stand there and tell me it's going to be *fine*. At least respect me enough to stop lying to my face. Because it's not fine. Nothing about this is fucking *fine*. It hasn't been fine for a long time, and there is no light at the end of the fucking tunnel."

Mac looked like she had slapped him in the face. The hurt that washed over his expression momentarily made her feel guilty. This wasn't his fault. She knew that, but she couldn't take the words back. He shook his head before he pushed off the dresser and left the room.

Marissa exhaled and felt a deserved punch of guilt. Running her hand over her face, she closed her eyes to stop the tears from falling.

She should have gone after him, but the house was far too small for that. They didn't need to put themselves on display for their other housemates. Instead, she tossed the bag to the floor and got off the bed, heading out of the bedroom.

Mac was sitting at the dining room table, working on a puzzle with Kate and Jacob, but LeBeau was perched on the couch, scrolling through the television channels. Mac briefly glanced up but dropped his eyes back down to the puzzle. Kate looked up and gave her a smile, bouncing contently in the chair she was sitting in. As they were settling in, Kate seemed to be handling it all the best. Jacob glanced at Mac before raising an eyebrow at Marissa and turning back to the puzzle.

Once she was sure they were focusing on the puzzle in front of them, she sat on the arm of the couch and looked at LeBeau, who was staring at her expectantly.

"I need to see my therapist," she said finally, quiet enough that only he could hear.

He shook his head, thankfully matching her volume. "That's not possible." When she just continued to stare at him, he threw up his hands. "It's literally not possible."

"Figure it out." She shrugged her shoulders. She didn't care how it happened, but it needed to happen. "Tell them I'm in crisis."

He looked her over, raising an eyebrow. "Are you in crisis?"

She paused, thinking about her answer for a moment before she let out a slow breath. "I'm about to be."

He stared at her for a moment before nodding his head and getting off the couch. "I'll be back," he said loud enough for everyone to hear, giving her one last look of irritation before heading out the front door.

Feeling accomplished, Marissa got back to her feet and headed back into the bedroom. She put the TV on and lay down on the bed. Ellie jumped up and stretched out beside her. She drifted off to sleep to the sounds of a *Law & Order* marathon.

Chapter 12

Two days later, Marissa was sitting in the middle of the bed with a new high-tech laptop on loan from the FBI, secured and untraceable. She was in the telehealth waiting room, thinking about the past couple of days. She and Mac hadn't continued fighting, but they also hadn't made up. He slept beside her, but with his back turned to her on the edge of his side.

And for what it was worth, she knew he was probably sleeping as much as she was. Which was little to not at all. She was still having nightmares and struggling to stay asleep. Not to mention, she was struggling just to fall asleep because nothing felt comfortable. Her body was flaring angrily.

She had known she was fixating on the bag, as though the answers were in there. But she also looked at it like the thing was just waiting to set off a trap.

The laptop in front of her dinged as Dr. Bailey came on to the screen. "Hi, Marissa. Can you hear me?"

Marissa nodded. "I can. Thank you so much for agreeing to see me on short notice and for meeting me this way."

Dr. Bailey shook her head. "Of course! I am so sorry that this is all happening right now." The FBI had to inform her of the situation because virtual telehealth appointments weren't something she normally offered through her practice. "Tell me how you're feeling."

Marissa paused. She wasn't even sure if she could put her feelings into words. "I'm ... overwhelmed. I'm scared. I'm anxious, and I'm angry." She was somewhat impressed that she'd been able to label any of it. "I'm also just so exhausted."

"You look tired," Dr. Bailey replied gently. "Are you getting any sleep?"

Marissa shrugged her shoulders.

Dr. Bailey knew her well enough that she didn't need a verbal response to her first question. "Is it the physical stuff or is it the mental stuff keeping you up?"

"Probably both," she admitted. "And it's made me irritable." She huffed.

Dr. Bailey nodded. "Then tell me about it."

This was why she had set up this meeting. She knew she needed this part; she just didn't want to dive in. "Mac and I got into a fight a few days ago. We haven't really talked since. Which is hard because we're all sharing smallish spaces."

"What was the fight about?"

Again, Marissa shrugged a shoulder. "It really wasn't about anything at all." She sighed. "I was just snappy and defensive."

"Can you tell me a little more?" Dr. Bailey pushed.

"I have all my files of the case—the stupid Couples Killers case, my case—all shoved in this duffle bag from home. I've been staring at it since we got here. The other day, he asked if I was going to open it. And I sort of … just went off on him. And we sort of just argued." She shook her head. "So it really wasn't about anything."

At that, Dr. Bailey nodded. "I see." Marissa could tell she was writing something. "So, just an escalation from exhaustion?"

Marissa nodded.

"I imagine Mac must be exhausted, too," she said. "I imagine that if you aren't sleeping, he's probably not sleeping either. Or at least not well. I know he helps you when you wake up from nightmares. Has that been happening?"

Again, Marissa nodded.

"I can't even begin to imagine what you must be feeling right now. With everything that's going on at home, with your family, with your mom. And then forced to be somewhere you don't want to be, even if it is for your own protection. I'm sure it's bringing up a whole mess of feelings for you." She paused, letting out a small sigh.

"Yeah…" What more could Marissa say?

"It's not surprising that you're having trouble sleeping," Dr. Bailey noted. "And I imagine all this stress has sent your body into a bit of a flare?"

Marissa nodded.

Dr. Bailey gave her a gentle smile. "And I have to imagine it must be hard for him, too. There is no control. And from everything you've told me about him, he's a bit of a fixer. And this isn't a situation he can just fix. He's probably really frustrated and exhausted, too."

Now Marissa was feeling guilty, and it probably showed on her face.

Dr. Bailey shook her head, her smile never wavering. "It's completely expected. You guys are in tight quarters, the stress level is through the roof, and neither of you is sleeping well." She summed it up so easily in one sentence. "You just need to remember where you're both coming from. You know, with Mac, it's always meant from a genuine and good place."

Marissa nodded. "I know. I do. It's just—." She paused. "Really hard right now."

Dr. Bailey nodded understandingly. "I can't even imagine." She sighed sympathetically. "Talk to me. About whatever you want to. What you're feeling.

What you're having nightmares about? Anything you need to."

Her muscles felt rigid as she adjusted herself and the laptop on the bed to be a little more comfortable. Insisting on a session was probably the best decision she had made since they left home, or at least close to it. The journaling time with Kate was proving to be a positive exercise they did once a day, too.

"I did take your advice," she started. "I've been writing down my feelings in a journal. Kate is doing it with me."

"That is wonderful!" she exclaimed. "How is Kate doing?"

"She's really been amazing. She's so much more grown-up than she should be," Marissa paused, guilt seeping back in. "She shouldn't be stuck here. I should have arranged for her to go to another family."

"Don't do that. You need to stop holding all the guilt of the world on your shoulders." Her voice was firm but still kind. "There's nothing you can do about the situation now, so just make the most of it. Enjoy your time together."

This was why she needed to be able to have therapy sessions. She needed a reminder to try to stay grounded, and it needed to come from someone on the outside. They spent the next hour talking about all of Marissa's pent-up feelings and her reluctance even still to remain in the safe house.

They talked about things she could do to try to relax, some of which included making LeBeau go to town and shopping on her behalf. At least there was some amusement to be had there. Poor dude, just trying to do his job.

They also discussed Marissa's family: her fear of what everyone must be thinking without her there. Without so much as a word or a goodbye. The fear that her mom would die before they made it out of the stupid forest.

Before getting off the call, Dr. Bailey again reminded Marissa, "You need to be kind to yourself and those around you. Remember, you are all in this together, and everyone is likely feeling just as overwhelmed or as stressed as you are."

Marissa felt lighter as she closed the laptop. They agreed to meet again in two weeks unless there was a crisis or a need to do so sooner. The FBI had insisted that she limit sessions if she could, but it had definitely been needed. She exited the room, brought the laptop to Luke LeBeau, and then walked over to the kitchen, where Mac was busy prepping dinner.

"Hey," she said, her voice a little softer than she had intended.

Without turning around, Mac replied, "Hey." His hands were breading chicken. If she had to guess, it was a chicken parmesan night. Most nights they ate easy, cheap dinners because that was what they were provided. But after some persuading, and after LeBeau had tried Mac's cooking, he'd agreed to get ingredients for full dinners at least once or twice a week.

"I owe you an apology," she said, hopping up onto the counter of the little island in the middle of the kitchen. She grimaced as pain shot up the spine of her back and arched uncomfortably, trying to stretch it out. "There's no excuse for my behavior the other day. And I'm really sorry."

At that, Mac stopped what he was doing and turned to look at her. She hadn't noticed the bags beneath his eyes until now, the exhaustion worn plainly on his face. "I'm sorry too... It's all been a lot. I just wish you would let me in," he said softly. "You can yell and rant at me, but you won't let your walls down. You won't let me in."

"It's not my intention." She blinked, dropping her eyes. She hadn't thought of it that way. She hadn't given him enough credit to begin with. "I'm just so tired," she admitted, giving him a weak smile. "I know you're tired, too, though. And I know you're probably getting as much, or as little, sleep as I am."

Now Mac gave her a small smile. "I know it's hard to see right now, but we're going to get through this," he assured her. Taking a step forward, he kissed her forehead, careful not to touch her with his chicken-covered hands.

Chapter 13

This wasn't what he had signed up for. He was trading one serial killer for another. Only this one didn't like to get his hands dirty; he had other people do all the work. Then again, Ben was making him do all the work right now, too. So was there really a difference? How the fuck did he end up here?

It had all started innocently enough. He had just been watching. Then he'd taken pictures to save for later. It had all been a victimless crime. A year later, and now he was a murderer.

Even when Ben had pushed him to the limit, when he had killed Brenna Thompson, there had been the smallest spark of hope that he would get out of this alive. Now, it was clear, more than ever, that wasn't going to happen. If Ben didn't flip a switch and kill him, Johnny O'Rourke, the most recent person he had stalked and taken pictures of, would. Mob boss, human trafficker, drug king, pimp ... the list went on. And he had followed him around for a week and taken pictures of him following other people.

At one point, they had made eye contact. He had been lucky enough not to have the camera out at that moment, but the cold sense of dread that filled him when he was spotted was enough to make him want to toss the camera into the water and run. Of course, there was nowhere to go where Ben couldn't reach him. Thankfully, O'Rourke hadn't been aware of what he was doing—or wasn't concerned about it.

He had done his research. Which was probably a mistake. Anytime he look something up on Google, nine times out of ten, he end up regretting it. This was a common problem most people had. That rash is cancer, or that sore throat is probably cancer! Or, in this case, he found the very long, detailed rap sheet of the dangerous man he was being forced into tailing. Johnny O'Rourke had started out small; it wasn't like Seattle was a city full of crime bosses. But Johnny wasn't actually from Seattle. He came from a crime family in Miami, of all places, and when he made the move to Washington, for a minute, he went legit. But there wasn't very much money in legitimacy, and he was used to living a certain way. He was the most sought-after bookie, the kind who gave huge payouts and was willing to give you a little extra ... for something in return. He had reinforcers everywhere who did most of his dirty work and made sure the payments kept coming. But he was a greedy son of a bitch, and he always wanted more. He started selling drugs, gathering up prostitutes, chasing off their abusive pimps, and promising them more. That was when he dipped his toes into human trafficking. And there was a disturbing fetish for children out there, which paid double if not triple what he could get off anyone else.

Murder wasn't beneath him either, obviously. He had his enforcers do most of his work, but there had been a number of times he had taken some people out personally. He had also taken out two inmates while he was in jail, although he had claimed self-defense. No one was willing to argue, so he wasn't charged with anything.

The man was a fucking nightmare, the kind of man they used to make mobster movies about. If he had been in O'Rourke's shoes, he would have taken his money and gotten himself out of the country. Start over. He probably had enough to buy his own island. But he had taken his arrest very personally. He insisted that the FBI, the police, and lawyers had all fudged evidence to get him sent away because it made all of them "look good." Each one of them had gained recognition, and some had even been promoted from that arrest. And *that* was the reason the man was taking them all out, one by one.

It had been a few weeks since Marissa had gone to the safe house, but he had been keeping an eye on O'Rourke, under orders. Ben knew where the safe house was, but he was still in town, floating between Port Townsend and Seattle and keeping up appearances. Appearances were very important. Ben had asked him to keep tabs on the mob boss while he prepared for the endgame.

Jack didn't see much left for him after that. He needed to continue to make himself valuable to Ben. So he would continue to do whatever was asked of him, keep his head down, and not argue. Even if that meant following a dangerous man around town.

It was almost baffling just how invisible this man seemed to be to the authorities. He and Ben had discussed calling in tips to the cops, but Ben had determined that O'Rourke gave them the space and time they needed to get things in order. Besides, Ben had it all under control.

Before she had been banished to the safe house, Marissa had begun digging deep into the photographs she had collected over the years. From the outside, she started to look paranoid. Ben thought this was a good thing, but Jack wasn't as sure. The closer she looked, the more likely she was to figure things out. She was a lot smarter than Ben gave her credit for.

The last year had been way more than Jack had bargained for. And what did he have to show for it? Another hotel room, the bathroom turned into a makeshift darkroom. He had some concerns and some anxiety. He had killed someone.

Grumbling to himself, Jack looked at the pictures he had taken of Caroline all those weeks ago. He should have never stepped foot back in Georgia, but he had told himself it was just for twelve hours. He had stopped by his storage unit to grab some things and then spent the rest of the day following Caroline around until it was time to hop on a plane.

She was the reason he was in this mess in the first place. If he hadn't spotted Marissa, and been reminded of Caroline, he could have been anywhere else in the world right now. By adding her into the mix, he had all but signed her death warrant.

They resembled each other enough that they could have been related. They were similar in personality, too, in some ways. He admired both women, for their looks, for their tenacity, and for their brokenness. Marissa used her damage like a shield, wearing it in the daylight and employing it to keep everyone at arm's length. Even with her FBI boyfriend, the walls were still standing. Caroline, on the other hand, kept her brokenness hidden from the world. Sometimes it would peek out in moments of vulnerability, but those were few and far between. Maybe it was because he knew it was there; it had molded her into something truly beautiful.

Jack put the pictures down on the nightstand and got comfortable on the bed, leaning back against the wall. He couldn't do much of anything without word from Ben. He just had to wait.

Chapter 14

Any excitement Marissa might have felt about leaving the house was immediately squashed when she thought about where they were headed. They had spent a month just sitting in the safe house, twirling their thumbs, but when no one else could get Fryer to talk, here they were. At first, they had discussed a secure video chat, but Fryer had refused the idea.

Marissa's state of mind was not the best. Weeks of being surrounded by the same walls, unable to go anywhere or talk to anyone, had left her feeling defeated, as though everything was lost.

She had tried asking if someone could tell her about how her family was doing, but she may as well have been talking to herself. Marissa managed to stay awake for most of the drive, her objective to obtain an idea of where the safe house was located. It took nearly four hours to get to Seattle, and she could feel her heart rate pick up as the car parked in the precinct lot.

Marissa stepped into the precinct and felt her stomach drop. Everything looked the same, but the feeling was different. Everyone was working as though nothing had changed. As though these people hadn't attended Cooper's funeral a month ago. Marissa hadn't been allowed to make the trip out to Seattle since, as they had been in lockdown since it happened. She had seen Dr. Bailey twice via private online video chats. And yet, here they were once again because Walker couldn't get Fryer to talk. He wouldn't talk to anyone but Marissa.

She was less than excited by the idea of sitting across from Fryer again, but she was grateful to finally be out of the house. They had left Jacob back at the safe house with Kate and LeBeau. Kate was less than thrilled, but Jacob had challenged her to a game of Phase Ten, which they were likely still playing, and Kate was probably wiping the floor with both agents.

When Marissa and Mac arrived, before walking into the room, Marissa turned and put a hand on Mac's chest.

"I'm going to do this one alone."

He shook his head without hesitation. "No, I think that's a terrible idea."

"I think he may give me more if I'm in there alone."

"I have to agree with her, Agent Mackenzie," Walker chimed in.

Marissa had to resist the urge to shudder when he spoke. He had become her least favorite person in the last couple of weeks, and that was a hard spot to take considering she knew serial killers and murderers.

Mac shoved his hands in his pockets, looking between Walker and Marissa before nodding reluctantly. "I will be right here if you need me."

She gave him a half smile and leaned up on the tips of her toes to kiss his cheek before she took Ellie into the interview room.

"You look tired, detective." Fryer watched her, his gaze cold as he shifted back into his chair, despite his wrists being chained to the middle of the table.

Marissa huffed, her eyes drifting down to the table as she shook her shoulders. "It's been a long couple of weeks."

"Tell me more."

Marissa fought the urge to roll her eyes. She had to remind herself she was sitting across the table from a murderer. "I see we are back to formalities." She sidestepped his question, not wanting to dig into her life, which, unfortunately, was no longer private. It hadn't been for a long time.

"You seem more comfortable when we're being formal," he said plainly, as though the answer had been obvious. "Considering everything going on since our last conversation, I thought I would be considerate."

She had almost forgotten. Marissa sucked in a breath, forcing the words out. More flies with honey. "I appreciate that. I haven't been in a great head space." It wasn't a lie.

"Tell me, what's been going on?"

"Not a lot. We've been in a safe house for the last couple of weeks." She adjusted in her chair. "But you already know that."

The murderer across the table nodded his head. "I knew you were otherwise indisposed. They kept sending different agents in here." His lips curved into a smile, but there was no amusement in his eyes. "How does it feel, knowing your only approved field trip is to see me?"

"You could say that."

He sucked in a breath and shook his head at her. "How many of you does that leave for his hit list?" He leaned forward on the table once more.

Marissa's mouth felt dry. "Not many."

He shook his head again. "I have to say, detective, I've never met anyone who attracts danger like you do."

"What can I say? It's a talent," she said quietly, with a sigh.

"What's the date?"

The question caught her off guard. Raising her eyebrow, she instinctively looked toward the one-way glass. Finally, she met that icy gaze again and shrugged her shoulder. "I don't actually know."

A moment later, Walker's voice boomed through the intercom. "It's October twenty-sixth."

"You're running out of time," he said without missing a beat.

Marissa rubbed her temples and closed her eyes, leaning on her elbows. Sighing as heavily as she could, she shook her head without looking up. "We aren't here to talk about me—."

Fryer dropped his fists on the table, causing Marissa to jump back, startled. She straightened in her chair and pulled her hands into her lap. Ellie was on her feet, hackles up, but she glanced at Marissa, nudging her knee. Marissa's eyes were wide, her mouth dry.

When Fryer seemed certain that he had her full attention, he continued. "Maybe we should be." His voice was low, and he dropped his eyes to the table.

She let the silence between them drag out, half expecting the door to open. Leaving Mac on the other side of this interview may have actually worked. "Why do you care?"

The killer across from her tilted his head to the side, the wheels in his mind clearly turning as he carefully thought through every implication of his words. "Do not misjudge my motives," he answered finally. "I don't want him to win." He adjusted in his chair, letting his handcuffed hands fall into his lap. "You and I aren't friends, though I do prefer you to the rest of those sheep in uniforms. Your visits have become the highlights of my weeks. I respect you. I would be disappointed not to have these lovely, little sessions to look forward to. But ultimately, I don't want him to win."

Marissa blinked, processing his words. She swallowed the lump that had lodged itself in her throat and nodded her head. "Fair."

His answer had actually given her a strange sense of ease. The threat she had felt moments ago had washed away, and in its place now sat something close to relief.

"Tell me who he is." She said it as a statement, even though it was really a plea. A plea he ignored.

"You tell me, what kind of security do you have?" His tone and voice were even again. "Cameras in and outside the house, I assume? Surveillance next door or across the street? The guard dog. Plus, you've got your very own personal FBI bodyguards." He motioned toward the one-way window before leaning closer toward Marissa, lowering his voice. "How are all these envelopes getting past all of that?"

Marissa went to answer, but the truth was, she didn't know. He had asked her this before.

His voice grew even softer. "Even though I owe this man nothing, I can't come right out and tell you anything, Marissa. Why not?"

Marissa blinked. Her brain had jumpstarted and was now rapidly running. She met his eyes, those empty gray eyes, and finally understood what he had been trying to say. Suddenly, her last meeting with Internal Affairs Agent Sean Boswell flashed across her memory. The thought that had been plaguing the back of her mind leaped to the forefront.

"It's an inside job," she whispered, her eyes wide.

A ringing erupted in her ears, and she could feel her heart racing against her chest. She was going to throw up, and she wasn't surprised in the least when the door opened behind her.

Mac and Walker came into the room, and Mac tossed her a look of defeat, letting her know he'd tried to keep Walker out.

"This interview is over." Walker stood at the door, waiting for her to get up and leave the room.

"We just started—."

Walker held up his hand. "It's not up for discussion."

Marissa blinked at him once before turning back to Fryer. He was frowning at the two uninvited men, but then he met her eyes once more.

"Think about it, Marissa," he said quietly, as she got to her feet. "I have *never* lied to you."

Once they were on the other side of the door, Walker led them to the office he had been using and closed the door behind him. It had been Cooper's office.

"He is fucking with you," he said finally, standing behind the desk.

Marissa glared at him. "Is he? Because it would make a lot of fucking sense."

"Marissa, this is why we urge you to stay on track! He's trying to make you crazy."

She was pretty sure *they* were trying to make her crazy. Sucking in a breath, she shook her head. "What does he have to gain by lying to me?"

"He wants to drive you crazy. To make you suspicious. To play mind games because he needs some kind of entertainment."

Marissa stared at him for a long moment before turning to Mac, who was standing beside her. "And what do you think?"

It was maybe only half a second, but Marissa saw him hesitate. It was all she needed to feel vindicated. "I-I'm not sure."

Walker shot Mac a scowl that looked like the equivalent of scolding him, of using his full name, and promising they were going to talk in private later. Turning back to Marissa, he shook his head. "You didn't even get us a name this time."

"Are you fucking kidding me?" Marissa snapped, shaking her head in full disbelief and hitting the desk with both of her hands for emphasis. "First of all, we had *just* started when you pulled me out of there. Second—." She was vibrating with rage. "What about *my* fucking name? Why don't *I* matter? *He has the fucking answers.*"

Mac tried to put a hand on her arm, but she yanked it away.

"I agreed to sit across from a fucking monster who held me for days and took part in things I can't even say out loud. To help *you*. But I'm a fucking victim, too. And I deserve fucking answers, too. Because I'm still here." She hit the table again. "But I won't be if I can't get some actual help."

"We have provided you with as much help as you have allowed us to," Walker said quietly.

"Bullshit." She snorted at him. "What you have provided is not enough. I'm still getting photographs and letters, and you are no closer to figuring out who it is. Why is that? With all the fucking surveillance and manpower you have 'helping' us. So tell me, why shouldn't I consider what he's saying? Because honestly, it makes a lot of fucking sense."

She straightened and let go of the table, taking a step back. The silence that followed was heavy and uncomfortable, but luckily Marissa was too angry to feel it. Before Walker could spit out some kind of excuse, she continued, "I'm not going back to that fucking house."

"Detective Ambrose."

If fire could have shot forth from her eyes, there would have been nothing left of Senior Special Agent Nick Walker. "I am not going back to that house. I want Kate and the cat and our stuff picked up right *the fuck now*."

They locked eyes for a long moment before both Marissa and Walker looked to Mac, who threw his hands up and took an actual step away from them.

Ellie huffed softly, nudging her nose into the back of Marissa's knee as her heart rate rose.

"I'm not going back to that house," she said again firmly, folding her arms over her chest.

There was another long stare down before Walker relented just a little, letting out a breath and relaxing his own posture. Marissa took it as a win, whirled around on her heels, and stormed out of the office.

Mac stepped out with her and gently put a hand on her arm. "Give me a minute."

Marissa stopped and nodded. She watched Mac walk back into the office and close the door behind him. She leaned against an empty desk and looked back toward the closed office. Ellie sat down beside her feet, looking up at Marissa with her mouth open in a soft pant. Marissa reached down to scratch the shepherd's ear as she took a look around the precinct. Clyde Bennet was sitting across the room at a desk, watching her, with a few agents that Marissa recognized but couldn't name. Further down were the detectives and the officers, all functioning as though everything was fine.

The way Marissa felt made her certain nothing was going to be fine. In place of the sadness and regrets she had walked in with, she just felt angry. She watched everyone, unease spreading through her. She didn't know who to trust. The people she had been putting her trust in, her safety, might have been part of the problem. Might have been the whole problem. She shook her head, trying to shove her doubts down.

Thinking back to all her visits with Fryer, all the information he had given previously could be proven. As far as she knew, he hadn't ever lied to her. Everything he had ever told her that could be fact-checked had been.

She watched as the office door opened, and Nick motioned for Clyde. The door closed behind him.

Marissa desperately wanted her phone. She wanted to call her mom; it had been an entire month since she'd spoken to her. She couldn't imagine what her family was thinking.

Again, she looked around the room. She missed Cooper. Fuck, she missed Tom. She missed the normalcy and comfort she used to find in this place. This used to be the place she would go when she needed to escape her life. She could throw herself into her work and into cases and escape from what felt like overwhelming personal problems. Back then, it was her second divorce, avoiding family, debt, and student loans, and feeling lonely. It felt like a different lifetime. Like something she had watched go by on a screen.

The door finally opened, and the three men appeared. Mac walked over to her while Clyde Bennet went back to his desk, looking more annoyed than bored, and picked up the phone. Walker stood in the doorway, watching her and Mac.

"Come on. Let's go home."

"Like, home-home?" she asked without moving from the chair she was sitting in.

Mac nodded his head. "Home-home." He pulled out Marissa's phone from his pocket. She excitedly accepted it from him, jumping to her feet. "Jake is bringing Kate and Wicket and will meet us at the house. We also have a meeting set up with Agent Boswell from Internal Affairs."

Marissa nodded, anxiously waiting for her phone to turn on. She was less excited at the idea of having to meet with Sean Boswell, but maybe it would be enlightening. It would be interesting to see what he thought of what Fryer had said.

Mac took her by the arm and led her out to the parking lot, Clyde trailing behind them. As they reached his SUV, Clyde tossed Mac the keys. "I'm probably out here for the night, but I'll have Madi pick me up from the ferry and grab my car tomorrow."

Mac nodded. "Thanks, man."

Clyde paused, glancing at Marissa. "Call your sister."

Marissa blinked, an ice-cold lump dropping into the pit of her stomach. She went to ask him why, but Clyde simply nodded his head and turned back to the police precinct.

Marissa buckled her seatbelt and rolled down the window. Walls that weren't really there still felt like they had imploded on her. She had replayed the last several hours over and over again. Ellie curled up behind the driver's seat, able to keep Marissa in her view. Marissa pulled her phone out of her coat pocket and stared at it anxiously. She had no doubt that there would be hundreds of messages and voicemails. They had been at the forest house for a lot longer than Marissa had realized. How could it already be the end of October?

Glancing at Mac, Marissa could feel anger radiating off him. Suddenly, she felt a tear in her rage and worried that maybe he was angry with her.

"I'm sorry..." she started, but Mac reached over, took her hand, and gave it a squeeze.

He checked the road before pulling out of the parking lot and onto a one-way street. Once he started down the road, he glanced over at her with an encouraging smile.

"You have nothing to be sorry for," he assured her, and while he was completely genuine, Marissa had to fight to swallow the anxiety.

She nodded and looked back out the window, but kept hold of his hand. Her mind was racing through all the possibilities. The consequences of an inside job were a lot to consider. She had lost her faith in the system a while ago, but she knew Mac valued and believed in that same system.

And this possibility was probably not sitting well with him.

Closing her eyes, her head felt heavy. She didn't want to do this anymore.

As though he could hear her thoughts, Mac gave her hand another squeeze, hopping on to the freeway, making the decision to drive the whole way home rather than take the ferry. "We'll get things figured out," he said without taking his eyes off the road. "We will go back through all the files, and if there is anything to find, we'll find it."

She shook her head. "If it's an inside job, covering their tracks is going to be a given."

"But if it's an inside job, that explains an awful lot," he said, as though he was rolling the words around in his mouth. "They can cover their tracks are far as the provided information, but we can look for holes." He paused. "And I'll show you whatever I need to, as well."

"I trust you," she said without hesitation, but he shook his head.

"And I love you for that, but we're going to go through everything, my files, too. I want you to have zero doubts."

"I don't have doubts about you," she said, again with no hesitation. And it was foolish, but it was honest. He may have been the last person on Earth she felt like she could completely trust, who had her best interest at heart.

Finally, Marissa's phone started making noise as it lit up. She felt frozen as she watched the messages pour in, but before she could start looking through them, her phone was ringing in her hand. It was Madilyn.

Chapter 15

Marissa opened her phone and felt her heart catch in her throat. "Madi."

She heard her sister breathe out a sigh of relief. "Where the hell have you been? I've been trying to get a hold of you. For weeks!"

Marissa winced, closing her eyes, but didn't say anything.

Madi hissed on the other end of the line. "You weren't here, and I couldn't get a hold of you. I had to make a decision." She could hear her younger sister's voice crack. "Where are you?"

"I'm coming home. I'm so sorry, I couldn't have—." She started to explain but stopped herself. "What happened?"

"Things aren't going well…" Madilyn started before there was a long pause. "We moved her to palliative care."

"Palliative care?" Marissa blinked, repeating the words and suddenly glad she was already seated as she reached over to grab Mac's arm. He glanced over, meeting her eyes for a moment before returning his eyes to the road. Marissa watched his brow furrow.

"She was struggling really hard, Marissa. She was frantic and uncomfortable. Chemo isn't helping anymore. All the doctors we spoke to thought this was the best course of action."

"Okay." It was all she could manage.

"How soon can you get here?"

Marissa looked at the clock on the dashboard and felt her heart ache. Any answer wasn't soon enough. "Maybe an hour and a half?"

Once she hung up the phone, she looked over at Mac, opening and closing her mouth repeatedly, but there were no words. Mac gave her hand a squeeze and pushed the SUV over the speed limit.

Marissa smiled at the nurse behind the counter. "Hi, I'm looking for Marilyn Ambrose?"

The older woman gave her a kind smile back, pointing toward the right. "Room 6032, dear."

"Thank you."

She hesitated, looking in the direction the older woman had shown her. Marissa had spent the last several hours anxious to get there and now that she was only a few feet away, she suddenly wished she was anywhere else. Pushing off the counter, she forced herself to walk the rest of the way. The room was at the end of the hall, and the door was open. As she turned to walk in, she saw Melanie sitting in the chair under the television by the window. As she stepped further into the room, she saw her mom sleeping on the hospital bed in the middle of the room. Madilyn was sitting in a chair on their mom's other side, holding their mom's hand. Madi noticed Marissa first, and after giving their mom's hand a squeeze, she let go, got to her feet, and pulled Marissa into a tight embrace. Marissa hugged her back, unable to take her eyes off of their mom lying in the bed. She looked so frail. Her face had grown thin and pale. The lines on her forehead and around her eyes had deepened. Her jaw was slack as she breathed.

As she let go of Madi, Melanie had gotten to her feet. Turning to her baby sister, she felt her heart drop further. She stood there with her arms folded across her chest, her head hanging down. Taking a step forward, she pulled Melanie into a reluctant hug, resting her chin on the top of Mel's head.

"I'm glad you're here," Madi said softly, rubbing Marissa's arm.

"I'm sorry it took me so long." She let Mel go and again, her eyes landed on her mom. She looked at the machines on either side of the bed, both of them pumping some kind of meds into her mom's IVs.

"She's comfortable now," Madilyn said finally, following Marissa's gaze. "Like I said on the phone, she was struggling so much. We spoke with her doctor, the oncologist ... everyone who was a part of her team. They really believed that this was the right thing to do. And..."

"It's okay." Marissa's voice was softer than she had intended, and her mouth felt dry. She saw the bright band around her mom's wrist with bold black letters. DNR. Do not resuscitate.

"She has pain meds and meds that keep her comfortable because she was panicking, so she's pretty much just sleeping." Madilyn paused, lowering her voice. "Um, do you think it would be okay if I took Mel to go get some food? We'll come right back. I just don't think she's eaten in two days."

"Of course." Marissa nodded, looking between her sisters and forcing a smile. "Of course. Take your time. I'll be good here." She was confident about that, too, until she was suddenly in the room alone. Madi had asked if she had wanted anything while they were out, but Marissa had said no. She told her to make sure to stay out for a while. Get some fresh air. They both looked so drained, so exhausted.

She sat down in the chair beside her mother's bed, looking back up at the IVs and taking a moment to glance around the room. It was nice, but really white and sterile. There were some pictures on the table sitting up in frames Marissa recognized from Mel's house. Taking her mom's hand, the tears she had been holding back finally fell down her cheeks. Her mom could have just been resting, but her eyes kept wandering back to that DNR bracelet.

"How did we get here, Mom?" she asked softly, looking down at the dog lying at her feet. "We never had that lunch. We were supposed to have so much more time." Marissa closed her eyes. "I'm so sorry I was late getting here. If I had realized…" She shook her head. Because that wasn't true. Because of everything happening around her, she would have been late getting there no matter what. But three and a half months ago, they had been talking about five years. And now this was it. It wasn't fair. There was so much more she wanted to say, but the words wouldn't come. She couldn't say them out loud.

There was a soft knock at the door, and Marissa wiped her eyes and tried to smile. A petite older woman came into the room with a kind smile. "Hi there. I'm Natasha, one of her nurses. I'm just here to check on some of her vitals." She got behind the computer, glancing back over at Marissa. "You must be the oldest daughter."

"I'm Marissa," she confirmed, nodding before she got to her feet. "We can get out of your way." Marissa gestured to the dog, who also got to her feet, and then stepped back until her back was against the window. She watched the nurse check her mom's pulse and then read some of her IV bags. Natasha glanced over at Marissa, pausing what she was doing. "Do you have any questions that I can answer?"

Marissa looked down at her mom before shaking her head. "Not really. Not that I can think of."

Natasha nodded, giving Marissa a sympathetic smile. "This one is for her pain, to keep her comfortable. The one over there is to keep her calm," she explained. "She is much more comfortable than she was when they brought her in yesterday."

Marissa nodded, grateful for the information she couldn't seem to ask.

"Will she wake up?" She was surprised by the sound of her own voice, and she was sure she really didn't want the answer.

Natasha's big, brown eyes, full of understanding and sympathy, met hers. "It's hard to say because she has a lot of medications keeping her calm." She paused, watching Marissa for a moment. "We keep an eye on her breathing and on her medications. We only check her BP once a day. This part of the hospital is about making this as comfortable and easy as possible, although there is nothing easy about it."

Marissa dropped her head, silent tears falling to the floor. Ellie looked up at her, gently nudging her side, concerned. Marissa scratched her ear with one hand, using the other to hold her eyes, willing the tears to stop, but they wouldn't.

"I am so sorry about your mom," she heard Natasha start again. "It's never easy." She finished what she was doing before she went back to the computer and input some data before logging back out. "If you need anything or can think of any questions, just let me know. Her doctor will be making her final rounds for the evening soon."

Marissa nodded. "Thank you so much." She watched the woman leave, closing the door behind her.

She stepped forward and sat back down in the chair beside her mom, leaning back. Ellie followed and curled up at her feet, huffing loudly as she did. Marissa looked over at her mom sleeping beside her and just watched her breathe, trying to find the words, but none came. What she needed in this moment was for her mom to tell her everything was going to be okay, and she couldn't do that. She would never do that again.

Her sisters eventually returned and remained for another hour or so, sitting together in the room in silence. They may have been in the same physical space, but they might as well have been in different rooms.

It was almost midnight when Mel got to her feet. "I need to go home for a few hours. See my kids, the baby. My husband."

Madi also got to her feet. "Yeah, a few hours of sleep isn't a bad idea."

"I think I'm gonna stay," Marissa said without giving it much thought. She was afraid to leave the room, to be somewhere else if her mom passed. Not that she would say that out loud, especially to her sisters.

"Are you sure?" Madi asked, concerned.

Marissa forced a smile, nodding. "Yeah. I'm sure."

"Call if anything changes."

"Of course." Marissa got to her feet to give them hugs. She watched them leave and sat back down in the chair. Instead of leaning back again, she pulled her phone out and called Mac. He answered on the second ring.

"Hey."

"Hey," she said before she started crying quietly again. "I'm going to stay here tonight."

"Okay," he said softly. "Do you need anything?"

"No, I just wanted to let you know."

"Alright, but you know you can call me no matter what time it is if you need anything at all, right?"

"I know." She sniffled, watching her mom's breathing. "I love you."

"I love you too."

She hung up the phone and blinked back tears, leaning back into the chair and putting her phone down on the table beside her. She plugged it into the charger that one of her sisters left. Folding her arms across her chest, she just continued to watch her mom breathe, her eyes beginning to feel a little heavy.

Marissa was startled awake when there was another knock at the door, and someone she hadn't seen yet entered the room. Marissa straightened in the chair, rubbing her tired, burning eyes. She noticed color outside the window, cold and gray instead of the darkness of night. Morning had crept in while she had rested. The woman who had walked in was tall with kind eyes that watched her.

"Hello. You must be Marissa. My name is Dr. Lin." She came over and extended her hand.

Marissa reached out and took it, her mouth once again feeling dry. "Hi. Yes."

"Are there any questions that I can answer for you?"

Marissa thought back to the information Natasha had given her and shook her head. What she wanted to ask, she also didn't want to know.

Dr. Lin seemed to sense it anyway. "I've been doing this a long time, and while I can't give you a projected timeline, I would say that we're pretty close. I wouldn't be surprised if tomorrow was it."

Marissa felt her whole body tense, feeling as though the wind had been knocked out of her.

"She is significantly more comfortable than she was when they brought her up here. I hope you can find some comfort in that."

Marissa nodded her head.

Dr. Lin dug into her coat pockets until she found what she was looking for. She offered the small booklet to Marissa. "You might find this helpful." She paused. "You can talk to her; she can hear you."

Marissa looked at the booklet and the words *At the End of Life*, and, again, felt like she couldn't breathe. Swallowing, she forced herself to try to smile and spit out words. "Thank you."

She was grateful when Dr. Lin left the room, disappearing into the next patient's room and leaving Marissa alone once again with her mom. She flipped through the booklet but couldn't bring herself to read through it. Putting it down next to her phone, Marissa turned back to her mom.

There was so much to say, and yet, Marissa couldn't say any of it. She folded her arms across her chest and leaned back in the chair, taking a deep breath. Glancing down at Ellie, who was stretched out at her feet, already softly snoring. She looked back over at her mom and closed her eyes, hoping she could get some rest.

The next time Marissa opened her eyes, Greg was letting himself into the room. She rubbed her eyes and got to her feet, offering him a small hug.

"Sorry, I didn't mean to wake you," he said, running a hand through his hair.

Marissa shook her head. "It's okay. I needed to get up, anyway." Ellie stretched out behind her and came to stand beside her. Marissa turned to grab her phone and shoved it in her pocket. "Ellie needs to go out, and I'm going to run home. Shower, eat. I'll be back later."

Greg nodded. The once bright, kind man looked sullen and fatigued; it was hard to witness. Grabbing her coat, Marissa headed out the door and into the empty hall. She rubbed her eyes and pulled her phone from her pocket. She went to her contacts, but as she did, her phone began ringing in her hand.

"I was just about to call you." She couldn't stop the small smile that formed on her lips.

"I just wanted to call and check in. How are you doing?"

"I was hoping you'd come get me? I just want to take a shower and change and then come right back."

"I can do that. Give me fifteen minutes, tops."

"Thank you." She paused. "I love you."

"I love you, too."

After Mac hung up, Marissa hopped into the elevator. She just needed to eat and stand in the shower for a minute. And then she would be back.

She opened her texts, opened Madi's message, and started typing.

[Greg is here. I'm going to run home and shower. I'll be back in an hour or less.]

As the elevator opened, she looked up from her phone, and there was Jared, standing beside Brian. They both stopped the conversation they were having and looked at her.

Her brain froze, but she managed to step off the elevator. She blinked, and Brian stepped forward and pulled her into a hug. "Hey," he said softly.

When he pulled back, unwanted tears had begun to form in her eyes again. "Hey." She managed weakly, glancing at Jared. "Is Mel here?" She looked around behind them, expecting to see her little sister.

"No, not yet. She and Madi were getting breakfast first. We wanted to come up and see your mom while Kirstie has her appointment."

Marissa had to let the words repeat in her mind before she nodded slowly, remembering. "Right. Congratulations, by the way!" She turned to Jared, who was now a new father. "She is beautiful." It wasn't a lie. She thought back to the picture he had texted almost two months earlier before the safe house.

"Hey, why don't you head up and I'll be right there?" Jared shot a look to Brian, who nodded in response.

"I'll see you later," he said to her, giving her shoulder a squeeze before stepping onto the elevator.

Marissa smiled and nodded in return before turning back to Jared, who stood almost awkwardly in front of her. Once the elevator doors closed behind her, she wrapped an arm around herself and used her other hand to wipe the tears threatening to fall.

"I wasn't sure if we were going to see you. I know you were MIA."

Marissa couldn't stop herself from sighing. She knew eventually everyone was going to start asking questions about where she had been. Her sisters had been too depressed to be bothered with it right now. But the sigh was enough to give Jared pause.

Running his hand through his hair, he looked down at the floor. "I'm glad you made it back in time," he said slowly.

All she could do was nod. She was certain that if she opened her mouth and said something in response, she would start sobbing.

"If there is anything you need … or anything I can do…"

She forced herself to give him a smile, shaking her head. "There is nothing anyone can do," she said, swallowing. She shook her head, directing her eyes to her feet for a minute before looking back up at him. "How's it feel to be a dad?"

"Terrifying," he admitted with a small laugh. "I have no idea what I'm doing."

Marissa couldn't help but smile. "You're going to make an amazing dad. I have no doubts." She paused. "I'm really happy for you."

There was a long silence, a lot left unsaid between them. She had meant every word she said.

"You know I'm here for you, right?" he spoke softly, stepping forward until he was standing directly in front of her. She brought her eyes up to look at him, and before she could stop herself, she leaned into him and started to cry. He hesitated but put his arms around her. There was so much grief in that moment, it could have strangled her. Her mom was upstairs, waiting to die. There were no words to convey what she was feeling. She felt his chin rest on the top of her head, and she relaxed into him, closing her eyes. She felt his fingers stroke her hair and his chest heaving with each heavy breath he took. For a moment, she felt calm. A calmness and stillness she hadn't felt in a while.

Her phone had begun ringing in her pocket, and she nearly jumped out of her skin. Taking a step back, she wiped her eyes and pulled her phone out to see Mac's name. "My ride is here," she said before looking back up at Jared. He looked back at her, a mix of conflict and sadness in his eyes. "Sorry for crying all over your shirt."

He shook his head, a charming smile gracing his face. She knew it was forced, though. "You have nothing to apologize for. It's fine."

Marissa nodded. "Congratulations again, Jared." She tried to return his smile as she made a move past him. She paused for a second, as though waiting for him to say something, but then continued on her way through to the lobby and out the doors.

Mac was waiting in the SUV right outside the doors.

"Hey." He gave her a small smile, looking her over as she got into the passenger seat. Ellie sat at her feet instead of jumping into the back.

"Hey," she said softly, buckling her seatbelt. "Thank you for coming."

"Of course."

Chapter 16

Just a few hours later, Marissa was back in the hospital. Greg had left, and Madi and Mel were back in the room. Brian had come by again, this time with Preston in tow. Marissa was finally able to hold her nephew.

The day was quiet, aside from the bustle of nurses coming in and out. At one point, Melanie asked about her mom needing food. The doctor came in shortly after that, explaining that as the body starts shutting down, the need for food also stops. This information sent her baby sister into a spiral. Madi took her for a walk outside, insisting some fresh air would do her good. When Madilyn came back, she plopped herself in the chair beside Marissa. She still looked stunning, even with her puffy eyes and pale face.

"I can't believe we're here," Madi said softly.

"Yeah. Me neither," Marissa whispered back as Madi rested her head on Marissa's shoulder. At least they were there together. No one deserved to go through this alone.

Marissa glanced over at her sisters, Madilyn sitting at her mom's side once again, texting someone on her phone. Likely Clyde. Melanie, who was sitting in the chair by the window again, was playing a game on her phone, frowning. It was already dark outside again; the day had gone by so quickly. Marissa glanced up at the television. Another episode of *NCIS* started before she looked back over at her mother. She was breathing significantly better than she had been the night before when they were alone.

Leaning back in her chair, she thought about the mess of the last few months. She rubbed her face and closed her eyes. Marissa couldn't quiet her mind: Cooper's death, the hunt for O'Rourke, the conversation with Fryer. It was too much. She turned her eyes back up to the TV as the show returned from commercial. She needed to turn her brain off, put the case out of her mind. She needed to be present. But even sitting there in the room with her sisters and her mom, it didn't feel real. It felt like a bad dream—or a bad joke. She glanced over at Madilyn, who had looked up from her phone to watch their mom. Drawing in a deep breath, she looked back up at the TV, sank into her chair, and tried to get comfortable.

"I don't think she's breathing." Madilyn's voice was quiet, but her words hung in the room.

Marissa's heart caught in her throat as she leaned forward, frantically searching her mom for any sign of breath.

Melanie got up out of the chair and walked over to their mom's side. Marissa got to her feet, too, but took a step back. Madi, with one hand holding on to their mom's, put her other hand on her chest, and after what felt like an eternity, she looked up at both of them and shook her head. Mel grabbed the hospital phone by the bed and called for the nurse, taking their mom's other hand. Marissa realized she had taken another step back, bumping into the chair that Melanie had been sitting in. Ellie was at Marissa's side, eyes trained on her as she nudged Marissa's knee.

It was the longest moment of silence of Marissa's entire life. She could feel her body beginning to shake as pins and needles spread across her nerves. She could feel her heartbeat pounding throughout her body. Finally, a voice came through the phone.

"How can I help you?"

When Mel wasn't able to speak, Madi took the phone from her and, keeping her voice low, managed to say, "I don't think my mom is breathing."

It wasn't like any kind of hospital response Marissa was familiar with. After her time in the ICU, she expected beeping, alarms, a rush. But then she remembered her mom's band. Do not resuscitate. She remembered where they were. A nurse arrived, giving just a quick knock at the open door but not waiting for a response to come in. She came over to Madi, who let go of their mom's hand and took a step back to get out of the way. The nurse checked her pulse and waited a minute. Took out her stethoscope and held it to her chest. After another minute, she shook her head, making eye contact with Marissa.

"I don't hear anything. She's gone." She glanced over at Melanie and then at Madi before looking back at Marissa. "I have to go get another nurse to confirm it, but I'm so sorry for your loss. I will be right back."

Marissa didn't even see the nurse leave the room. The bile was rising in her throat when Melanie's open sobs brought her back into the room and to the moment. She stepped over and put her arms around her, pulling Mel into a hug as she looked at the body that had been their mom. She was gone, and Marissa couldn't breathe. By the time Madilyn had come over, Marissa felt like all the air had been sucked out of her lungs. Melanie had buried her head into Marissa's chest and was squeezing Marissa so tightly that she was sure it was the only thing keeping her on her feet. Marissa had one arm wrapped just as tightly around Mel, holding her close. She extended her other arm and Madilyn fell into her, burying her wet eyes into Marissa's shoulder.

Marissa watched as the second nurse came in and confirmed their mom was gone. Madilyn turned around and spoke with them. As the oldest, it should have been Marissa's job, but all she could hear was a ringing in her ears, her own erratic heartbeat, and Mel's softening sobs. She watched as Madi nodded and even thanked them as they left the room, closing the door behind them. She walked back over and leaned over their mother's body, kissing her forehead.

"We can have some time, however much we need," her sister said.

Marissa just nodded and felt herself wobble as Melanie let her go. She collapsed in the chair Marissa had been sitting in and took their mom's hand in hers.

Marissa watched them both, feeling like she should have been doing something. Saying goodbye. But her mom was already gone. The body lying in the bed wasn't her mom anymore. As the thought drifted across her mind, she again felt like the air had been knocked out of her. She felt dizzy. She grabbed hold of the chair Mel had been sitting in, the one furthest away from the hospital bed, and lowered herself into it. Ellie immediately rested her head on Marissa's lap, whining softly. She watched her sisters, wanting to will herself back to them, but she was frozen in that chair.

Instead, she pulled out her cell phone and made the call to Greg. After the second ring, she glanced at the time. It was almost 10:30 p.m. He answered on the third ring.

"Marissa?" His tone was panicked. When she released soft sobs instead of words, he said her name again. "Marissa." This time, the panic was gone, replaced with audible heartbreak.

"She's gone," Marissa finally got out over her own sobs. She tried to stay quiet, not wanting to disrupt the goodbyes her sisters were in the middle of, but the pain and grief forced their way out. "She's gone," she said again, unable to form any other words.

She heard him crying softly on the other end of the line. "I'm so sorry," she said to him as a sudden numbness began spreading through her.

Eventually, Greg managed a thank-you and said he would call her in the morning and that he was so sorry for her loss. When Marissa hung up, the words sat heavily against her. *Sorry for your loss.* She had heard it a few times in her life, but this was completely different.

Next, she went to call Mac, hitting the button and putting the phone to her ear. It rang for a long time. It wasn't until Jared's voice came through the other end that she realized she had selected the wrong name.

"Marissa?"

She blinked, glancing at her sisters, who barely seemed to notice her there, both crying. Mel's sobs were loud enough to be heard over the phone, she was sure.

"Jared." She said his name quietly, trying to get her mouth to connect to her brain again. "I'm sorry to call you but…" She glanced down at Ellie and rubbed the shepherd's ear, beginning to cry again.

"Hey, you don't have to apologize. Do you need me to call Brian?" he offered after a moment, his voice quiet.

She glanced over at Mel and nodded her head like he could see her, trying to find her voice again. "Yes, please," she whispered.

"Okay." He paused. "I'm so sorry, Marissa."

"Thank you," she managed before she hung up the phone. She waited a minute before looking at her phone again, this time making sure she hit Mac's speed dial. He answered on the second ring.

"Marissa?"

At this point, she was right on the edge of hyperventilating. She needed to breathe slower. "Mac," she started. "My mom's gone."

"I'll be right there."

Before Marissa could respond, he had already hung up. She pulled her phone away from her ear and put it on the table beside her, pulling her legs into the chair with her. Ellie groaned at her in disapproval as she began closing into herself and shoved her cold, wet nose into Marissa. Marissa nodded, acknowledging what the dog was doing, and dropped her legs back off the chair. Every part of her felt numb. She got to her feet but found herself sliding down to the floor beside the chair she had just been sitting in, right below the window. Ellie dropped herself into Marissa's lap, not letting her pull her legs up to her body like she had intended. She wanted to curl into a ball right there on the floor and just stop the moment.

The next half hour was both the slowest and also the fastest of Marissa's life. Mac arrived in less than ten minutes. Clyde was with him, and he immediately went to Madilyn's side. Brian arrived a few minutes later, apologizing for taking so long to get there. Mac sat down on the floor beside Marissa, seeming bigger than ever while she felt so small. He spoke to her gently, wrapping his arm around her and trying to relax her muscles, which had her frozen in place. Once he was able to get Marissa to her feet, he started to lead her from the room.

She looked over at her mom's body, again processing that her mom was no longer there. It looked like her, but she was gone. At some point, the nurses had come back and fixed her. She looked truly peaceful and comfortable. Like she was just sleeping. As they left, Marissa stopped to ask the nurses what happened next. They spoke to her about the next steps, and she nodded her head but heard none of it. She was grateful Mac was there, confident he'd been listening.

Her sisters reappeared in the parking lot with their significant others, everyone sort of just awkwardly coming back together. No one said anything; they just stood in the middle of the mostly empty parking lot, feeling the cold breeze sweep between them.

"What do we do now?" Mel asked, huddling into Brian for warmth as he wrapped his arms tightly around her.

Madi, who was leaning against Clyde and holding his hand, asked, "Do you want to go get something to eat?"

She was doing all the big-sister stuff Marissa should have been doing, but when Marissa opened her mouth to do any of it, no sound came out. So instead, she shook her head at Madilyn's question.

"I'm not hungry," Mel said. "I just want to go home."

"Do you want company?" Again, Madi was stepping up. And Marissa was just standing there, wordlessly.

Mel nodded, and Marissa found herself sighing. She no longer felt welcome. Mel wouldn't even look at her.

"Alright, we'll meet you at the house." Madilyn gave Mel a hug before Brian led her to their car.

Turning to Marissa, Madi gave her a hopeful look. "You coming?"

Marissa had to clear her throat to find her voice and shook her head. "No, I think I'm just going to go home. I'll call the funeral home in the morning and make sure that everything is taken care of." She could at least do that. Her mom had left her with all the instructions.

"Are you sure?" Madi looked disappointed.

"Yeah, honey, I'll see you tomorrow. I promise." She pulled Madi close for a hug. "I love you."

"I love you too." Madilyn let go and turned to head to her car, Clyde staying close beside her.

Marissa watched them, waiting until the cars were gone from the lot before she turned to Mac. She went to say something, but again, words didn't come out. He put his arm out and caught her, holding her.

"Let me take you home," he said finally, turning but still holding on to her as he led her to the car.

Chapter 17

I t had taken forever for Marissa to get any sleep
that night. She told Mac before getting out of the
car that she just wanted a normal night. What she
had wanted was routine, but because they had just
spent a month and a half in lockdown, they couldn't
even have that. But the night came pretty close.

When they walked in, Kate was waiting up for her
in the living room, Wicket stretched out across her
lap. The teenager got to her feet and gave Marissa
the biggest hug she had gotten from her since they
had met. She noticed Jacob sitting in one of the
chairs, looking lost in the book he was reading. He
paused to give her a sympathetic smile. Mac disappeared and reappeared with a bowl of spaghetti
and ushered her to the couch. She settled into her
corner and started flipping through the streaming

services on the television after Kate gave her the remote. She didn't really want to eat or watch anything, but she felt like indulging the two of them was the right thing to do. Eventually, she stopped on *How to Lose a Guy in 10 Days*, a movie she had seen a thousand times over, and started pushing the pasta around in her bowl.

Once the movie was over and the dishes were all in the kitchen, they said their goodnights and went to their corners of the house, Jacob included. He had just about gotten situated in the guest room, a room that had been Madi's when Marissa and her sisters were growing up, when they were rushed out to the safe house. It was almost comedic how Jacob was just part of the home unit now, despite the fact that Marissa had made it clear that she no longer trusted the FBI. And he had been in the house when things were tampered with; he had just become another member of the household. Even Wicket had taken a liking to him, sleeping on Jacob's chest when Kate was busy or otherwise occupied. He also had a regular running game of chess going with Mac. Marissa did not see the appeal, nor did she have the patience, for that type of game, so she was grateful Mac had a partner for it.

While she had been in the hospital with her sisters, Walker had told Jacob he could come back to the office, but Jacob had declined. Marissa wasn't sure what that meant, but she felt like he was still on her side. It felt good.

Mac closed the bedroom door behind them as Marissa tossed her shoes into the corner and sat down on the edge of the bed.

"What can I do?" he asked.

She felt like she had been asked that a lot lately. She couldn't fault him for it; he was trying to be there for her. To be supportive and helpful. But the kindness made her want to scream.

Instead, she shook her head. "Nothing," she responded softly, getting back to her feet. "I think maybe I'll just soak in the tub a little bit."

She saw his disappointment, but he shook it off quickly enough.

"Okay," he said finally, stepping toward her and away from the door.

"I just need a minute." She sighed, closing the space between them, leaning up on her toes to give him a quick kiss before disappearing into the bathroom.

Ellie followed her in, recognizing what was happening, and curled up on the mat beside the bathtub. Marissa started the water and left the door cracked as she turned off the lights.

As she submerged herself into the tub, the hot water left pins and needles against her skin. Marissa lowered herself in, filling the giant tub up to the brim before turning the water off. She rested there, staring at the ceiling, the only light coming from the cracked open door and the moon through the window. Rubbing her temple and closing her eyes, she tried to bring herself to terms with this new reality.

Marissa had lost people. Hell, she had lost a few recently. But this was not the same. Despite the air filling in her lungs, she felt like she couldn't breathe. Her chest felt constricted. There was a hole where something had always been, something she could count on. Her mom was gone. And nothing was ever going to feel right again.

This was how it was supposed to go. You were supposed to say goodbye to your parents. But when they were in their eighties and nineties, passing away peacefully after a completely full life. Not because of fucking cancer.

She knew she should have gone to her sister's tonight. But she couldn't bring herself to be in that space. She needed to be alone with it for a minute. If she had gone to Mel's tonight, it would have been all about Melanie. Not intentionally, but it was just how things happened. Marissa was too tired and too numb to be in that space, and she didn't trust herself to come out of it not saying something she would regret.

When she eventually left the bathtub, the water, which had started out scalding, had turned cold. Marissa had spent hours just staring at the ceiling. She was exhausted, unable to quiet her mind. She couldn't focus, couldn't relax, and couldn't do any-thing. She was just numb. Marissa crawled into bed, curling up against Mac, who was already sleeping.

He groggily put an arm around her, pulling her close and letting her cry herself into a state close to sleep.

She woke up early, feeling like she hadn't slept at all. Mac hadn't even left for his morning run yet when she sat up. Her head felt heavy, and her body ached.

"Do you need anything?" Mac asked as he finished tying his shoe.

"No." She rubbed her eyes with one hand, the other propped up behind her, keeping her in the seated position.

"Can I do anything?"

"No," she said again and gave him a weak smile. "But I appreciate you asking."

He got to his feet and walked over to give her a kiss. As he left the room, Marissa felt a stab of guilt. But as she picked up her phone, the guilt washed away, and a feeling of dread replaced it. She needed to call the hospital and see exactly who she needed to be in touch with. The assumption was the funeral home.

Swallowing, she Googled the number for the funeral home first. A woman answered after a couple of rings.

"King Funeral Home and Crematory. How may I help you?"

She had to force the words out of her mouth, but eventually got there. Marissa needed to call the hospital next to give them permission to release the body. She needed to go in and finalize all the plans her mother had already put in place. Marissa was able to give them the information for the obituary over the phone. The phrase "survived by" made the bile rise in her throat again, and as soon as she hung up the phone, she ran into the bathroom to vomit.

Once she was sure there was nothing left to spit out, she dropped to the bathroom floor, rolling to her back to once again stare at the ceiling. Two days ago, she had been in lockdown in a house somewhere in the middle of the forest. Then she'd been told that maybe everything that had been putting her life on hold and under a microscope had been an inside job. And now her mother was dead.

"How the fuck is this real life?" she mumbled, closing her eyes momentarily and taking a deep breath. Her heart was still pounding a mile a minute, and it felt like maybe it would pop right out of her chest. She hadn't noticed when, but Ellie had joined her in the bathroom, lying alongside her while resting her head on Marissa's stomach. Marissa stretched out a hand to pet her, breathing in through her nose. While she considered sitting back up, her phone started to ring. She hadn't realized it was still in her hand. Jackson's name flashed across her screen.

"Hey, Jackson," she answered the phone weakly.

"Hey, kiddo. Good to hear your voice." He paused. "I heard you were back. I, um." He stumbled over his words, and Marissa knew what was coming next.

"I'm really sorry to hear about your mom, Marissa. I'm so sorry. If there is anything I can do..."

"No, but I appreciate it." She sighed.

"I know this is terrible timing," he continued, "but I received a call this morning from that Internal Affairs agent, Sean Boswell. He was hoping—." Another pause. "He actually insisted on meeting with you. Today."

Marissa resisted the urge to groan. "Yeah. Okay." What else was there to say? "Do we have a time? Is he meeting us here?"

"I did explain everything you have going on, so he's coming here. He was leaving while we were on the phone. So two hours, tops?"

"Okay. I appreciate it." She glanced down at Ellie's big, brown eyes.

"I really am so sorry, Marissa," he said again. "If there is anything I can do, please don't hesitate to ask."

"Thank you, Herb. We'll see you this afternoon."

By the time Mac had returned, Marissa had managed to sit up but hadn't moved very far. She told him about the meeting. He helped her to her feet, and she headed over to the sink, splashed cold water on her face, brushed her teeth, and attempted to get ready for the day. It had taken her a lot longer than it should have, but she managed it, and mostly by herself. She had shooed Mac down the stairs, insisting she could take care of herself.

And then she spent ten minutes just staring at her reflection and remembering the photos she had received of her breakdown in that very bathroom when she'd tried to tear herself apart. Every time she thought she had hit rock bottom, there was a basement, a crawl space, and now a whole underground system.

By the time she was dressed and downstairs, Ellie and Mac were ready to go. Kate was sitting in the living room. They needed to get her back in school. There were so many things she needed to get back in order, Marissa knew, but … one thing at a time. She was slipping on her shoes when her phone started ringing again. Grabbing it from her back pocket, she sighed.

"Hey, Madi," she answered, stepping into the living room and motioning to Kate that they were leaving. She got to her feet, giving Wicket one last pet, before following them out the door. Jacob was already waiting by the SUV. She had planned on taking her car, but in that moment, Marissa realized the crew she was leaving with was too big to fit comfortably in the Mini Cooper. It was strange to think that, just one year ago, it had been only her.

"Hey." Her sister sounded so far away. "I just wanted to check in, I guess."

She almost asked how Madi was, but stopped herself. "I called the funeral home. I need to call the hospital." She started rattling things off because the silence was too heavy.

"Okay," Madilyn said on the end of the line. "I'm going to be at Mel's all day. I was hoping you would come by?"

Marissa closed the door behind her and locked it, lingering there. "Later, maybe?" She almost asked if Mel even wanted her there, but decided not to. "I have a meeting I have to go to but after," she said with more certainty.

"Okay." Madi paused, sighing heavily. "Where have you been, Riss?"

Marissa closed her eyes. "I'll tell you everything this afternoon. I promise." She bounced on her feet, not making a move off the porch yet. "I just need to get through this meeting."

"Okay."

Marissa ended the call and put the phone back in her pocket, taking a minute before she walked down to the car, Ellie following at her heels. Everyone was loading into the black vehicle, and as she sat down in the driver's seat, Mac handed her the keys.

"I figured you might want to drive."

Marissa nodded, giving him a weak smile before she turned on the car and pulled out of the driveway.

Once they arrived at the station, Ronnie met Marissa at the door, waiting to hug her.

"I am so sorry, Marissa." Ronnie gave her a sympathetic smile. "But it's really good to see you."

"It's good to see you, too." She knew she was going to have to brace herself against an outpouring of condolences and sympathies. And, of course, it was all coming from the right place; that didn't make it any easier to hear.

Even Jackson gave her a hug as they walked into his office. "I am—."

"I know." She cut him off as gently as possible. "Is he here yet?"

Jackson shook his head. "Not yet. Should be any time now, though." He sat back down in his chair, running his hand over his face. "I know you're hearing it already, but if there is anything I can do, just ask." He looked down at his desk before continuing. "I can't help but notice that O'Rourke is still evading capture. There haven't been any sightings of him in weeks. So, if you don't mind me asking, how did you get out of lockup?"

Mac closed the door behind them, folded his arms across his chest, and sighed.

Marissa glanced out to see Kate sitting with Ronnie, talking excitedly about something before shrugging her shoulder. "I sort of refused to go back. I met with Daniel Fryer again, and he made a suggestion that maybe this—" she used her hands to motion at her surroundings, indicating *everything*, "—is all an inside job."

Jackson raised his eyebrow. "Interesting..."

When he didn't offer any other commentary, Marissa nodded. "It was a strong suggestion. And honestly, it makes sense to me. A year of going unnoticed despite surveillance, he's either a ghost or..."

"No, that does actually make sense." The sheriff adjusted in his chair, a deep frown over his expression. "So no more FBI then?" He glanced at Mac, who just shrugged his shoulders.

Marissa nodded. "I assume that's what Sean Boswell is coming to discuss." She looked at Mac, too, realizing he'd never actually spoken to her about the conversation he'd had with Walker and Clyde after she had left the room the day of her last Fryer interview.

"What's that mean for you?" Jackson looked over Mac, who again shrugged.

"We'll see."

In all the madness that had followed that meeting, they hadn't had a chance to decompress or take it all apart. And Marissa hadn't actually considered what this all meant for Mac. Thankfully, before she could feel too bad about it, Sean Boswell walked through the front door.

"You can use the conference room." Jackson got back to his feet, looking between her and Mac. "You want me to go in with you?" He directed the question to Marissa, who couldn't help but smile and shake her head.

"No, but thank you."

Jackson walked them out of his office, then escorted all three of them to the conference room. Before Marissa could walk into the room, Jackson took her by the arm. "This is for you. Read it later." He gave her a soft smile. "You aren't the only rule-breaker around here."

Marissa looked down to see a white envelope addressed to her. In her mother's handwriting. Her heart skipped a beat, tears instantly pushing against her eyes. She folded the envelope and put it in her pocket before turning to give Jackson a hug. "Thank you."

"I'm sorry about the timing of all this," Boswell said, glancing from Marissa to Mac. "But there are just a couple of things we need to go over."

Marissa nodded but continued to stare at the top of the table. All she could think about was the letter in her pocket.

"I reviewed the tape of your last interview with Daniel Fryer." He was flipping through notes from his file folder. "And I know that after this interview, you refused to go back to the safe house."

"Yup," she said with very little enthusiasm.

"Unfortunately, that comes with some paperwork. And we need to be very clear on what you are refusing the FBI's help with."

"Am I wrong?" She straightened in her chair, meeting the man's eyes for the first time.

He paused, glancing at Mac before looking back down at his notes. "I can't say one way or another, and I'm not here to give you my opinion—."

"But you *are* here, which says that you must be looking into something."

He let out a sigh and stopped fiddling with his notes. "First, I'm here on behalf of the FBI to close out whichever case you want to with the FBI." He paused again, sliding a packet of papers in her direction. "Moving forward, I need to know exactly what you are refusing from the FBI."

"I will not go back to a safe house."

"Do you still accept FBI guards with Johnny O'Rourke still evading capture?"

She hesitated, glancing between Boswell and Mac, unsure. "I do," she said tentatively.

"Are you sure? Because I need you to be sure."

"Yeah, I'm sure," she said finally, picking up a pen to sign the papers.

That part made sense. Even if what Fryer said was true, keeping the FBI around while O'Rourke was still on the loose seemed like a good idea. Glancing at Mac, it again occurred to her that if she sent them away, she would also be potentially sending Mac back to DC.

Boswell watched her for a minute and then nodded to the papers.

"Alright. What I wanted to talk about today were the accusations that Daniel Fryer made." He sat across the table, watching their expressions. "As you know, I was already looking into things with Daniel Fryer. I have some theories but nothing conclusive and nothing of note that I am at liberty to share. I want to know what your takeaway is."

"I think it's possible," she said plainly. "It makes everything make so much more sense. Why we never catch anyone on camera, why we can't match prints, why three years later, we are no closer to identifying the accomplice. Why Daniel Fryer won't come right out and give me a name."

Boswell looked over at Mac, the IA agent's expression still and unchanging. "And what about you? What do you think?"

"I think it's possible. Although I can't imagine anyone who goes through weeks of training and takes the oath of the position could do something like that."

Marissa felt an ache in her chest as she looked at the conflict on his face. He believed in what he did and in helping people. The idea that someone in the same position could have been a serial killer would be shattering to him.

"Neither can I." Boswell nodded in agreement. "Another thing we need to consider is not just the FBI, but the police force. I want you to know I'm doing extensive checks on everyone."

They spent two hours in that conference room, going over everything in her stalker case again. Had Marissa thought about it, she would have grabbed everything she had in that duffle bag back at the house. By the time they left, for the first time in a long time, Marissa actually felt almost hopeful. She had also forgotten about the letter that was in her pocket, distracted by details of the case and the inside job accusation. It felt like it could be the answer, and Boswell seemed to agree.

Kate was in a good mood, too, talking a mile a minute. Ronnie had promised to come over on her next day off, and they would have a movie day or a girl day. It was refreshing and comforting to see her opening back up.

Instead of driving home like she really wanted to do, Marissa went up through the neighborhood to Mel's house.

Chapter 18

She pulled the Mini Cooper right alongside Jared's Chevy Impala in the driveway. She also saw her former in-laws' car and what she assumed was probably Clyde's SUV.

"Full house," she mumbled under her breath. She pulled the keys out, turned to face her body toward Mac, and looked back at Kate. "Thank you guys for coming with me. It means a lot." She had offered to take them back to the house first, at least Kate. Mac looked offended at the idea. Kate had given her a big smile and said they were going to stick together.

They made their way to the front door, but before Marissa could even knock, her former mother-in-law was there, pulling her into a hug. Up to this point, and since she had left her bathroom floor, Marissa had managed to keep her composure.

Now in Amanda Shaw's arms, the walls she had put up that morning immediately crumbled back down, and she shuddered as the tears came pouring out of her.

"I'm so sorry, sweetheart," Amanda said gently.

Growing up, Amanda had always been what Marissa called her "bonus mom." Now she was the only mom she had left.

They stood there in the doorway while Marissa sobbed for several minutes before Amanda's husband, John, came and ushered everyone into the house, giving Mac, Jacob, and Kate a warm greeting. "No need to stand out in the cold and wet."

Marissa hadn't even noticed that it was drizzling out.

Wiping her eyes, she pulled herself away from Amanda as Mac took her hand and gave it a squeeze. Before she could take in the room, four little girls came running to her. Well, two of them ran to her. Brianna and Blaire came up slowly, with tear-stained cheeks. Marissa knelt on the floor and opened her arms, pulling them all in for the biggest hugs she could manage. It had been hard when Mel had kept her nieces from her. Now, after so many weeks in lockdown, she had no desire to let them go.

"I missed you guys so much," she said.

"Where have you been?" "We missed you too." They were all talking at once when she heard Madilyn laugh softly.

"You should probably let her up, though."

Brie was the first one to notice Kate and gave her a hug before grabbing a hold of her hand. "Come on. You can come see my room." She stopped and looked at Amanda. "Is it okay if we go upstairs?"

"Of course, honey. Just keep the noise down."

Kate looked at Marissa, unsure, but Marissa gave her a small smile and a nod of her own. Brie turned and headed up the stairs, Kate and her sisters in tow.

Getting off the floor, she wiped her knees off and pulled Madi into a hug. She was pale and her eyes were red, but she looked good.

"Where's Mel?" She glanced around the room. Her former in-laws were on the couch in the room with them, engaging with Mac. Clyde came into the room behind Madi and put his arms around her waist.

"She's lying down upstairs. She's tired."

Marissa nodded. She understood; she had also just wanted to stay in bed.

"Kirstie is with her. Jared and Brian are in the kitchen." She took Marissa by the hand and started leading her to the dining room. "Come on."

Marissa glanced over at Mac, but he was fielding all the questions from Amanda. Madilyn didn't let go of her hand until they reached the table. "Do you want something to drink?"

Marissa shook her head, but Madi continued. "I have tea, I have coffee. In the car, I have wine…"

Marissa snorted and shook her head, sitting down. "Mads. Sit with me."

"I don't know if I can," she said, rubbing her hands anxiously. "I feel ... I feel like I should be doing something."

"Sit," Marissa said gently.

Madilyn sat down at the head of the table and let out a heavy sigh. She glanced into the living room, and Marissa followed her gaze to Mac and Clyde, who were still conversing with Amanda and John. A moment later, she turned to look back at Marissa.

"Where have you been?

Marissa winced. "Do you watch the news?"

"What?" Madilyn was clearly confused. Honestly, she didn't really seem like the type to watch the news. But Marissa couldn't think of any other way to start this conversation.

"The news. Have you seen Johnny O'Rourke on the news? The mobster who escaped custody a few months ago?"

Madilyn looked confused, but after a minute, she frowned and tilted her head. "I think so?"

"Well, five years ago, that was my case. And when his lawyer got him into the appeal process, he escaped custody." Marissa looked at the table top. She needed to watch what she said, not mention Mac or the reason for the appeal. "He started taking out everyone who helped get him arrested and sentenced. The prosecutor. The CI who testified at his hearing. One of the arresting officers who was on scene that day." She looked at her sister. "I was the one who arrested him. That was my case."

Madilyn listened and nodded, the expression shifting over her face as she started to understand.

"So we spent the last several weeks in a safe house under the FBI's insistence. I didn't have a choice, and I couldn't tell anyone." And she had missed the last weeks she could have spent with her mother.

"Holy shit, Marissa." Madilyn blinked as Clyde and Mac came over to the table.

"What's going on?" Clyde asked, sitting down in the chair at her other side. Mac took a seat beside Marissa and put his arm around her shoulders.

"But he's still out there," Madi continued. "They haven't arrested him, right?"

Marissa shook her head. "They haven't. But we're done with the safe house."

"What changed?"

She paused, glancing over at Clyde, who raised an eyebrow. "It's really complicated, and honestly … it doesn't matter." She dropped her eyes back to the table. "I just wish we had left sooner."

"What are we talking about?"

Marissa looked up as Jared and Brian entered the room, Brian holding a tiny baby girl in his arms while Jared had a glass of water in his hand.

"Marissa was just filling us in on where she's been the last few weeks," Clyde answered without bothering to look at either man, irritation in his tone.

"Wait. Does that mean you knew where she was this whole time?" Madilyn turned to look at Clyde, whose expression turned stiff.

"This may not be the time—."

"Oh no. We're going to have a conversation. Right now." She snapped at him before getting to her feet and giving Marissa a small smile. "Excuse us. We'll be right back." And a moment later, she was dragging Clyde off to question and scold him behind closed doors.

"I don't envy him," Brian said, glancing at Jared before walking over to the chair Madi had just left. "Here." He handed the baby girl in his arms over to Marissa. "This is Kayleigh Diane, my niece."

Marissa took the baby in her arms and felt her heart swell. She was perfect in every way. She looked up at Jared, suddenly feeling as though she was doing something she shouldn't be. But Jared only gave her a reassuring smile.

"She's absolutely perfect," she said softly.

"Yeah, I'd have to agree." Jared grinned, sitting down where Clyde had been a moment before.

"She's almost three months old now?" She looked at Jared, who nodded and gazed at the little girl in her arms.

"Yeah, can you believe it?"

Marissa heard Madilyn's voice briefly come through the kitchen, an argument definitely taking place somewhere.

"Her pictures don't do her justice," Marissa whispered, looking down at the baby cooing back at her.

"So, did I hear something about a safe house?" Brian said finally, and Marissa just nodded.

"Yes, sir, you did." She felt a pang of sadness as she looked at the bright-eyed, beautiful baby and let out a sigh. "I would have been here if I had been able to."

When no one said anything, she automatically assumed that they had probably thought the worst, considering what happened the last time she was in this house.

"So, is it safe for you now?" Brian finally broke the silence.

"Safe enough," Marissa answered without much feeling. At her tone, Ellie shifted at her feet, raising her head from the laying down position she had been in to stare at her for a long moment before huffing, possibly in judgment, and laying her head back down.

"Not really," Mac mumbled, just a little louder than she had.

Glancing up, Marissa noted mixed emotions all over his expression, and what followed was an uncomfortable silence around the table that lasted way too long. Thankfully, Kayleigh started fussing in her arms. Jared jumped up and was next to Marissa before she could blink. Gently, she handed the baby over and gave him a smile. "Congratulations. She's truly beautiful."

"Thank you," he said, beaming.

There was something both beautiful and hard about seeing new life when they were together to mourn the end of another. Marissa wrapped her arms around herself, feeling cold.

Madi eventually came back, red-faced and with fire in her eyes. Clyde followed, looking much more irritated than Marissa had ever seen him. Jared disappeared, taking Kayleigh to her mother, and slowly the rest of the men dispersed. Mac gave her a kiss on the cheek before following Clyde out of the dining room.

"I was so angry at you," Madi said softly when it was just them. "We—*I* thought you just bailed."

Marissa bit the inside of her cheek and sucked in a breath. She wasn't sure when she had given everyone the impression that she was this selfish, awful person, but it didn't seem to be going away.

"I would never just fucking bail, Mads. I have *never* been that person," she snapped quietly. "I don't know when everyone started thinking the fucking worst of me."

"I-I—," Madilyn stumbled over her words, but Marissa shook her head.

"Did Mom think the worst of me, too? Did she think I just bailed like everyone else? Is that what everyone told her?"

Madilyn opened her mouth and closed it again, unable to confirm exactly what Marissa had said. Instead, tears started rolling down her cheeks.

Marissa was too angry to cry, at least right at that moment. She dug her chewed-on nails into the palms of her hands and looked down at the table.

"No one knew what to think," Madilyn said finally. "I called the sheriff, thinking we needed to file a missing person's report, and he assured me that he didn't, but wouldn't say anything else. You were just ... gone. Your stuff was gone, the dog, even the cat."

"I didn't want to leave. I never even got to say goodbye." She shook her head. "Not really. We didn't get to have a conversation. The last time I spoke to Mom was weeks ago, and it was another canceled visit because she wasn't feeling up to socializing. And I was so upset with her about it." She clenched and unclenched her fist on the table, letting the jagged nail break through the skin of her hands. "And she probably died angry and disappointed in me."

Madilyn went to put her hand over Marissa's, but she pulled it back, again shaking her head.

"Don't." Marissa's voice was shakier than she had meant it to be. "It is what it is, and there's nothing that can be done now." She got to her feet. "I need to go."

She looked around, trying not to look frantic as she searched for Mac. He was back in the living room, sitting with Amanda, John, and Brian. Turning back to Madi, she swallowed the lump in her throat. "Would you go grab Kate for me?"

Madilyn watched her for a long moment before letting out a deep breath, only nodding and heading toward the stairs.

Marissa entered the living room quietly, forcing a small smile to her face. "We need to go," she said, her voice suddenly a little hoarse. She needed to get out of there before she completely fell apart. Mac got to his feet, and they all started saying their goodbyes.

Ten minutes later, they were on the front porch, and they had given everyone multiple hugs. Amanda insisted that Marissa call later, and to remember she was there for her. Melanie never got out of bed. But on the plus side, she didn't have to see Kirstie. Jared hadn't returned downstairs, though. Saying goodbye to all her nieces was the hardest, but she promised she would be back sometime that week just to visit.

Marissa turned to give Madilyn a hug. "Tell Mel I was here. I'll give you guys a call later." She strained to keep the emotion out of her voice.

Madilyn looked like she had been slapped across the face, but she nodded as she pulled back from the hug. "I will. I'm sorry, Riss. I love you."

"Love you too."

She turned to follow Mac and Kate down the steps, but Jared appeared in the doorway.

"Hey, you're leaving already?" He let Madi walk by before he stepped out the front door, closing it behind him.

Marissa motioned to Mac to give her a minute and turned back around to Jared, stepping up on the porch.

"Yeah. I need ... I just need to go." She shoved her hands in her back pockets and did her best to keep the emotion out of her voice. It didn't work very well. She felt the envelope in her back pocket then. How could she have forgotten?

"I know you're already sick of hearing it, but I really am so sorry," he said after a moment, looking her over. "If there is anything you need, anything I can do, call me."

It was the sincerity in his voice that broke the dam, and the tears and sobs came out in one big wave. He stepped forward and pulled her into a hug, keeping her on her feet when she felt like she was going to collapse right there on the porch. He held her until she was able to get her breathing under control. She nodded, not trusting herself to say anything at all.

Pulling back slightly, he kissed her forehead. "Seriously. Call me if you need to."

She managed to nod and stood there for an extra moment before she wiped her eyes and nodded at him, then turned to walk to the car, Ellie on her heels. Mac sat in the passenger seat, an expression on his face that Marissa wasn't sure she had seen before. But she knew Mac's feelings toward Jared. At the moment, she couldn't worry about it. She had appreciated and needed the comfort. And Jared understood this loss.

Chapter 19

"I am so sorry to hear about your mom," Dr. Bailey said gently.

"Everyone keeps saying that," Marissa said, leaning against the arm of the couch. Ellie lifted her head to look at her before laying back down with a huff. Marissa let out a sigh, looking down at the shepherd. "And I know what they mean. And they mean well. It's just … I don't know."

"I can understand that," Dr. Bailey said in her soothing tone. "And we don't have to talk about it. Or we can. We can talk about whatever you want."

"I don't know," Marissa said honestly, letting out a long breath. She didn't even know how to start the conversation. The last time they had spoken had been in the middle of her safe house lockdown breakdown, but that had been a couple of weeks ago.

Marissa had known that this was going to be a rough session. She almost didn't come, but she also couldn't just sit around the house. She had kept herself as busy as she could, making phone calls, going over arrangements, and making plans. But a week later, all that was left was the funeral itself.

She had also spent the week avoiding seeing her sisters in person. She had spoken to both of them on the phone, but every time they wanted to get together, she found a reason not to. Madilyn was so apologetic, but it didn't make anything better. Mel hadn't mentioned anything about Marissa's absence at all. In fact, she was pretty sure that Melanie was only calling because Madi and Brian insisted it might be a good idea.

Her family just thought she had left. Assumed that when things got hard, she ducked out. As though she would purposely have missed time with her mom, knowing that she was dying.

At the point where the silence in Dr. Bailey's office felt like it was lingering too long, Marissa adjusted on the couch again and sighed. She might as well start there. "They all just thought I left. While my mom was sick. That I would leave without saying a single word to anyone."

Dr. Bailey didn't say anything, giving her the room to talk, but Marissa noted the surprise on her face.

"'Almost everyone, anyway." She shook her head and looked at Dr. Bailey's sympathetic expression.

"My mom knew the reason. I don't know how she knew, and I don't really know what she knew, but she understood that if I could have been there, I would have been. We hadn't talked in almost two months. And before that, it was all superficial, talking about how she wasn't feeling well but being careful not to talk about the fact that she was dying."

She rubbed her face and pulled at her hair, which was tied back in a ponytail.

"And all those years, I kept her at an arm's length, because things weren't safe. Or maybe it was just an excuse to keep my distance. Because things are a lot less safe now than they have been the last few years."

She paused, finding a spot on the floor to stare at.

"And you know, even before that, before everything happened, our relationship was complicated. But she knew." Marissa let the words hang in the air for a minute.

"Was it complicated?" Dr. Bailey asked.

She nodded. "We were really close when I was growing up. It was just us and our mom. But when I got married the first time, she was less than thrilled with me. Jared and I had eloped but didn't tell anyone. And after that, we sort of never got back to where we had been. I lived two hours away, and we barely ever saw each other. We never really talked. And when we did, it was hollow at best. I mean, I didn't even know my mom was dating anyone. And they had been dating for *nine years*."

"What about recently?"

Marissa sighed. "It had gotten better. She gave me the house, and she was being as supportive as I would let her. But without being able to tell her things, it was hard." She wiped her eyes from the tears that had started to fall. "But then, I just disappeared. And my sisters were telling her that I was just gone. Everyone was fucking angry at me like this was my fucking choice." She shook her head. "I haven't always been an easy person, or the best sister or the best daughter, but this is exactly what happened when I broke up with Jared. Everyone assumed the worst. Like I just broke up with him after all those years for someone else. Everyone is just ready to think the absolute worst of me."

She had to wipe her eyes again, and now she felt a lump lodge in her throat.

"And it was killing me to think that my mom thought I wasn't there because I didn't care or because I didn't want to be. Or even because I was too scared to be. But she left me a letter."

Dr. Bailey raised her eyebrow but said nothing as Marissa swallowed the lump in her throat and leaned back on the couch and let her eyes drift to the ceiling. Letting out a deep breath, she leaned forward again and pulled the letter out of her bag, which was on the floor at her feet. She leaned back against the couch again, holding the folded letter in her hand that rested on the arm of the couch, and stared at it.

"She gave this to Herbert Jackson before she entered the hospital that last time. And I've read it so many times now. I can't stop reading it."

"What does it say?" Dr. Bailey asked after Marissa paused.

Marissa tried to keep her composure together. She was so tired of crying, the skin beneath her eyes raw from rubbing them so much. She unfolded the paper and took a deep breath.

To my baby girl,

I don't know the details of where you are, but I know that you would be here if you could. I only regret that we didn't have more time. That I didn't spend all the time I could and had with you. I'm sorry that I didn't take this more seriously a few years ago. I don't know that it would have made a difference, but I'm so sorry that now we'll never know. All the apologies and regrets won't and can't change anything.

I know things have been unspeakably hard for you these last couple of years. And I know that if you could be here right now, you would. I don't have the details, but Herb assures me that you are okay and that you are safe.

I love you so much, and I hope that you know how proud I am of you. I wish I could have told you one more time. I hope more than anything that I get to. But I can't make any promises. So just in case, I love you so much, baby girl. You and your sisters have been the best parts of my life.

Here is to hoping that we'll talk soon.
I love you, sweetheart.

Marissa wiped her eyes with one hand, folding the letter back up with the other. By then, the letter was covered in tear stains from the repeated times she had read it. It didn't make her feel better, but it was something to hold on to. Even still smelled like her; the letter had been written on one of the many stationary pads that she owned. Dr. Bailey offered Marissa a tissue and a smile. "You got to see her before, right?"

Marissa nodded. "I did, but she was on so much medication, keeping her comfortable, she was sleeping. The whole time. She never woke up." She bit her lip. "I was there. I spoke to her. I told her I was there. That this wasn't how it was supposed to be. That I loved her. And then she was just gone."

"I'm sure she knew you were there," Dr. Bailey offered gently.

"I have to believe that. Because the alternative…" She let her words drift off. She tried to swallow and coughed. "And you know what makes it so much worse? Once she was gone, I couldn't do anything." She shook her head as Ellie sat up and rested her chin on Marissa's lap. "I was frozen. Mel and Madilyn held her hand, said goodbye, and I just sat there. I couldn't … because it wasn't her anymore."

"That's not an unusual response."

Marissa knew that was the truth. She remembered Allison panicking at her parents' funeral because, even though it looked like her parents, she melted down over the fact that it wasn't them.

"I'm just so angry." She let out a long, slow breath. "I'm not even sure why. I'm just … angry. I have seen so many dead bodies in my line of work at this point, but it doesn't compare. One minute, my mom was there. Sleeping, breathing a little bit easier. And the next, she was just gone. There was just a body in her place."

"Again, not an unusual response." Dr. Bailey wrote something down before meeting Marissa's gaze. "It also sounds like you have some very valid things to feel angry about."

"Maybe," Marissa said unconvincingly with a shrug. "I don't know how to do this."

"Do what?"

"Go on with my day like everything is fine? Get up in the morning knowing my mom isn't here anymore. That I can't call her when I want to hear her voice?" She tugged at her hair in frustration. "Not resent my sisters for thinking the literal worst of me. Not resent everything that has happened that landed us in a safe house that kept me from my mom during her final days."

Dr. Bailey nodded but didn't say anything, giving Marissa the space she needed to get the words out.

"Like, it's because of my relationship with Mac that O'Rourke was out in the first place, and everything that has followed. Cooper's death, the safe house. And that was just awful for me. And I put Kate in that position to be in danger."

"How is Kate doing now? Before the safe house, I know you had really gotten into a good routine. And we spoke a little bit about it while you were in the safe house, but you said she had started journaling? And she had started to settle into a routine again."

Marissa started picking at her fingernails, looking down as she spoke. "She's better. She's a lot better now that we're home. But having to pack up and rush out like that, I think it really brought up some unpleasant things for her. But she's a strong girl. She's doing really well. Better than me, if I'm being honest." Marissa looked back up to meet Dr. Bailey's gaze.

"Well, that's good to hear, considering everything you've had going on since you got home."

Marissa nodded, looking back down at her hands with a sigh.

"So back to your relationship with Mac. You said you have resentment."

"No." She shook her head but frowned. "Yes? I don't know. I hate knowing that our relationship was the catalyst for everything that has happened with O'Rourke and continues to happen. Because nothing has changed. And that's part of the problem, too. Because I could have just refused the FBI and the safe house and been here for the last six weeks with my mom."

"But who's to say that you would be here and okay today if you hadn't been in the safe house?" Dr. Bailey asked.

Marissa shrugged. "We'll never know." She paused. "There are a lot of things we'll never know. And it's just another thing I'm angry about." She felt the knot in her chest tightening up. "I don't resent Mac. And I don't regret our relationship. I love him. But I hate that we kept it a secret long enough to cause all the trouble that has followed."

Shaking her head, she adjusted her legs beneath her, and Ellie grumbled, as she had to adjust her head in Marissa's lap. "The choices we made are what I regret. And I've spent a lot of time wondering … if we had just been honest from the beginning … if things would have played out differently. But again, we'll never know."

"What else have you been feeling? You've mentioned a lot of anger. Has there been anything else?"

"Sadness. Guilt. Hopelessness." She shook her head. "But being angry is so much easier. If I let myself feel all the other things, I can't push myself to get out of bed. To eat food. To move forward with my day. Being angry means I can function throughout the day."

"That must be exhausting."

"It is," Marissa admitted. "It's exhausting, and at the end of the day, everything hurts so much more than it normally does. But I don't know how else to get by."

"Have you been able to journal? And try to get some of those feelings down on paper?"

"A little bit here and there. It's mostly words. Not even full sentences." She shook her head and offered an awkward smile. "I'm not a writer."

Dr. Bailey smiled. "That is perfectly okay. Whatever it takes to get that out. Even if you make it bullet points. It's not for anyone but you, so it doesn't need to be well-written."

Marissa nodded. She felt weird when she went to journal. It felt unnatural to sit down and put feelings to paper. "Kate has really helped me be consistent about it, though. We still make time to do it nightly."

"So going forward, what's going on next?"

"My mom's funeral is Sunday." Just three days away. "After that, I don't know." She shuddered, feeling a chill from a draft that most likely wasn't real.

"It's okay to take things one at a time." Dr. Bailey closed her notes and leaned forward on her desk. "I do think you need to find a way to give yourself space to feel all the other things you're trying to keep buried under all that anger. Because if you don't, they *are* going to come out anyway, whether you're ready or not. And you're going to burn yourself out."

Marissa felt so much worse by the end of the session. She didn't know how to let herself feel those feelings. And she felt panic just thinking about the funeral. Not because of the funeral itself, but the worry about what came in the days after. When there was no longer something she needed to organize and work on. She would once again have to focus on serial killers and mobsters—and remember that she was actively being stalked.

"Hey, do you want to go get something to eat?" Mac offered as she came out of the therapist's office.

Shaking her head, she leaned against him as they waited for the elevator. "No. I'm not feeling very hungry."

"I know, but you still have to eat," he said, but he didn't push her any harder.

"Do you want to talk about it?" he asked gently, again, once they were in the car. He had been asking her that a lot. And she knew it came from a good place, but the question sort of made her want to scream.

"What is there to talk about?" she asked numbly, getting on the road and trying to feel the contentment that driving usually brought her.

"How are you feeling? How did your session go?"

Marissa could hear him trying to keep his voice even, but there was frustration in the questions.

She shook her head. "Not really," she answered with a sigh. "I'm just tired."

Mac let out a sigh of his own and turned to look out the window, his frustration hanging heavy within the little car.

"I'm sorry, I just … I don't know." She was already feeling so talked out, and now she felt guilty, and then angry about feeling guilty. "Please don't take it personally. I'm just kind of talked out."

"I just wish you would talk to me at all. I keep saying it, Marissa," he said finally, turning back to look at her. "It feels like you've just shut me out completely."

She made the decision to drive the whole way home rather than get on the ferry. Once she was on the freeway, she glanced his way. Marissa was glad that Jacob was following them today in his own car rather than tagging along to listen to this conversation. Again.

"I'm not trying to shut you out. I've told you: I just don't know what to say. I don't know how to talk about my feelings or even what I'm feeling. I'm just..." She tried to find the words but couldn't. Instead, she tightened her grip on the steering wheel. "I don't know."

"You don't need to tell me how you're feeling. You just need to talk to me."

Marissa had to think back, certain that he was wrong and that they had talked. The fight in the safe house didn't count; that had been because of exhaustion. "I don't know how to do this."

"To do what?"

"Any of this." She gestured to the air around her with one hand. "I'm tired of being a victim. I'm tired of other people being in control of my life. My mom just *died*, and I don't know how I'm supposed to feel or function on a day-to-day basis."

"Then don't *be* a victim," he said. It wasn't an attack. It was encouragement. But now it was Mac's turn to sigh. "I just want to be here for you, but it feels like you're pushing me further and further away."

"It's not intentional." It also wasn't about him.

"I can't help but worry that you blame me for not being there. For being stuck in the safe house for all those weeks."

There it was. Marissa shook her head. "I don't blame you," she said gently. "I do worry our choices made it happen, but I don't blame *you*. I love you."

She dropped one hand off the wheel to reach out for his.

"I love you too." He took her hand and gave it a squeeze.

The rest of the ride home was silent. She turned some music on and cranked the heat up. He fell asleep about halfway through the drive but kept hold of her hand the rest of the way home. She glanced over and felt a punch of guilt. Mac was just as tired as she was. His life was being threatened, just as hers was. He was in just as much trouble, and he spent most of his energy trying to make sure *she* was okay. This wasn't fair to him, but she didn't have any answers.

Chapter 20

Marissa looked at her reflection in the mirror with a heavy sigh, trying to smooth the bottom of her dress. She had labeled it her funeral dress, and she had worn it far too many times in recent years. Marissa hadn't slept at all the night before, and it showed. She needed to use extra coverup to hide the dark circles beneath her eyes and grabbed a black sweater to wear over her dress, hiding the scar that ran down her chest. It was probably all in her mind, but today it felt irritated, and she found herself trying to scratch it.

Glancing at the clock, she found it had only been three minutes since she had checked it last. She wasn't ready for today. And she needed to get to the funeral home early to make sure everything was in order.

Her phone buzzed, and she picked it up from the bathroom counter, seeing her dad's name flash across the screen. She had been texting him since the day after her mom died.

[Hey, honey. Just wanted to let you know I'm thinking about you today. I wish I could be there with you. I love you, honey.]

She hated that she was relieved he wasn't coming. He would have been there if she had asked him to be. But because of Melanie and Madilyn, she asked him not to. And she was angry about that, too. Her dad should have been able to be there with them. He had the right to grieve their mom, too.

[Love you, too, Dad]

With a heavy sigh, she took one last look at herself in the mirror and turned to leave the bathroom. She was startled to see Kate sitting on her bed, already dressed in her own black funeral clothes.

Marissa had offered to have Kate stay with Ronnie or Meredith Parker for the afternoon, so she wasn't forced to go to a funeral. But the teenager just gave her a hug and told her she would be there.

"Sorry," she apologized. "I didn't mean to startle you."

Marissa gave her a reassuring smile. "Don't worry, it's not just you. I'm a bit jumpy today." It was probably the lack of sleep. "I appreciate you coming with me today. It means a lot."

Now it was Kate's turn to give her a reassuring smile. "Of course. It is the least I can do. And I really liked your mom."

"Me too," Marissa said softly. She looked around the room, knowing there wasn't much more she could do to waste time. "Alright, let's go."

She and Kate headed down the stairs, Ellie following at Marissa's heels. Mac was already ready to go and waiting for them.

By the time they arrived at the funeral home, Marissa's heart had lodged in her throat. She felt like she couldn't swallow, and her chest was knotted up tight. They were two hours early, but she had wanted to make sure everything was exactly how her mom had wanted it.

The assistant met them at the door. "Hi, Mrs. Berkeley—."

"It's Ambrose, Andrea. But you know you can call me Marissa." They had gone to high school together.

Andrea Bowen nodded her head and gave her a small, sheepish smile. "Sorry, Marissa. Old habits." She glanced at Mac, not unimpressed, before she looked back at Marissa. "Can I talk to you for a second?"

She sighed and nodded. "That's why we're here early."

"Follow me."

Marissa gave Mac's hand a squeeze and followed Andrea to the funeral director's office. Closing the door behind them, Andrea sat down at the desk that belonged to her father and gave Marissa a sympathetic smile. "I'm really sorry for your loss. I remember going to your mom's shop after school when we were writing papers together, and she always made the best cookies."

Marissa smiled. "Yeah, she did … What did you want to talk to me about? Is everything okay?"

"Oh, I'm sorry. Yes. Everything is okay. I just wanted to return your check."

Marissa frowned. "The check that was paying for all of this?"

"It's already been taken care of."

Marissa's frown deepened. "What do you mean, 'It's already been taken care of'?"

Andrea shrugged her shoulders. "The services have already been paid for."

"Who the hell paid for it?" Marissa blinked, confused.

"Someone who wished to remain anonymous." Andrea met Marissa's gaze with her best impression of a poker face.

"Come on, Andrea. Just tell me."

"I can't tell you," she said with a sigh, but she pulled out a piece of paper from the door and slid it across the table. "I'm not at liberty to say or show you the receipt or anything, but here is your check."

Marissa looked down to take the check and noticed the receipt beneath it. Taking the check, she looked at the receipt, inspecting the signature at the bottom. Recognizing it immediately, she caught Andrea's eyes and was met with a look of understanding.

"You can see why I made the mistake this morning with your name," she said gently. Sliding the receipt back and dropping it into the drawer, she gave Marissa a small smile. "Everything is taken care of. You have nothing to worry about."

Marissa wanted to say thank you but was at a loss for words. Andrea obviously understood her position.

"Take all the time you need. You can have the office. I will see you after." She gave Marissa's arm a squeeze and exited, closing the door behind her.

Once she was alone, Marissa let out a breath that seemed to release tears from her eyes that quickly streamed down her cheeks. She grabbed her phone from her pocket, fumbling blindly for a moment, went to her speed dial, and put it up to her ear, listening for the ring.

After the eighth ring, she hung up. She swallowed, trying not to shake as Ellie nudged her knee.

Jared had paid for everything. She suspected he had also paid for the hospital, since the billing department had also refused to let her pay for that, too. But they were less forthcoming than Andrea had been. He had paid for everything and had said nothing. She really shouldn't have been surprised; no matter what they had been through together, they had been family. Nothing changed that. Of course, it was typical that he hadn't told her either.

She sat down in the chair and let out a heavy breath. Her head hurt. She sat there for a long time, knowing she needed to leave, but she couldn't bring herself to move.

Nearly twenty minutes later, she finally got on her feet and left the little office. She found Mac and Kate standing with Madilyn and Clyde, who had also arrived early.

"Hey," Madi said, pulling Marissa into a hug.

"Hey." Marissa folded her arms in front of her as she pulled away.

"I tried calling you this morning," Madi said when it became clear Marissa wasn't going to say anything else.

"Sorry, it's been a rough morning." She had seen the call come through. She was still feeling a heavy wave of resentment and anger toward both of her sisters.

"Yeah." She looked down at the ground and clasped her hands in front of her.

"How's Mel?" Marissa asked finally.

"She's doing better," Madilyn said unconvincingly. "Amanda and John are helping Brian with the kids while Kirstie is helping Mel."

Marissa nodded. She wasn't in the mood for small talk. "Can you guys excuse me? I just need a minute."

She didn't wait for any responses, although Mac followed her for a couple of feet. "Do you want any company?"

Shaking her head, she leaned up to give him a quick kiss on the cheek. "No, but thank you. I just need a second. I'll be right back." When he nodded, she gave him a small smile. "I love you."

"I love you too."

Marissa took herself for a short walk away from the church and into the neighboring cemetery. She wasn't alone; she knew Jacob was behind her somewhere, keeping watch. Marissa didn't bother looking over her shoulder to confirm it anymore. Holding her sweater close, she found herself standing in front of Allison's tombstone. It hadn't been intentional.

"I remember the day we did this for your parents," Marissa said softly, letting out a sigh as she spoke. "Pretty sure the weather was just as shitty." She glanced up at the dark, overcast sky and shook her head. "It's absolutely going to rain."

She sat down on the grass in her dress, folding her legs beneath her. Ellie sat beside her before stretching out all the way.

"I fucking wish you were here." She shook her head. "I feel like I can't talk to anybody. I'm too angry at my sisters. Everyone just keeps telling me how sorry they are, and it just feels..." she trailed off.

"It probably feels empty, even though you know it comes from a good place."

She turned to see Jared standing behind her, hands in the pockets of his slacks. He gave her a small smile. "Sorry. I didn't mean to startle you. Or interrupt."

"You aren't interrupting. I'm literally just talking to myself."

"No. I imagine she's out there listening to you somewhere." He leaned against the tree beside him. "And if she were here, she'd be telling you all your feelings are normal."

Marissa raised an eyebrow. "You sound like my therapist."

"I mean, it's probably true." He shrugged a shoulder, watching her for a moment. "Honestly, though, how are you doing?"

Marissa shrugged, turning back to face Allie's grave again, unable to look him in the eyes. "Not great," she said honestly. "I sort of don't know what to do with myself."

She paused, wiping the tears from her eyes before looking back at him. "You paid for everything." Her voice was barely above a whisper, but he must have understood what she was saying.

Pushing off the tree, he sat down right next to her. Ellie wagged her tail and wiggled over to him, excited to see him. "Of course I did. It was the least I could do," he answered softly.

She went to answer, but words didn't come out. Instead, a new wave of tears began. He inched closed and put his arm around her. She fell into him, openly sobbing against his chest while he held her, just letting her cry.

They sat there like that for a long time. She cried until she felt like there were no tears left. As she forced herself to calm down, it started to lightly drizzle.

"Come on. We should head back anyway," he said finally, pulling away from her gently and getting to his feet before he helped her to hers. As she stood, Jared helped steady her before giving her what felt like the most comforting hug she had received in a long while and kissed the top of her head. She didn't want to move, so she held on to him for a lingering moment before letting out a breath and then nodded.

"Okay."

The service was beautiful and long, and everything her mom had wanted. So many locals were there. Greg, of course, was there. The only people Marissa could tell were missing were her father and her cousin. She knew why her dad wasn't there; he hadn't wanted to make Melanie and Madilyn uncomfortable. Another piece of resentment Marissa felt deeply. She could only imagine the tantrum Mel would have thrown. Her cousin, Charlotte, though, she hadn't heard from in a while. It wasn't unusual—she was always on the move, always busy. But when she had reached out about her mom's funeral, she had expected her to be there.

The family made their way through the cemetery, stopping at the open plot beside her late aunts. Thankfully, the rain had stopped.

"I need a minute," Marissa said softly, giving Mac's hand a squeeze. Marissa had to walk away. She needed space, just needed to put a bit of physical distance between her and the coffin that held her mom. Mel was standing between Kirstie and

Madi, with Brian right behind her with his parents and kids. They were all grouped together, while Mac and Kate were just off to the side of them.

Marissa felt crowded and closed in, despite the fact that they were in an open space. She didn't want to feel swallowed up … claustrophobic. Marissa dug her fingers into her arms, knowing there would be bruises later.

She could just imagine what her mom would say, seeing her isolate herself from everyone else. And she knew what her mom would say about holding on to the anger and using that feeling to get through the day. That it took more energy to be angry than to just forgive what was clearly a misunderstanding.

Marissa couldn't keep doing funerals. Hell, she hadn't even attended Cooper's. But this was her mom. The person who had always been there for her, even if she didn't want her there, and she was gone. Watching the casket disappear into the ground knocked the wind right out of her.

Chapter 21

S he watched from a distance, leaning against a tree, and eventually closed her eyes.

There was a sigh. "It was a beautiful service … How are we going to afford this?"

Marissa opened her eyes to see Madilyn walking up beside her. Swallowing the lump in her throat, she cracked her neck to the side. "We don't have to." Her voice was hoarse.

"What do you mean?"

"Jared paid for everything," she said, tears welling back in her eyes as she watched people begin to walk away. "The funeral. The hospital. All of it."

"Oh … wow." It was all Madi could say.

And what else was there to say? Jared had been a part of their lives for the last two decades. For as long as Marissa could remember, Jared had always been there. It shouldn't have been as surprising as it was. Jared had never been one to flaunt his inheritance from his own late mom, but he had been smart with his money. He wasn't one to flaunt his kindness, either.

Before Marissa could respond, she realized that Mac had also walked up alongside her. The expression on his face filled her with instant regret.

Madi could apparently read the room, so she gave Marissa's arm a squeeze. "I'll see you guys at Mel's." She didn't wait for a response and headed off in the direction of Mel, Brian, and the kids.

"Why didn't you tell me?" Mac asked.

"Because I didn't even know." That had been the truth. She started walking, pausing long enough to make sure he was following her. "I went to pay for what I thought the service was going to be, use the money my mom put aside specifically for it, and was told that it had already been paid for. Just like when I asked the hospital who I needed to talk to about the bill. But this time, I got to see the receipt." And she knew Jared's signature.

She looked up as they came to the crosswalk and stole a quick glance at Ellie, who sat down to wait.

Mac's expression was unreadable.

"Please don't read into this like it's something, because it's not."

She sighed, glancing back toward Jacob, who was lingering behind them, trying to give them some space. They crossed the street and continued walking for a minute before Marissa finally spoke up again. "Where is Kate?"

Mac was still frowning. "She's with your nieces."

Marissa nodded and waited, but when the silence dragged, she asked, "Why does it matter?" She dropped her eyes to the ground and then out to the street where they had come from. Ellie was also looking back toward the street, staring intently at something Marissa couldn't see.

"Because, Marissa." There was a sharp inhale and a long sigh, but Marissa couldn't bring herself to meet his eyes. "I need to know if I'm wasting my time here. I want to know that I'm not just here for convenience. I love you, and I want to believe you love me. But it always comes back to *that* asshole."

"Mac, my mom just died..." She swallowed and wrapped her arms around herself, looking up at him without meeting his gaze. Ellie started whining, still staring across the street. Marissa followed her gaze but saw nothing.

Mac closed his eyes and ran his hand through his hair, frustration all over his face. "Marissa." His voice softened, but when he opened his eyes, she saw the pain within them. "There is never a good time for this. I'm sorry. I just … I just need to know that *I'm* the choice you're making and not the choice you're stuck with. I need to know where I stand. That this isn't just a waste of my time. Because I've been here. Giving you everything I have."

Marissa felt a sharp ache in her chest, tears now freely flowing down her cheeks. She let go of herself with one hand to wipe the tears away. The last year flashed before her, thinking of every time he had been there for her and how little he got back from her in return. He deserved better. He deserved so much better.

"For fuck's sake." Mac's low growl snapped her back into the present as she turned to follow his gaze and saw Jared. Ellie's focus broke as Jared approached, wagging her tail and letting out a bark before searching again for whatever had kept her attention moments before.

Marissa took a step back, stepping off the sidewalk and into the street. She glanced over at Jacob, who stood just off to the side of where they were, hands clasped in front of him and sunglasses hiding whatever he thought of the situation unfolding in front of him. His expression remained unchanged. She wondered at what point this had become her life.

"What do you want?" Mac snapped, his normal cool, even-tempered self at a boiling point.

"Amanda wanted me to let you know Kate is riding with them and the girls." Jared glared at Mac, but his eyes fell on Marissa. Eyes full of concern. "But I also wanted to see if you were okay."

"She's fine," Mac snapped before Marissa could answer.

"I didn't fucking ask you." Jared shot a glare in Mac's direction.

"Look, asshole—," Mac started, but Marissa put herself between them.

She put her hands up. "No, I'm not alright." She intentionally raised her voice a little louder than both men had been. "But I will be."

She looked at Jared. "I can't thank you enough. For everything. Truly." She met Jared's eyes, and he looked at her with an understanding meant only for her.

Turning her gaze to Mac, she softened further. "Let's finish this at *home*. We can go to the wake after." She made sure to emphasize the word *home* for Mac's sake.

Time seemed to halt and flash by all at the same time. First, Marissa heard Ellie's snarl and bark. Then, the sound of gunfire exploded in Marissa's ear, and she felt Jared shove her—hard. Before she could react, she saw him fall to the ground.

The sound of people screaming rang in her ears. Instinctively, she dropped low to the ground, grabbing her gun from her boot holster and forcing herself to focus on where the shots were coming from.

Ellie let out another low snarl Marissa wasn't used to hearing before she lunged forward and ran toward O'Rourke, who was standing out in the open across the street, gun in his hand. Marissa felt a cold sensation slam into her, but aimed her gun at the murderer in front of them and didn't hesitate on the trigger.

Marissa had heard several pops around her, each crackling in her ear. She saw Ellie lunge at his side and pulled him down to the ground. He didn't move.

Everything had happened so fast.

Glancing around her, her eyes grew wide in horror at the scene. All three men who had been standing with her just moments earlier were all on the ground. People had started gathering around. Marissa saw Jackson across the street, standing with Clyde over the body of Johnny O'Rourke. Ellie still had O'Rourke's clothing in her mouth, holding him to the ground because she expected him to get up.

"Ellie! Here!" Marissa shouted, watching the dog drop O'Rourke and dart across the street back to her, wagging her tail proudly. Ronnie ran across the street, following the shepherd over to Marissa. Glancing to her right, Marissa felt her heart lodge in her throat. Jared was lying there, perfectly still on his side, his face on the pavement. Blood pooled beneath him, although Marissa couldn't see from where without moving him.

Carefully, she put her hand on his shoulder, feeling for some sign of life. When nothing happened, she moved to feel for his pulse. It wasn't until she felt his heartbeat beneath her fingers that she let out her own breath.

He was alive.

"We need medical!" she yelled across the street as Ronnie knelt beside her.

"Are you okay?"

Marissa could hear Ronnie, but her voice was muffled. Marissa's ears were still ringing as her eyes frantically searched the scene.

Ronnie offered her arm to help Marissa up. "Marissa, you're bleeding."

"I'm fine." She barely paid any attention to Ronnie once she was back on her feet and turned.

Mac was slumped against the building behind them, gun at his side, holding his shoulder with his left hand and panting, his eyes following her. Marissa could see the blood all over his hand and shirt. He was injured, but he was alright.

Marissa turned her gaze to Jacob, just off to the side of Mac. Ronnie had moved over to him, checking for a pulse. She winced and shook her head. He was dead.

"Fuck." Marissa looked around at the rest of the scene. Officers were trying to get bystanders to move along. Clyde had made his way over as Jackson continued to stand over O'Rourke. Jackson met Marissa's gaze and nodded in her direction.

Ronnie was suddenly beside her again. "Marissa, you're still bleeding."

This time, Marissa glanced down, following Ronnie's eyes. Her shirt was wet and sticky with blood from her right side, but Marissa couldn't feel it. She shook her head, starting to move again.

"It's fine," she insisted, kneeling beside Jared again and looking over at Mac.

"Are you okay?" Her eyes took all of him in, searching. He was holding his shoulder, where he was clearly bleeding. But Marissa could see the bottom of his shirt was also covered in blood. "Where are you hurt?"

"I'm alright." Mac winced as he adjusted himself. "It's my shoulder. My side." He paused. "Are you okay? You're bleeding."

Marissa just nodded, swaying on the balls of her feet as she remained crouched uncomfortably between the two men. "I'll be fine," she said, inhaling deeply. She watched as EMTs finally appeared, splitting up to take care of everyone. She moved out of the way and watched as they turned Jared over to examine him. Marissa could see the blood had been coming from his abdomen. He was still unconscious. He had pushed her out of the way.

"Marissa." Mac's voice brought her back to the moment. Turning back to Mac, she couldn't hide the tears from her eyes. "Everything is going to be okay."

She nodded, but she wasn't sure he was right.

It had felt like hours since they had been taken to the hospital. A bullet had grazed Marissa's side. Her right side, where the deep scar from the warehouse was. She hadn't even really felt it between the adrenaline and the scar tissue that had built up. But now her muscles ached just about everywhere, as the tension had finally given way. They had bandaged her up and, thankfully, they had given her a good dose of Dilaudid, so the aches were easing. Her mind was also moving significantly slower. She looked up at the clock and groaned. She was halfway ready to pull the IV out of her arm and go find someone, anyone, when there was a knock at her door. Ellie, who had been lying on the hospital bed with Marissa, stretched out alongside her legs, lifted her head curiously.

Jackson appeared, one hand in his pocket, as he walked into her room. "How are you feeling?"

"Fine." She shrugged her shoulders. "Ready to get out of this stupid gown and go check on everyone else."

"Well, you'll be happy to know that there was no serious damage to you. It was a clean shot and not deep."

"Perfect," she said with little enthusiasm. She paused, opening her mouth to ask, but, instead, Jackson held up his hand.

Jackson hesitated. "I believe they are both out of surgery. And stable."

Marissa closed her eyes briefly, relief coursing over her. "Thank God," she muttered before shaking her head. She swallowed uncomfortably. Her mouth was so dry. "What about Kate?"

"She's alright. She had already left with Amanda before any shots were fired."

Marissa let out a heavy breath, instantly regretting the movement as pain shot through her. "This was a fucking clusterfuck."

"I know, kid," he spoke gently, pulling up a chair and sitting down beside her bed. "But at least O'Rourke is off the streets. And for the most part, everyone is okay. You did an amazing job today." He paused again, lowering his voice. "Why don't you lean back and rest? You've more than earned it."

Marissa straightened, frowning. Something about the way he was talking to her seemed off. It could have been the painkillers messing with her mind. She blinked and shook her head, moving to throw her legs over the bed. "No, I can't just lay here—."

Jackson rubbed his jaw with one hand and shook his head. "Yes, you can. They want to keep you overnight. Just to keep an eye on you."

"What about Kate? I can't just leave her alone—." She started to protest, but then she suddenly felt very tired.

"Veronica is already at your house and has ordered pizza for the both of them. Promised Kate a new movie marathon. She'll bring her by tomorrow."

Marissa tugged at her mind for the words to push back, but her eyes fell on Ellie, who repositioned herself on Marissa's legs. Turning her attention back to Sheriff Jackson, she frowned. "There's something you aren't telling me." She raised an eyebrow at him, but even that took too much effort. "Why are they keeping me overnight?"

He put up his hands defensively. "Just to keep an eye on you. Nothing major. Make sure bandaging you up was enough. Keep an eye on your pain management."

That turned on a lightbulb somewhere in her mind. While she and Jackson had never spoken about the quantity of alcohol and pills she had grown accustomed to last year, she was sure he had known about all of it. This just meant they were going to let her have the pain medication here, under watch, and would hand her some ibuprofen when she was finally discharged. She nodded in understanding, though her lips were still in a thin frown.

"And what are you doing here?" she finally asked, breaking the thick silence.

"I figured I'd keep you company while I can." He leaned back in the chair, getting comfortable.

Marissa wanted to ask where her sisters were, but she couldn't bring the words to her lips. She was afraid of the answer. Unfortunately, Jackson knew her well enough to know where her mind was.

"Your sisters were here. So was Kirstie Miller. After talking with the doctors, they decided it would be best if they all went back to Mel's. There wasn't a lot more they could do here. Madi sort of had to force them to leave at the nurse's request."

Marissa nodded, but a feeling of emptiness spread through her. She was pretty sure she had been awake most of the time since her arrival at the hospital. No one had come to see her. Because it was her fault.

Leaning back, she felt the weight of defeat. She adjusted her head on the pillow. "Today was my mom's funeral."

"I know." He shifted uncomfortably. "I'm so sorry." She watched him for a moment as a deep sadness flashed across his face. Marissa had known that there was a moment in time when her mom and Jackson had become close. He had been friends with her dad, but Jackson had stepped up when her father had left.

She let out an unsteady, heavy sigh. "I fucking hate hospitals, Herb." All the formality was gone. If he was going to keep her company, it wasn't going to be formal.

"I know," he repeated, his tone again soft.

"You promise that they're okay?" She kept her eyes on him.

Herbert Jackson was a great sheriff, and Marissa had known him for the better part of two decades now. He was a good man with a tough exterior. But one thing Jackson wasn't good at was lying.

He rubbed his hands together, looking down at the floor as he sat back up in his chair and let out a long sigh before he met her eyes again. "They are going to be fine."

Marissa wanted to argue, but she could feel the exhaustion washing over her, all the adrenaline gone. "I'm so tired."

"Then sleep. I'll be right here." He gave her an encouraging smile.

"But I don't wanna," she mumbled.

As she was drifting off, she heard him say, "You really did do a great job today, kiddo. And I'm so sorry about your mom."

Chapter 22

Marissa felt a sharp pain in her side as she tried to adjust and groaned. Opening her eyes, it took her a moment to remember where she was. She was still in the hospital. Sounds filled her ears: beeping, voices over the intercom, commotion outside the room. Her room was dark. The blinds were closed. Jackson wasn't there anymore, but Madilyn was, sleeping soundly in the chair next to her.

With effort, Marissa forced herself to sit up, the machine beside her bed beginning to beep. She glared at the machine attached to her IV and adjusted her arm back to the way it had been. It was enough to make the beeping stop, but not before waking Madi, who straightened up in the chair and yawned. Even half-asleep, Madilyn looked so put together. Marissa was sure she looked as rough and terrible as she felt.

"Hey." Madilyn suppressed another yawn. "How are you feeling?"

"Like I've been shot," she responded dryly. The truth was, her side felt like it was on fire. "What time is it?"

"It's..." she glanced at her phone, which had been resting in her hand, "...eleven a.m. And my phone is almost dead."

"When did you get here?"

"I've been here a while. Jackson had to go to work. And we agreed we didn't want you to wake up alone."

"How is everyone else?" She watched her sister try to keep her expression still, but Madi wasn't a poker player, either.

"They're fine," she said calmly, clearly believing that she was doing a good job.

Jackson was a terrible liar, but he was very good at keeping the truth to himself. Maybe it was a law enforcement trait. But Madi was a bad liar, and telling Madilyn a secret was as good as broadcasting it.

"Madilyn Lorraine." Marissa's voice was soft, but her eyes were hard. After a moment, though, those softened too. "Please. Just tell me the truth."

Madilyn tried to glare at her but dropped her shoulders with a heavy sigh. "Mac and Jared are both ... better." She hesitated. "Mac went through surgery. The gunshot to his side was clean. The one in his shoulder was a little harder to remove. They're talking about permanent nerve damage. But he's stable."

Marissa waited, but Madi was looking down at her hands. "And Jared?"

"Jared is still in the ICU." Madilyn took a deep breath. "According to what I was told, he coded, and he stopped breathing on the way here. They did revive him, and he made it through surgery, but he's having a hard time."

Marissa had known Jackson was lying to her, but not to this extent.

"It's going to be okay," Madi said with very little confidence behind it.

"It doesn't feel okay." She adjusted, dropping her legs over the bed. She sucked in a breath as pain radiated throughout her entire body. The adrenaline was gone, and she could feel *everything*. The area around where she had been shot was on fire, and the pain pulsed through her, making each breath something she had to force out. Her chest was tight, and every inhale felt like a stab to her rib cage.

"What are you doing?" Madi got to her feet and looked around helplessly for someone else to try to make Marissa lie back down. At least Madilyn knew she couldn't tell Marissa what to do.

"First, I'm going to go to the bathroom. Then I'm going to put my clothes on." She winced, the sharp pain causing her to pause. Nausea was taking over, and she felt lightheaded. Gritting her teeth, she continued to try to ease herself to the floor. "And then I'm going to leave this room."

"Can't you at least wait until we can get a doctor in here?"

"Mads, I'm going stir-crazy in here. I need to see them with my own eyes. I need to go home for clothes. Because I will be damned if my choices are a fucking hospital gown or a dress that I wore to my mother's funeral service *and was shot in*."

Madilyn looked down at the ground. "I did bring you some clothes."

Marissa sighed, feeling instant regret. "I'm sorry. I just … don't do well being idle. And I *really* hate hospitals." She could feel herself closing up.

"I get it." Madilyn gave her a sympathetic look. "Let me see if I can find a doctor. Let's see if it's actually okay for you to go."

Marissa stared at her sister for a long moment before she gave a reluctant nod, and Madi darted out of the room. She wouldn't admit it, but she wasn't sure she had enough momentum to get to her feet. The pain was excruciating. While it wasn't something Marissa should have taken personally, Madi and Mel had been at the hospital right after she arrived, and Marissa hadn't seen either of them the day before, so it was hard not to feel like Madi had drawn the short straw on who should stay with Marissa.

Marissa stared at Ellie, who was staring back at her. Swallowing, Marissa fought not to break down as she watched the shepherd tilt her head to the side, trying to figure out what was wrong. She was replaying Madilyn's words, thinking about the conditions both men were in. Letting her eyes wander around the hospital room reminded her of the last time she was in one. It had only been a few weeks. Marissa was numb, and she had to keep herself that way. She could not allow herself to feel it right now.

There was a knock at the door and the doctor appeared, with Madilyn close behind. "Ms. Ambrose, good to see you awake. How are you feeling?"

Marissa sighed, really sick of the question. "A little uncomfortable. Like I was shot."

He looked through her paperwork for a moment before nodding his head and meeting her gaze. "Your sister says you're anxious to go. As I'm sure you know, we can't force you to stay, but if nothing else, I would insist on taking it easy. You can expect to be sore and should probably limit most activities."

"So I'm good to go?"

"You are good to go if that's what you want. I can get you your discharge papers. But I can't prescribe you anything more than ibuprofen."

Marissa nodded with zero surprise. "That works."

The doctor wrote down some notes on her chart, glanced at her vitals, and nodded his head. "Alright. Someone will be back in with those papers shortly."

Marissa nodded and sighed as the door closed behind the doctor. Madilyn had sat back down in the chair beside the bed and was leaning forward, her elbows on her knees, frowning. It suddenly dawned on Marissa that Madi wasn't around last year, so she had no idea how bad things had gotten.

"What was that about?" Madi asked the predictable question.

With a heavy sigh, Marissa rubbed her face. "I may have been overusing certain prescription medications. And drinking a lot of alcohol." She shrugged her shoulder. "It's fine. I'm good now. But it's in my charts."

Madilyn stared at her wordlessly for a long moment, processing the information. "May have been? You're good now?" she repeated after Marissa in disbelief.

Sighing heavily, Marissa let her shoulders drop. "It's a long story, Mads. I don't need your judgment or disappointment."

"I'm not judging you." Madilyn seemed taken aback by the accusation. "I just didn't know." Her voice dropped. "I feel like I'm always playing catchup."

Marissa again had immediate regret. "I'm sorry. It's just … things have been really hard. And for a minute, pills made it … tolerable. Chasing it with alcohol made it comfortable."

It was the first time she had admitted it out loud. They had removed most of the alcohol from the house and nixed the opioids. But she had never put it into words.

"It wasn't as bad as it sounds. It could have been so much worse." She started tugging on her hair. "It reached its peak right around the time Mac arrived."

"Got it." Madilyn nodded, and for a moment, she thought she saw a familiar sadness wash over her sister's face. "I'm sorry I wasn't here."

Marissa shook her head. "Please don't be." She turned her body to face her sister, speaking genuinely. "I mean it. You have nothing to apologize for."

"I missed a lot," she said quietly.

"I'm glad you did." She meant it. Letting out another sigh, she glanced toward the door, wishing someone with discharge papers would come through. "I'm glad you're here now, though." She still felt angry that Madilyn, that both of her sisters, had just assumed she'd bailed on them and their mom. But she had meant what she said. She was grateful and glad Madilyn was back home.

Madilyn's eyes had grown glassy as she tried to keep the tears from falling down her cheeks. Opening her arms, Marissa barely had a moment to brace herself before Madi was wrapped around her, definitely hugging too tight.

She winced. "Remember, I was just shot." She let out a breath of relief as Madi let go.

"I'm sorry!" Her eyes were wide with horror. If Marissa's side wasn't screaming at her, she would have laughed.

"You said something about clothes?" She was trying to push the pain she was feeling down. Pain was part of her everyday life, but the feeling of fire spreading through her stung. Every part of her screaming, burning. She shivered and wrapped her arms around herself, trying to hide the trembling in her limbs.

Madi nodded, rummaging through the bag beside the chair she had been sitting in. She pulled out a T-shirt and sweatpants. "The doctor suggested loose clothing."

Once the doctor came in with her discharge papers, Marissa insisted that Madilyn go home. While Marissa wanted to leave, part of her knew she was not likely to leave Mac there alone. He didn't have anyone else, not on this coast. Once her sister left, Marissa headed to the desk to get the information for both Mac and Jared.

While walking, she could feel every step as the wound beneath the bandage stretched and receded, her movements short and stiff as she tried to breathe and move through it. Maybe she should have stayed in that hospital bed one more day.

Mac's room was on the same floor as hers had been. So at least she didn't have to go far. She didn't even bother knocking on the door as she walked into Mac's room. He looked like he might have been arguing with the nurse when he noticed her.

"Thank God," he said quietly, no longer paying attention to the nurse jotting things down on her chart.

She had to push the tears back, overcome with sweet relief. "Hey."

She unsteadily walked over to the other side of his bed, away from the machines and the nurse, as fast as she could manage, which wasn't very fast. As she approached his side, she looked him up and down, her heart lodging in her throat. His shoulder was wrapped, bandaged, and in a sling across his chest. She could see that the nurse was poking around his side, which was also bandaged. His hair was a mess, and he looked pale and tired, with dark circles under his eyes appearing even darker against his colorless skin. She couldn't even manage words and felt unable to form cohesive thoughts. She just needed to be still and let the relief continue to wash over her; it almost outweighed the pain she felt all over.

Marissa pulled a chair right up against his bed and sat by his side as the entire scene flashed before her eyes again. The sound of the popping in her ears, the sight of both Mac and Jared on the ground.

Mac put his hand out over hers and gave her a gentle smile. "Hey."

His touch brought her back, and as she met his gaze, the tears flooded out of her eyes and down her cheeks. She felt stupid.

"Hey. Don't cry."

"I'm so sorry." She wasn't really sure where it was coming from. The relief, the worry, the guilt.

"Why?" he asked gently, bringing his hand up to her cheek.

Marissa shook her head, at a loss for words. She took his hand and wrapped both of her hands around it, dropping her head.

She felt him squeeze her hand. "Everything is going to be okay now. He's dead." She heard him wince and looked up to see him trying to adjust in bed while the nurse gave him a disapproving look.

Marissa swallowed the sobs back down, nodding her head and forcing a smile for his sake. There was real relief in that moment. She wanted nothing more than to curl up beside him and hold him close. The reality of how close she had come to losing him raced across her mind, sucking the air out from her lungs as it did. Swallowing, she shook her head at no one in particular and just gave his hand a squeeze. Marissa wasn't sure that anything was ever going to be okay again, though.

She definitely had regrets about leaving the hospital bed too soon. The hospital chair was so uncomfortable, and her whole body simply ached. The site of the gunshot wound felt like maybe it really was on actual fire, as opposed to just a burning sensation. She placed her fingers just above the bandage and winced, her skin clammy and warm to the touch. It was worth it to be beside Mac, to see him, hold his hand, and talk to him. Seeing him with her own eyes brought so much relief that she couldn't put it into words. He asked about Kate shortly after her arrival, just as relieved to hear she had already left before the first shot was ever taken.

"I owe you an apology." He held her gaze for a moment but dropped his hand back into his lap and let his chin fall to his chest. They had sat in silence most of the afternoon, just glad to be in each other's company. "For my behavior after the funeral and for the things I said—."

"Mac," she started, but he shook his head, looking back up. Marissa wondered if this had anything to do with the pain meds he had received within the last hour.

"No. There is no excuse for how I behaved. I was out of line. I'm not proud of it, but when it comes to your ex-husband, I feel less than adequate. Forever the runner-up." His gaze dropped from her eyes to the floor. "I always go back to that time you broke it off. I remember exactly what you said." He paused, letting out a heavy breath. "Do you?"

Marissa frowned, shaking her head. She couldn't remember what she had said. She remembered the ache it had left, but then she had been so sure Jared was it for her.

"It wasn't anything I had done or not done, that I was wonderful and amazing, and any girl would be lucky to be called mine. But you wouldn't be able to forgive yourself if you didn't give your marriage another chance. That at the end of the day, you still loved *him,* and he still had your heart. It wasn't fair to me to pretend otherwise." Mac shook his head, his body shuddering slightly at the memory as though he was trying to shake it off. "Murderers. Stalkers. They don't concern me as much as your ex-husband."

She felt a stab of guilt, the words bringing back the memory. He had been so gracious and kind, even as she broke his heart. It added to the tightness she already felt in her chest. And here he was, lying in a hospital beside her. The idea that she could cause him more physical harm, just by being close to her, wasn't lost on her. It was the very reason she had broken it off with Jared in the first place.

Marissa saw the opportunity, and she hated herself for it. "I do remember," she said softly, dropping her eyes to the floor. "And it will always be true."

She could feel his eyes boring into her as the room grew so still, the only thing she could hear was her own breathing.

"W-What are you saying?" The tone in his voice made her flinch.

"I don't know." She shook her head. She suddenly doubted herself, unsure she could go through with it. "I just … want to be honest with you."

She half expected lightning to strike her down where she stood. What she wanted to say was that she loved *him*, and after this experience, she couldn't imagine ever losing him. But if she let him stay, that would be exactly what would happen.

"Marissa…" His tone was low and quiet. It was a warning. "Don't do this. I know what you're doing. This whole thing had nothing to do with that. This was O'Rourke." He got to his feet, but she kept her eyes on the ground.

"That's not what I'm doing." She lied. "I can have—." She almost said *Jacob Starr* until she remembered he was dead. "A different agent stayed at the house. Or we can set you up on the couch. But I think this is for the best."

"No, you don't," he said with a sigh. "Look at me."

He waited, but she didn't move.

"If you're telling me you don't love me, that you don't want me, at least look me in the eye and tell me to my face." His words were harsh, but his tone hadn't changed. He wasn't buying it; part of her was relieved.

She swallowed before she forced herself to look up and meet his eyes. He took a step toward her, stepping right in front of her. She had to look up to hold his eyes. She clenched her jaw and tried to repeat her words.

"I-I..." Her voice trembled as she tried to spit the words out. "I don't want to do this anymore." Mac searched her face while the words hung in the air between them before he leaned over and suddenly kissed her. At first, it was soft as his lips brushed hers, but it soon deepened, and he wrapped his good arm around her waist, pulling her into him. Her arms went around his neck as she kissed him back with a desperation that hadn't been there moments before. Her body was screaming, trembling with pain, but she did her best to ignore it.

He finally let go of her when they were both breathless, but he remained where he stood. He took a moment to catch his breath before shaking his head at her. "Don't do that. Don't use your ex-husband against me. I'm not going anywhere."

Marissa looked down at the floor. "I just don't know what I would do if anything happened to you. Anything worse than this." She gestured to him.

"You can't control everything, Marissa," he said gently, unable to stop himself from yawning. His pain meds were working at least.

"Let's not have this conversation now. Just rest." She leaned forward and kissed him before she slumped back in the chair with a heavy sigh, squirming a little in discomfort.

Chapter 23

It had been a week and a half since the shootings, and they were all still in the hospital. Marissa had spent every night there next to Mac, although she had been home and checked in on Kate multiple times by this point. Madi and Ronnie had taken turns staying at the house with her. When Kate asked for Jacob, Ronnie had to break the news that he was gone. Kate had pretty much gone quiet since the day of Marissa's mom's funeral. Madi had heard her crying herself to sleep on several occasions. When Marissa came home, Kate didn't want to talk about it. She just held Marissa in a hug, not wanting to let go.

Jared had spent most of that time in the ICU, having only been moved to his own room and no longer in critical care in the last couple of days.

Marissa still hadn't seen him. There hadn't been any real opportunity to do so. But today was the day. At Mac's urging, she finally made her way to Jared's room.

Marissa had paused in the hallway, though. *What do you say to someone who took the bullet you were the intended target of? Someone whose heart you had already shattered. Someone who almost died pushing you out of the way.* Maybe the right words didn't exist. She just needed to go in. As she took a step forward, her path was suddenly blocked by a petite blonde.

Kirstie folded her arms across her chest, popping her hip out in dramatic fashion, firmly planting herself in the way of the door. "No."

"No?" Marissa questioned, raising an eyebrow. Ellie sat down, anticipating they wouldn't be moving anytime soon.

"No," she repeated as though Marissa was supposed to know what she was talking about. Kirstie shook her head. "Don't you think you've done enough?" There wasn't any emotion in her tone, but a storm raged in her eyes.

Marissa gaped at her. "What—?"

"He wouldn't be here right now if it wasn't for *you.* He wouldn't have been shot if someone wasn't trying to shoot *you.*"

Marissa was so caught off guard that she actually took a half-step back, placing a hand over her stitches at her side. The area was still warm and sensitive to the touch.

"He could have died. He DID die on the way here. Because of you."

Marissa noticed for the first time the small blonde was shaking.

"He has a child now. A life that has absolutely nothing to do with you. Why can't you just leave him the fuck alone?"

Marissa was floored. It took her a moment longer than she would have liked to find her words. "Kirstie, I haven't—."

The blonde threw up her hand. "Don't. Don't lie to my face. Keeping him so close that he thinks there's still a chance." Kirstie shook her head, wrapping her arms around herself. Marissa realized she was shaking out of anger. "You don't have to like me or respect me, but Jared and I have a daughter together. She is going to need her dad growing up. And just by being near you..." Her words trailed off as an unsteady breath came out in their place.

Marissa went to defend herself but stopped. Swallowing, she glanced passed Kirstie to the door. "I just wanted to make sure he was okay." The pain from her wound and the stitches had begun to radiate through her body, or at least, she had become very aware of it.

"He's not okay!" she said without hesitation. "But he will be. You don't need to see him, and I don't want him seeing you."

"Kirstie—."

"NO." She raised her voice and held her ground. If Marissa had been on the outside of this conversation, rather than the target of Kirstie's anger, she would have been impressed. "I'm not even saying this is your fault, but the people around you aren't safe. They are just collateral damage. And now, you are putting my family at risk. And my friend." Kirstie's voice gained more backbone the more she spoke. "I don't know if it's true, but if you are, in fact, the target of some crazy psycho, how can you stay here? How can you put the people you supposedly love at risk, just by being there?"

Marissa was speechless. Her eyes had grown wide, and again her gaze drifted past Kirstie, but the blonde adjusted, blocking her view of Jared's hospital door.

"I think it would be better if you just left. Leave the town, leave the state, and leave everyone alone. We would all be better off without you."

Marissa's eyes dropped to the ground. She was at a loss for words, and she could feel the tears welling in her eyes. Wiping her eyes with the back of her hand, she swallowed any form of defense that she had been building up. Biting her lip, she gave a half-nod of her head.

"I don't disagree," she said softly, finally breaking the silence. "Can you at least tell me what they said?"

"The bullet ripped through his large intestine. No exit wound. They had to fish it out. Thankfully, he's finally stable." She looked back at the closed door as though she could see him on the other side before glaring back at Marissa. "He's got a long recovery ahead of him, but he will be fine. But only if you stay the fuck out of his life."

Marissa blinked, took a breath, and then another before she nodded slowly. "Take care of each other," she managed before she turned and headed back to Mac's floor, trying to hold herself upright. In that moment, it felt important to keep that brave face, even as she walked away.

She did make a detour, however, to one of the bathrooms, locking the door behind her. She sank to the floor, leaning against the door, hands over her face. Ellie sat down by her side and rested her muzzle on Marissa's shoulder.

The worst part about what Kirstie had said was that she wasn't actually wrong. It *was* Marissa's fault that both Jared and Mac were in the hospital. The danger was present because of her, and they were all just collateral damage. Technically, O'Rourke had been after both Marissa and Mac, but it didn't change the danger she put everyone in.

Ellie nudged her nose between Marissa's hands and her face, licking her face. Wrapping her arms around the shepherd's neck, she buried her head into Ellie's fur and tried to silence the sobs that were escaping. Trying to keep them back only made her body hurt more. Even on the ground, Marissa was holding herself stiffly and in an unnatural position, doing her best to ease as much of the physical pain as she could.

They stayed like that for a good ten minutes before Marissa clumsily got back to her feet. She glanced at her reflection for a second before she dropped her eyes to the sink, watching the cold water run down the drain. She splashed her face a few times before she straightened, grabbing a paper towel to dry her face before leaving the bathroom and gritting her teeth while she walked.

A few moments later, Marissa pushed the door open and stepped into Mac's room. He was sitting up, with his legs over the bed, in the pair of sweatpants she had brought from the house but no shirt. The doctor appeared to be finishing up bandaging his shoulder, a stern expression on his face.

He turned that stern expression on Marissa. "While I would advise another night or even a few in the hospital, Mr. Mackenzie has refused. So we've bandaged the shoulder, cast the arm, and given him a sling. We also checked the stitches and bandaged his side. He has also refused pain medication."

Now it was Marissa's turn to frown. She looked from the doctor to Mac and back to the doctor. "Do you think we could have a minute?"

"Of course. I need to pull up the discharge paperwork, anyway." He shot a disapproving look at Mac before turning back to Marissa. "Good luck talking him into anything."

Marissa watched the older man leave the room before turning to Kate, who was sitting in a chair against the wall, looking anxious. "Hey, you okay?"

Kate mustered a nod, but her bloodshot eyes and wet cheeks said differently. Once Mac's condition was more stable, and he and Marissa had been able to better mask the pain and discomfort they were in, Kate had been allowed to visit the hospital. She'd been in quite a bit over the past week, but that didn't make things any less scary.

"I know you wanted to be here when we leave, but why don't you head back to the house? Ronnie is wandering the halls, and she can get you back and you guys can watch a movie while I get him all packed up and ready to come home."

Ronnie had come to get the last of the statements and retrieve the evidence—the bullets that had been dug out of both men.

Kate blinked, a look of relief flashing across her expression before she looked over at Mac and got to her feet. "Are you sure?"

Marissa nodded. "Of course. There's a spare key under the ceramic gargoyle at the bottom of the stairs of the porch." She hesitated for a moment before pulling Kate into a hug. She felt Kate hesitate, too, before the girl tightened her grip around Marissa.

"I'm sorry, I just really don't like hospitals," Kate said through tears.

"It's okay. You have nothing to apologize for."

Kate let Marissa go and hurried over to Mac, giving him a hug that caused him to wince. "I'm sorry," she whispered, her eyes growing wide.

"Don't ever be sorry." He hugged her back tightly with his good arm. "Especially about hugs."

While Mac hugged Kate and reassured her it was okay, Marissa texted Ronnie, who appeared moments later. Marissa tried to ignore the look of sympathy Ronnie gave her before giving Kate a big smile.

"Ready to go?"

Once they were alone in the small hospital room, Marissa folded her arms and looked Mac over. The sight of him on the ground flashed before her eyes, causing her to shudder. He reached out and put his good hand on her shoulder.

"Hey," he said with concern, but she shook her head.

"I can understand wanting to leave. We all hate hospitals. But why are you refusing pain meds?" The second the question left her lips, and she met his eyes, she suddenly knew the answer.

Mac swallowed and gave her the best smile he could muster. "I'll be fine, Marissa."

She shook her head. "If you're saying no because of me..." Her voice trailed off.

The memory of the struggles she had endured with pain medications when he'd come back into her life flashed before her eyes. It hadn't been nearly as bad as it could have been, and her behavior had been manic and out of character because of the meds her crazy murderer therapist had prescribed. Regardless, they had cleared her house of most of the alcohol and pain medications that she absolutely hadn't needed.

"Marissa." He brought his hand up to her cheek, making sure she looked at him. "It's because *I* will be fine without them. This isn't the first time I've been shot. I heal faster without them. Ibuprofen will be fine."

Marissa held his gaze, but she didn't believe a word of what he was saying.

"Can you help me get my shirt on?"

Marissa looked over his bandages and nodded. "We'll have to take your arm out of the sling for a minute."

He nodded and did just that. It was a slow process, but they eventually got the plain blue T-shirt on, and Marissa helped him get the sling back into position, too.

Once he was completely dressed, he started working on getting his shoes on, and Marissa sat down on the hospital bed and watched him quietly, still running the last couple of weeks through her mind. Mac looked up at her from the chair he had sat down in and sighed, bringing her back into the moment.

"How is Jared?" he asked softly.

Marissa felt tears sting her eyes at the mention of his name, but she willed them back. She half shrugged one shoulder. "I don't know."

"He'll come around," Mac said reassuringly, but Marissa shook her head.

"No. I don't think he will." Kirstie certainly wasn't going to, and Marissa couldn't blame her.

Mac hesitated, wincing a little as he sat back in the chair. "Speaking of Jared…"

Marissa's eyes lifted to meet his, and she opened her mouth to speak, but he held his hand up to stop her.

"We aren't going to have a repeat of the same conversation we've already had. I just want to tell you I'm sorry for being an insecure asshole." He sighed. "I understand you had a whole life before me. And that doesn't just go away. I love you, and I'm sorry."

Marissa felt the anxiety and frustration momentarily wash away as she met his eyes. "I love you, too."

Chapter 24

What a fucking mess this had all turned out to be. The last couple of months had not gone according to plan. At all. Thankfully, he was flexible. While Marissa and company had been in the safe house, he had used that time to his advantage. He had spent that time cleaning up the rest of Jack's mess back in Chicago, looking for a way to pin that on a reasonable suspect. He got the cabin ready, bought the van, and got all of his shit and Jack's in order. When the time came, no one was going to be able to find a paper trail. O'Rourke had provided him with the perfect ability to get everything ready.

What he hadn't planned on was Daniel fucking Fryer giving Marissa the key to figure things out. Thankfully, the timing of that had also worked in his favor. Her mom's passing to the shootout at her funeral had kept everyone busy enough that he knew no one was looking. This was why he was a planner.

O'Rourke had taken Marissa and Mac's reappearance as some kind of insult, like coming out of hiding was them saying he was nothing to be afraid of. They were among the last on his hit list. He needed to make a statement. Idiot. Now he was dead.

Okay, maybe not everyone had been too busy. The Internal Affairs agent, Sean Boswell, was another loose end he had to deal with. And Boswell was something that needed to be dealt with sooner rather than later before he dug too far.

The clock was running now. They had maybe two weeks at most to get things in order. He was almost excited, but everything had to go just right. There was still a lot of risk something would go wrong, and most of that landed on fucking Jack. He had a plan for him, too, though. The only potential issue with that was the next pieces of the plan relied on Jack to follow the instructions.

Working solo was definitely the way to go. It took too much of the excitement out of everything, having to plan every single detail and keep all his puppets in line.

O'Rourke had been a positive, unforeseen distraction. With everyone out of the house, he was able to remove all the surveillance he'd used over the past year. He was also able to take a few things to plant on their fall guy, who he was sure would be found soon enough, and that enabled him to twist Fryer's claims to his advantage, too. He had to make it all happen a lot sooner than he'd meant to, but that was okay. Again, he was flexible. He was a little concerned about the bullets at O'Rourke's crime scene, though. It had been a public spectacle, after all. The gun he'd used was unregistered, but he just needed to get rid of it quickly.

It was surreal to think that they were finally here. A year of buildup had given him more excitement than he could've imagined. Maybe his grandmother had always been right: Patience was a virtue.

He thought about the cabin and grinned. He had set it up to look a lot like the warehouse, not that Marissa would notice. She had been blindfolded the whole time. He had marked the spots for the van and keys, each separate and a decent distance away. He had also set traps around the perimeter. Everything was perfectly set up. He only had to wait a little longer.

He took a long, last drag off his cigarette before tossing it out into the street. He put on his game face and walked into the crowded house.

Chapter 25

A few days after Mac was discharged, they shifted into a new routine. Marissa had set up the living room for them, so Mac could either sleep in the recliner or on the pull-out, avoiding the stairs until he felt more comfortable. He was visibly pushing through pain but insisted he was fine.

Kate was back in school just in time for Thanksgiving break the next week. Marissa was frustratingly aware that December was only a couple of weeks away, and she felt the weight of the unspoken deadline that Fryer had pointed out. But she kept it to herself, focusing all of her energy on Mac. To the point where she was driving him crazy.

"I'm not completely helpless. I'm just a little sore," he'd finally snapped at her. What he didn't understand was her need to stay busy.

She had gone into her home office multiple times, thinking she could at least be productive. But every time she stepped inside, she was immediately overwhelmed by the mess of files that were contained in the duffle bag in the middle of the room. She couldn't bring herself to open it. Still. It felt like everything they thought they knew was wrong and no longer mattered. It was like they needed to start from scratch. And the idea of that was just daunting.

She would walk past the guest room that had become Jacob's, his stuff still inside. He hadn't been local, and he apparently didn't have much family. Just a brother who had thanked them for giving him the news of his brother's passing and never answered the phone again. They had tried to fly him out and offered to transport Jacob's body. He wasn't interested in hearing any of it. While Kate was in school, Wicket spent her time in that room, lying across Jacob's bed or on top of his suitcase, which had been left open at the foot of the bed.

Marissa would lean against the doorframe of the room, still not ready to disturb anything in it, and replay that day over and over and over in her mind. It had all happened so fast. Everyone had dropped to the ground in the blink of an eye. Marissa felt responsible. He had died because of her. He had been there to protect her. And now he was gone.

The day Clyde and Madi came by for a visit, Marissa was actually relieved for the distraction.

"Haven't talked to you in like a week. Just wanted to come by and see how you guys are doing," Madi answered when she asked about the reason for the visit. They made themselves comfortable in the living room while Marissa leaned against the wall in her living room, folding her arms in front of her.

"Do you guys want anything to drink? Or to eat?" She hoped they'd say no because there wasn't a lot of food in the house. The amount of takeout they had been eating recently was shameful.

"Do you have tea?" Madilyn asked, looking at her hopefully.

"Of course." She pushed herself off the wall. "Clyde, you want anything?" He shook his head and went back to the conversation he was having with Mac.

Turning, Marissa headed into the kitchen, Ellie at her heels. Playing hostess was not Marissa's strong suit. She put the kettle on the burner and let out a sigh. Madi came in behind her.

"How are you?" she asked gently, leaning against the counter beside her.

Marissa just shrugged her shoulder.

"You know you have to talk to me eventually, right?"

"Not now, Madilyn," she said after a few beats of silence.

Glancing over, she saw the hurt in her sister's face. A few weeks ago, she probably would have felt guilty over making her feel bad, but today, she didn't care. The moment they had shared at the hospital hadn't erased the fact that Madi believed Marissa had just left. While their mom was dying.

With no filter left, Marissa let the words come out. "No matter what has happened, you still assumed I just walked away." She shook her head angrily. "I'll be out when the tea is done."

"Rissa. Please. I don't know how else to say I'm sorry."

"You haven't tried to say sorry, Madi. You were angry because you just thought I bailed. Just like everyone else, you were okay to just think the absolute worst of me. There isn't an apology for that."

"But—."

"No. I don't want to hear it. Go sit down, and I'll bring your tea out when it's done. I'm not going to have this conversation right now. I love you, but it fucking hurts, Madi."

Her sister lingered there for an extra moment before turning and leaving the kitchen. Marissa knew she was being harsh, but her feelings still hurt. Just the understanding that everyone could assume the worst stung and ached, and it hadn't dulled over the last couple of weeks.

When the tea was ready, she came back out to the living room, and Clyde was on the phone, frowning deeper than usual. Mac was also frowning, his face pale. Handing the tea over to Madi, she leaned down.

"What's going on?"

"I don't know. Clyde got a phone call from his boss, and he's been making that face the whole time."

Marissa glanced at Mac, who met her eyes but shrugged his shoulder, indicating that he knew as much as she did.

"Yes, sir, I understand. We'll be there." He ended the call and got to his feet.

He looked directly at Marissa. "That was Nick. You and I need to go to Bellevue. Now. It's about," he paused, "*the case.*" He emphasized the last two words, causing Marissa to raise an eyebrow. This had to be about Ben.

Marissa straightened back up slowly but nodded her head. "Yeah, okay." Her brain was having trouble catching up, but a moment later, she turned to grab her shoes.

"I'm going with you," Mac said, trying to get to his feet.

"No, you're not. You are going to stay right here," Clyde said, glancing at Madilyn. "Would you be good to hang out here until we get back?"

Madi nodded quickly. Marissa frowned but agreed that someone else should stay with Mac since he had difficulty moving around.

He glared at his partner before looking at Marissa with pleading eyes. "I should come with you."

"No, he's right. You need to stay and take it easy." She glanced at her sister. "Thank you for staying."

"Of course." She was still dejected and pouting from the kitchen, but she wasn't petty. "I can have Mel grab Kate when she gets out of school?"

"That would be great," Marissa answered before she walked over and gave him a kiss. "I will call you when I know something. I love you."

"I love you too. Be careful," he said, unhappy with the situation.

Almost two hours later, Marissa ducked beneath the yellow Do Not Cross police tape that Clyde held up for her before following. The car ride out had been heavy with silence. Walker was standing at the open door, leaning against the wall and shaking his head. Ellie trotted up behind Marissa, nose in the air.

"It's a fucking lot in there," he said before they could walk inside. "But the good news is that this is over."

Marissa didn't respond but took a breath before stepping over the threshold and heading inside.

She wasn't sure what she expected, but she walked into a messy apartment, dark because of poor lighting, with clutter everywhere. A familiar, sickening smell wafted through the air. Clyde hadn't given her a clue as to what she was walking into or what Walker had shared over the phone.

She saw an officer standing next to what Marissa assumed was the hallway. He motioned for her to keep going. Without waiting for Clyde, she walked down the hallway and found the young officer she recognized as Sam Trotter coming out of a room to the left. Ellie paused at the young officer before stopping at Marissa's side. The shepherd liked him.

"Hey, detective." He sounded as uncomfortable as he looked. "Um. It's all in there."

Marissa frowned but nodded, stopping right in the doorway. The room was dark, with only a single lamp, but she saw the body first. Boswell was slumped back in an office chair, completely drained of color. He had clearly been there a minute. The gun was on the ground beside him, clearly having fallen from his hand. It was hard to deny the assumption that this was self-inflicted. Following where his gaze would have been before he took his own life, she turned to face the wall that was absolutely covered in photographs. Her breath caught in her throat as she scanned photo after photo of her face on his wall.

Clyde came into the room behind her quietly, examining the wall sans snarky comment. Marissa assumed it was taking a lot for him to stay quiet in the moment. Ellie nudged Marissa's leg, alert to what was probably her raised heart rate in that moment.

Looking over to the desk, she saw more photos, copies of the letters she had received, a few photos of O'Rourke, and a letter addressed to him. Stepping closer to the desk, she read the letter.

Sean,

I'm done. I've sent the information to the authorities—both Port Townsend and Seattle police and FBI—so they will know what you've done soon enough.

I won't be your puppet any longer. They are going to know everything.

-Veronica

Marissa blinked, holding her breath until Clyde took a step over to the desk. She went to pick up the letter, but Clyde offered her a pair of gloves.

"Maybe don't touch anything without these."

She didn't respond, but she took the gloves and put them on, lifting the letter up to take a closer look at the handwriting. She had started shaking her head, trying to process what this implied.

"Veronica?" Clyde raised an eyebrow. "You mean—?"

"Don't," she said, pulling out her phone and taking a picture of the letter. She took one last look at Boswell before she turned to Clyde. "I need some air."

She didn't bother waiting for him to respond and left the room, passing Officer Trotter by the door and the unfamiliar officer at the top of the hallway before walking straight out the front door. She was walking fast enough that Ellie had to trot alongside her to keep pace.

There was bile rising in her throat, and her hands felt completely numb. It was cold, but it wasn't *that* cold. It was panic. She started shaking her hands, pacing in a tight circle.

"Are you okay?"

Marissa had forgotten that Walker was standing there, cigarette in hand, taking a minute for himself.

She didn't trust herself to answer but shook her head, forcing the vomit back down, trying to keep her breathing at a level pace. She wasn't doing a great job. Ellie had been keeping up with her, nudging her, but she was sick of Marissa ignoring her, so she jumped up on her.

After that moment, at the urging of her working dog, Marissa dropped to the ground and sat in the grass. Ellie insisted that she stay there and lay across her lap.

"Is that Veronica Rivera?" he asked, taking a quick, final drag of his cigarette before dropping it and stepping on it with his shoe.

"It can't be," she said softly, trying to run the last year through her mind.

"I did call Sheriff Jackson and to update him on the situation. He was going to pick her up." He let out a long sigh. "I would have never suspected Sean Boswell." He paused and then added apologetically, "I'm sorry for doubting what Daniel Fryer said. It was hard to consider anyone on the inside being capable of such things." He paused again, shaking his head. "I'm sorry."

She wanted to say the apology was not and could never be accepted. This was worse than anything she had considered before. Instead, she just said, "Thanks."

Clyde appeared in the doorway. "We should probably get you back home."

They weren't there to work the case; they were there so she could see the evidence with her own eyes. Because she would have never believed it any other way.

"We'll debrief in a few days. Go home, rest. Take care of my agent." Walker shook his head, still clearly irritated by that situation. "At least this is over."

Marissa kept hearing that phrase the whole car ride home. *At least this is over.* It didn't feel over. It felt like the world had opened up beneath her ... *again* ... and swallowed her whole.

"He's right, at least." Clyde broke the silence. "This should be the end of it."

Marissa shook her head. "Maybe."

"You don't believe it?"

"I don't know. I'm having a difficult time imagining Ronnie having anything to do with this." She shook her head. "Even Sean Boswell. It doesn't make sense. He doesn't know me. The *why* doesn't make any sense to me."

Clyde shrugged. "I mean, even if we knew the reason, we probably wouldn't understand, anyway. He was a psychopath."

Marissa sighed. "Maybe. But I know Ronnie."

"Maybe he had something over her?" he offered without taking his eyes off the road. The sun was already setting, and it was getting dark. "Blackmail or something?"

"Maybe," she said with zero conviction. "I need to call Mac." She wished he was there instead of fucking Clyde Bennet.

"Before you do..." Clyde started, glancing over at her, hesitating. "He seems like he's struggling a little bit."

"What do you mean?" she frowned.

"I mean, with the pain. He seems really uncomfortable."

"Oh." She sighed. "He is. He refused the pain medications."

Clyde shook his head. "Stubborn man."

At least they agreed on something. "Yeah, I don't know what to do."

"Do you know if his doctor put the prescription in?"

Marissa tried to think back to when he was getting discharged and everything the doctor had said. "I don't remember."

"You can always see if his prescription is in and pick it up for him. Tell him it's aspirin."

Marissa opened her mouth to say something but then closed it again. "Yeah, maybe." It wasn't a terrible idea. Putting a pin in the thought, she grabbed her phone and called Mac.

He answered on the second ring, clearly waiting for her call. "Hey."

"Hey," she responded softly. "We're on our way back."

"Jackson called me and filled me in on everything," he said, keeping his voice low.

"Yeah. It was a lot." That was all she could manage. "We can talk more when I get home. I just wanted to give you the update that we're on our way home. I love you."

"I love you too."

Marissa closed the call and looked out the window, letting the feeling of complete overwhelm and helplessness wash over her. The idea that all of this was over, what? Some obsession that was built off of two days in the warehouse? From someone who was mostly a stranger? And the idea that someone who she had known since middle school could be in on it? Someone she trusted with not only her life but with Kate's... Her blood ran cold.

"Do you need the heat on?" Clyde asked suddenly, and she realized she was actually shivering.

"No, thanks. I just need to close my eyes."

Clyde nodded. "Okay. Just let me know. I'll get you home as soon as possible."

Marissa adjusted in the chair and leaned against the door, wrapping her arms around herself and closing her eyes. She couldn't settle her mind, but she couldn't hear the thoughts if she was unconscious.

The next time she opened her eyes, Clyde was parking the car in her driveway. "We're back," he said.

Marissa sat up straight and wiped her face, remembering where they were coming from. She saw Mac and Jackson sitting on the front porch, waiting for them. Getting out of the SUV, she waited for Ellie before heading to the porch. Mac rose and met her at the top of the stairs. He pulled her in for a hug and held her there for a long moment as Clyde made his way past them. "Is Madi inside?"

Mac nodded. "Yeah, she and Kate are watching something." Marissa hadn't even thought about how this would affect Kate. She and Ronnie had grown so close over the last several months; this would be devastating.

Letting out a breath, Marissa reluctantly pulled back and glanced over at Jackson, who shook his head.

"We couldn't find Veronica anywhere. We did find something in her apartment, though." He held a piece of paper out. "We will find her."

Marissa pulled away from Mac to take a step toward Jackson, reaching out for what he was trying to show her. It was a piece of a paper—a letter. Marissa read it over four times before she looked up.

Marissa

I am so sorry for everything. I didn't have a choice. I hope you can forgive me, but I can't forgive myself.

Ronnie

Marissa blinked. The handwriting was the same. But she shook her head, looking frantically at everyone, but all they just could give her was sympathy.

"I don't care what this says. This doesn't make any sense."

"You took a picture, right? Of the note at Boswell's?" Clyde asked.

Marissa nodded and pulled it up on her phone, hoping there would be enough of a difference. But they appeared to be a perfect match.

"It doesn't make any sense," she repeated, desperate for someone to listen, but they were all giving her the same look.

"Why don't we go inside?" Mac tried, putting a hand on her arm.

Marissa pushed it away, still shaking her head.

"Marissa, he's right. Let's go inside," Jackson said as gently as he could muster.

Marissa sighed, wanting to argue. Maybe scream. But instead, she followed them. Since it was a school night, Marissa sent Kate to bed without giving her any information. She knew she had to eventually, but not right then. Once they were sure the teenager was in her room, Madi and Clyde said their goodbyes. Marissa sat motionless on the couch, not listening to Jackson and Mac as they talked about the implications of everything they had learned.

Eventually, Jackson left, too, promising to keep Marissa updated but insisting she stay out of it.

The next morning, Marissa offered to take Kate to school and, as a treat, she'd pick up coffee. But between dropping off Kate and grabbing coffee, she found herself at the pharmacy. Marissa chewed on her thumbnail, anxiously standing in the line. She couldn't remember the last time she had actually slept. Between the pain, the stress, and everything in between, sleep had eluded her for a while. She had convinced herself that she was doing this for

Mac, even though he had declined. The doctor had said once he was out of the hospital, it would be hard to manage his pain. Having painkillers on hand was just the smart move. At least, that's what she was telling herself. Ellie huffed dramatically, sitting at her side. Marissa could recall now that Mac's doctor had told her he put the prescriptions in, in hopes that maybe if Mac determined he needed it, he would take it. The doctor hadn't known why he was refusing.

Marissa moved up in the line, biting her lower lip as she dropped her hand. When she reached the counter, she smiled and gave the pharmacist all of Mac's information. She shifted her weight from one foot to the other and let out a deep breath. Since getting home, Mac kept the brave face on, but she could see that every single time he moved, he was in pain.

A minute later, the pharmacist came back with a bag and handed it over to her. And just like that, after signing the little screen, she walked back to her car with a bottle of Percocet.

In the car, she stared at the bag and felt immediate regret. But it was too late now to do anything about it. She looked over at Ellie in the passenger seat before letting out a sigh. She put the bag to the side, started the car, and headed for the coffee shop.

Chapter 26

After getting back from the pharmacy, Marissa had spent the day trying to reconcile the information she had been given the night before. She still didn't believe it. They still didn't have so much as a sighting of Ronnie; it didn't make any sense.

She had fought for permission to go look through Ronnie's house, but Jackson wouldn't let her anywhere near the vicinity. He had given her a copy of the note, but that was where the sharing ended. He insisted it was for her own good.

Mac tried to keep her distracted and wanted to make them food, as he was sick of all the takeout they had been living on. She was about to try talking him out of it when her phone started ringing. Pulling her phone from her pocket, she frowned when she saw the medical examiner's assistant was calling her.

"Hello? Kennedy?"

"Hey, Marissa." Kennedy's voice sounded weird over the phone. "Do you have a minute to talk?"

"Of course," she said, glancing at Mac before stepping out of the kitchen.

"I shouldn't be sharing this information." Kennedy hesitated. "But the bullets we pulled out of Jacob Starr, and the one from Mac's shoulder and Jared's gut ... those three matched bullets from the gun they found at Sean Boswell's home." There was a sigh on the other end of the line. "The rest of them were matched to O'Rourke's. And we pulled matches out of O'Rourke to your gun, Mac's gun, and Boswell's gun."

Marissa blinked. "So you're saying Sean Boswell shot Jacob, Mac, and Jared in all the chaos, and then he shot O'Rourke, as well?" That didn't seem realistic. Bellevue was not a short drive away. He couldn't have known the chaos with O'Rourke would ensue, and coming during the funeral was a risk. It didn't make sense. None of this fit.

She heard Kennedy clear her throat, snapping her back to the present. "The other reason I'm calling..." She was whispering now. "They found Ronnie."

"What? Where is she?"

"She's here, Marissa. They brought her to me," she said, still speaking softly but in a much gentler tone.

Marissa blinked, taking in Kennedy's words. Her chest heaved, feeling a heavy weight that hadn't been there a moment before. "Wait. Sh-she's in the morgue?"

"I'm afraid so." Kennedy was speaking at a normal level again. "They found her on the beach this morning."

Marissa felt like she was going to throw up. "But ... I don't understand."

"She washed up on the beach this morning," she repeated. "I haven't had the chance to do an in-depth exam yet."

Marissa wasn't sure how to respond or how to process the words she was hearing. Thankfully, Kennedy knew what Marissa was thinking.

"I don't have cause of death yet, but after a preliminary look, it appears to be self-inflicted." Her voice dropped to almost a whisper again. "Jackson ordered me not to tell you. But you had the right to know."

"Thank you, Kennedy. Call me as soon as you know anything else." Marissa had stepped back into the kitchen, unable to stand still.

"I will. Take care of yourself, please."

"Thanks."

Marissa hung up the phone and used the kitchen counter to brace herself, suddenly dizzy.

She glanced out toward the living room, where Kate would be later that evening, and fought to push down the bile rising in her throat.

"What's wrong?" Mac came out of the bathroom, frowning at her.

"They found her. Washed up on the beach this morning." She shuddered involuntarily. Marissa leaned down to scratch Ellie's ear, aware the dog was nudging her to alert her. Mac also became aware as he walked over and pushed the stool over to her.

"Please, sit."

Marissa didn't argue and sat down quietly, shaking her head. "I still don't believe it. It doesn't make any sense."

Mac rubbed her shoulders and kissed the top of her head. "Sometimes things don't make sense." She could hear the rest of his thought, which was that it didn't make it not true.

"Okay. Hear me out," she said after a minute, wiping her eyes. She was not going to cry again. She couldn't. "If it is what everyone says it is—if Sean Boswell was the mastermind, and Ronnie was following his orders—who was in Chicago?"

Mac sat down on the stool next to her and turned to face her, meeting her eyes. "We weren't keeping track of Boswell's moves. He could have been in Chicago." Mac sighed. "Marissa, we're not always going to have the answers." He shook his head, running his hand through his hair. "I'm sure someone is looking into all of that right now."

She sighed heavily. "Maybe not, but I feel like we should have more than what we have. Things should make more sense, fall into place."

"You know that's not how it works, Riss." Mac gave her that sympathetic look that made her want to scream. She was over everyone's sympathy.

"Well, it's dumb," she said, pouting.

Mac got back on his feet and put an arm around her. "Come on, let's go into the living room." She turned just in time to see him wince.

"Are you okay?" she asked with a sigh. She knew what his answer would be and what the actual answer was, and they were not the same. His shoulder and his side were still causing him problems. He was set to start physical therapy the next week.

"Yeah, I'm fine."

"I wish you would take something for pain," she said softly.

"I'm fine, Marissa. I just need to stretch out a little. Come on. Come to the couch with me."

Marissa sighed and nodded, heading to the living room with him. They settled onto the pullout couch, which was still set up like a bed, with a mass of pillows to help him get comfortable. Marissa let him settle into his spot before sitting down next to him, resting her head on his good shoulder.

"Do you really believe that it's over?" she asked finally. She didn't believe it was over. She wished she did—it would have been some kind of silver lining—but it just felt like it was more of the same. A setup. A cover-up to conceal the real bad guy.

"There is no reason to think it's not," he said after a moment. "The evidence is pointing us to the answers. Don't borrow trouble where there isn't any."

Marissa frowned. She hated that phrase. But instead of arguing, she just sighed and closed her eyes.

They stayed like that until Marissa left to pick up Kate from school, leaving Mac sleeping on the couch with Ellie sprawled out beside him. It was a quick ride, so she didn't need to make Ellie get up.

Kate got into the blue Mini's passenger seat and pulled up her backpack onto her lap.

"Hey, how was school?"

"It was alright. It's nice to be back, I guess." Kate shrugged a shoulder. The teenager never wanted to admit it out loud, but she enjoyed school. It had become obvious when they were in the safe house; it was the social stuff Kate wasn't big on. "How are you doing?"

Marissa had tried really hard not to say much about the situation, but she had explained that there was something going on that involved

Ronnie. Shrugging her shoulder, she gave Kate the most genuine smile she could muster. "Alright, I guess." She glanced over at the concerned teenager. "Honest. I'm okay."

Kate didn't look convinced, and Marissa knew there wasn't much behind it, but she let the answer hang there.

"Are things … going to be normal now?"

The question caught Marissa off guard. "What do you mean?"

"I mean, we don't have to go into hiding again?" She sounded so young in that moment, Marissa was thrown.

"No, honey, we don't." Especially if everything was "over." Not that Marissa believed it.

"Does that mean I can stay with you now?" Kate asked, dropping her eyes and hugging her backpack. "Could we just be a family?"

Marissa inhaled and thought about the question for a moment; that would be the real silver lining to this being over. Actually *over*.

"I would love that, Kate…" Marissa started.

But her gut told her this wasn't over.

"We'll see, okay?" She glanced over at the sullen-looking girl. "I promise. I'll meet with Ms. Parker and see."

At that, Kate perked up a little. As they pulled into the driveway, Marissa frowned at a gray Kia parked in front of her house that she didn't recognize. She spotted a dark-haired woman walking up the porch steps.

"Wait here."

Getting out of the car, Marissa walked toward the porch. "Hi. Can I help you?"

The brunette turned, and Marissa instantly recognized her from the photographs she had received. When she saw Marissa, she was sure the woman's expression mirrored hers.

"Hi." She seemed to hesitate, a Southern drawl coming through her soft voice. "My name is Caroline Grimes, and I was looking for you..." Her voice trailed off for a moment as she pulled out a folded photograph of Marissa from her jacket pocket. "Marissa Ambrose."

Marissa turned to motion to Kate, sending her inside. Kate hopped out of the car and threw her backpack over her shoulder. She paused, watching Marissa for a moment before closing the front door behind her.

Putting her hands in her back pockets, Marissa made her way up to the porch. "It's nice to meet you, Caroline." It was good to see she was still alive. "I received pictures of you, too. The FBI was searching for you. How did you find me?"

Caroline looked uncertain before she straightened herself. She stood maybe an inch or two shorter than Marissa, but other than that, it was hard to see her other features as she was bundled up, clearly not used to the cold.

"I'm a reporter for the *Atlanta Tribune* and I have a true crime podcast, *Crime with Grimes*." She let out a breath. She was nervous. "So I have my sources. I've been getting pictures like this, but of me, for months now. But I've gotten two of you the last two times. In this picture—," She showed Marissa the photo in her hand again. "there were some landmarks of the town in the background, and I was able to go from there."

Marissa blinked, surprised and impressed by the answer. "Alright then." She nodded. "Let's go inside and talk."

As she opened the door, she found Mac heading toward the entryway from the living room. He frowned as she held the door open. "Everything okay?"

"It is." Marissa smiled as Caroline came in behind her. "Mac, this is Caroline. Caroline, this is Mac."

"Oh." Mac paused, clearly trying to figure out why she looked familiar. "Hello."

"She is the mystery girl from the batch of photographs," Marissa explained, as though it wasn't a big deal.

Marissa looked around and saw Kate grabbing food from the fridge. "I'm going to go upstairs and do homework. I have a paper I want to get started on."

She gave Marissa a genuine smile before wrapping her in a quick hug and running up the stairs. The stress of the safe house and everything that had been happening the last couple of months seemed to be dissipating.

"We can sit in here." Marissa smiled gently at Caroline, pointing to the kitchen table. "Do you want anything to eat or drink?"

"No, thank you. I'm good," she said, her accent sounding somewhat familiar.

"Did you say you were from Atlanta?" Marissa asked, to which Caroline nodded.

Mac had followed slowly, going past them both to the back door to let Ellie back inside. She hurried over to greet Caroline, interested in the stranger sitting in her home, before running over to Marissa excitedly. "This is Ellie."

"She's beautiful," Caroline said before turning her attention back to Marissa. "I came because I was wondering if you had been getting pictures, too."

Marissa nodded and let out a sigh. "For the last three years and some change." Caroline's eyes widened in surprise. Marissa gave Ellie's ear a scratch and sat down at the table. "So, when was the last time you received pictures?" Mac raised an eyebrow at her, but Marissa ignored him.

"I think three weeks ago?"

Marissa let out a sigh. "Okay. Well. Theoretically, it's over. As of yesterday, there was a confession and a suicide, and the supposed accomplice was found dead this morning." Speaking it into words did not make it seem any more real, but she gave Caroline the facts as she had them.

Caroline listened, frowning and nodding slowly, her own disbelief mirrored in the woman's expression. "Theoretically?" she said finally, with a raised eyebrow of her own.

Marissa twitched her nose and looked down at the top of the table, tapping her fingers on it. "The evidence points to it. But…" She shook her head. "I don't know. It doesn't feel … right. Or finished."

It was the truth. With a sigh, she met Caroline's gaze.

"Internal Affairs Agent Sean Boswell and Port Townsend Officer Veronica Rivera." There was no recognition in Caroline's eyes at their names. She didn't really expect to see any. But then again, if she had been receiving photographs for a few months, there should have been some connection. "You said you've been receiving them for the last few months."

Caroline nodded. "Almost a year. They started last January, I think?"

"I assume neither of those names a ring a bell?"

Caroline shook her head and Marissa frowned. It didn't make any sense. She glanced down at her phone and considered messaging Jackson, but he was trying very hard to keep her on the outside.

"Do you get letters, too?" she asked suddenly.

To that, Caroline nodded.

"I brought everything with me if you want to see." She shrugged her shoulder. "I'm not really sure what I was expecting when I got here, but I just..." She trailed off, but Marissa nodded.

"Yeah. I get it."

Over the next couple of hours, they compared their letters and photographs and talked about their theories. Mac had gone and grabbed the duffle bag out of the office for her, but then left them to themselves.

Caroline was sweet, opinionated, and really smart. Another strong brunette to add to the list of victims that the Couples Killer already had. Her letters were the same as Marissa's, but also different. They read almost like high school love letters. More than ever, Marissa was convinced that this wasn't over.

As they both packed their things back up, they made a plan to meet with Sheriff Jackson. Having someone who had been enduring the same thing she had been dealing with for so long felt like a relief in a way.

"I'll meet you at the station Friday morning," Marissa confirmed as she was saying goodbye. They had planned on the day after tomorrow because Jackson didn't have availability until then, according to his receptionist, at least. He wasn't in the office, and he wasn't answering her calls, so she had to schedule with Shelly like everyone else.

Caroline smiled, also looking more relaxed than she had for most of the visit. "Perfect." She paused. "It was really good to meet you."

"It was good to meet you, too." Marissa waved and watched her pull out of the driveway. She had checked into the Tides Inn. They had exchanged numbers and made plans.

Chapter 27

Marissa felt strangely vindicated after meeting with Caroline the evening before, and it left her in a weird mood. Something about someone really understanding what she was going through, because they'd gone through it too, was almost comforting. And with Caroline's letter, she was sure she could reopen the conversation about whether Boswell and Ronnie were being set up. She was more sure than ever. There was something scratching at the back of her mind. Something familiar to her about Caroline's letters, the phrasing of things. But she couldn't put her finger on it.

"How are you feeling?" Mac asked from the recliner. They had been struggling to get him comfortable the last few days, but the chair seemed to help more than the couch.

Marissa made a face at him. "I should be asking you that. You're the one who's gone through surgery and won't take anything for pain."

"I'm not taking anything for pain because I feel okay." He shook his head. "So my question stands: How are *you* feeling?"

Marissa shrugged her shoulders. "Fine, I guess." Dr. Bailey had reached out twice since the funeral, but Marissa couldn't bring herself to make the drive. She couldn't leave Mac in the condition he was in. She also really didn't want to talk; it felt like that had been all she had been doing lately. She had rescheduled their appointment for next week.

"You know it's okay to not be okay, right?" he said after a moment, to which Marissa shot him a glare. Throwing up his hands, he shrugged his shoulders. "Listen, the last three years for you were already a lot. The last year was especially hard. And the last couple of months have been hell."

Marissa let out a sigh. "Mostly, I'm just tired." She was deflecting, and she knew it. She felt tired but also numb and broken and, physically, everything just ached. But dwelling on it wouldn't make anything better. Changing the subject was much easier. "What time is Clyde coming to pick you up?"

"He should be here any minute." Mac glanced at his phone. "I wish you could come with me, though."

She shook her head. "It's okay. I wouldn't be allowed in that meeting with you, anyway." She shrugged her shoulder. She did hate that she wasn't going with him, but she wasn't sad to miss out on Walker and Clyde. "Besides, I have to pick up Kate from school."

Mac sighed and nodded his head. "I know. But still." He glanced out the window and got to his feet. "Speaking of, Clyde is here."

Marissa also stood and brushed her hair out of her face. "Okay," she said sadly as he came over, put his good arm around her waist, and pulled her close for a kiss. She had to stand on the tips of her toes, but she pressed into him as she did, reminding herself not to put her arms around his neck despite how much she wanted to. "Just hurry home."

"I will. I promise." He gave her another kiss before he released her waist and headed out the door.

When the door closed, Marissa turned to Ellie, who was lying on the floor looking unimpressed. "Well, it's just you and me, kid."

It was surreal and a little weird that Marissa was alone. It was the first time in nearly a year that there wasn't someone nearby, somewhere. No bodyguard, no FBI, no police officers. After O'Rourke's death, there had been two FBI agents always lurking around. Marissa hadn't even bothered to learn their names. Once Boswell's body had been found, they had been recalled as well, and all the surveillance that had been in place was just gone. Glancing around the house, her eyes stopped at the window. She was certain that someone was still out there and watching, though.

Marissa walked over to the dining room and opened the glass door to her hutch where she had hidden the bottle of Percocet. She looked at it but then put it back. She didn't need it. Mac wouldn't accept it, and he would definitely be disappointed in the fact that she had gone and picked up the prescription. Closing the hutch, she shook her head at herself before going back into the living room.

It was so weird to be alone. Marissa wasn't sure what to do with her time. She sat down and started flipping through the television channels, but the doorbell rang. Ellie barked once, as though to make sure Marissa was aware, and then whined anxiously. Marissa froze at first, wondering who the hell would be ringing the bell. She looked down at her phone and opened the Ring app to see a delivery driver. Marissa got to her feet and went to the door, feeling suddenly uncomfortable.

Marissa opened the door to the delivery man with a thick envelope.

"Marissa Ambrose?"

"That's me," she answered more cautiously than she had meant to.

"Perfect. Can you sign here?" He offered her his phone for a digital signature. She signed, gave him a small smile, and took the envelope from him.

"You have a good day, ma'am."

"You too." She watched him turn and head back to his truck. She waited until he closed the door and then closed her own door. This was a thick manila envelope, heavy with whatever contents were inside. The return address was the post office on Main Street.

No one else was home, so she didn't need to run off to the office. Instead, she stood over the dining room table, opened the envelope, and dumped the contents on the table. Dozens of photographs fell onto the table. Without touching them, Marissa just scanned what she could see of the pictures that were facing up. Her blood turned to ice.

Just on the top, she saw pictures of her nieces, of Kate, of Madi, of Jackson. Flipping the rest of them over, she saw photographs of literally everybody. Jared, Brian, Mel, even fucking Kirstie. And the babies. Beneath the photographs of her family and friends was a letter, folded over. She grabbed the paper and carefully unfolded it to reveal its words. She read the first sentence over and over.

It's time.

Beneath that were instructions. A lot of instructions. The message was clear. If she didn't follow his carefully laid-out instructions, everyone was fair game. The words at the bottom of the letter sent chills running through her.

See you soon.

Marissa swallowed, feeling absolute panic wash over her. She looked around, her eyes landing on Ellie.

"Fuck," she said softly, letting out a very shaky breath. She looked at the pictures before rereading the letter again.

The implication was obvious, even before she saw it in writing. She needed to do what she was told, or everyone could be a target.

"Fuck." Tears filled her eyes, and she walked back to the hutch and pulled out the Percocet. If she was going to follow these instructions, she was going to numb everything first.

Chapter 28

Caroline was seriously questioning her decision to come out here. She was so far out of her element. But once she had identified the location of Port Townsend and found Marissa Ambrose, there hadn't been any other option. She had told Emma it was a work assignment, not wanting to worry her girlfriend more than she already had.

She grabbed her bags from the car, tossed them on the bed, and took a look around. The room was nice enough and small, nothing fancy, but right on the beach with big windows that opened right up to it. Caroline sighed, looking out at the ocean as the sun was setting before pressing the call button on her phone. The phone rang five times before it went to voicemail. Caroline winced, hoping she wasn't still upset.

"Hey Emma, I just wanted to let you know I did make it. This should be a quick trip. My return flight is Sunday. I left the information on the refrigerator. I hope that work wasn't bad. I realize it's..." She glanced over at the alarm clock. "It's almost ten there, so you're probably soaking in the tub ignoring this phone call because you're still mad at me, but I promise, this trip is absolutely going to be worth it. And I can't wait to tell you all about it when I get home." She sighed. "Please don't be mad, Em. I love you."

Caroline ended the call and shook her head. She knew she'd needed to come. She just wished it hadn't been in the middle of a fight.

It was going to be okay, though. Especially if she could go home to tell Emma that it was all over. The last few months had just been so much. It was taking a toll not just on her, but on their relationship, too. She tossed the phone onto the bed and grabbed her jacket, deciding to step outside. It was dark now, but she could still see the ocean. Grabbing her cigarettes out of her jacket pocket, she put one between her lips and lit it, inhaling. Once it was lit, she dropped her lighter back in her pocket and took a long drag, watching the waves coming in and out.

Even though she had been told the bad guys were dead and gone, she still felt like she was being watched. Not that she could remember the last time she *didn't* feel like someone was watching her. She rubbed her shoulders and took another drag of her cigarette. It was a pretty place, but it was much too cold for her warm blood. She finished the cigarette quickly, dropping it and squishing it with her shoe.

Turning, she walked back inside and locked the door behind her. She tossed her jacket on the chair and leaned over the bed to check her phone. As she reached out, someone put a heavy hand over her mouth from behind and grabbed her arm, twisting it behind her back and throwing her hard onto the bed.

"Sorry, Caroline" was the last thing she heard before something hard connected with her head and everything went black.

Book Club Questions

1. Has your opinion of Marissa changed at all throughout the series?

2. Were you surprised at the new accomplices' reveal?

3. Was there too much going on to follow or were the two cases clearly defined enough?

4. How do you feel about Jared and Marissa's relationship at this point?

5. Was this book too heavy? Was it too much of a tonal shift?

6. Which characters would you like to see more of?

7. How did you feel about Marissa standing up for herself? Was the timing right?

8. What do you think of Caroline? Were you surprised by her appearance?

9. Who do you think the mastermind is?

10. Any predictions for the next book?

Author Bio

.K. Ramirez is a mystery writer tucked in a corner of the Pacific Northwest. She likes to weave mystery and family drama with a little bit of romance all in one. She has been writing for as long as she can remember, before publishing the *Marissa Ambrose Witness Series*, in both the mystery and fantasy genres. When she isn't writing, she runs a dog training, boarding, and daycare facility as the head trainer and spends time with her husband, kids, and pack of dogs. She also trains service dogs and is an advocate for those suffering from chronic illnesses. You can find her and all her socials at www.akramirezwrites.com

Discover more at
4HorsemenPublications.com

10% off using HORSEMEN10